EXTRACTION

___

STONEWALL SERIES
BOOK 1

J.L. DRAKE

EXTRACTION

J.L. Drake
Book 1

To Paul,
You might be fictional, but I'm sorry for putting you through this.

I promise I got you…eventually.

CAST OF CHARACTERS

A Friendly Reminder

- **Daniel:** Cole's father, first generation Blackstone. Married to **Sue,** Cole's mother.
- **Abigail/Abby:** Mark's adopted mother, Cole's childhood nanny, house aide. Sister to **June.**
- **Dr. Roberts:** House psychologist. Dating **Abigail**.
- **Frank:** Blackstone contact for the Army. First generation Blackstone member.
- **Zack:** First generation Blackstone member. Restaurant owner.

FAMILIES

- **Cole:** Owner of the Shadows safe house. Leader of the Blackstone special ops team. Married to **Savannah**. They have two kids, **Olivia** and **Easton**.
- **John:** Blackstone member. Married to **Sloane.**
- **Mike:** Blackstone member. Married to **Catalina.** Daughter **Gabriella.**
- **Keith:** Member of Blackstone. Was married to **Lexi.** They have two kids, **Brandon and Reagan.**
- **Mark:** Blackstone member. Married to **Mia.** They have a set of twins, **Liam** and **Ethan,** and a daughter, **Tabby.**
- **Paul:** Blackstone member. Deceased. *Well…I won't ruin this one for you.*
- **Dell:** North Rock member. Dusk Safe house in North Carolina.

- **Davie:** North Rock member. Dusk Safe house in North Carolina.
- **Steve Chamness:** North Rock member. Dusk Safe house in North Carolina.
- **Denton Barlow:** The American. Deceased.

ANIMALS/PETS

- **Goats:** Friendly reminders of home
- **Chickens:** Annoying and always in the way
- **Scoot:** A-hole house cat
- **Butters:** Mark and Mia's husky
- **Tripper:** John and Sloane's German shepherd

CARTEL PLAYERS

- **Martin Castillo** – Dead (From Dark Water Series)
- **Eric Noah** – Martin Castillo's right-hand man, "Dead"
- **Talya Canos** – Eric Noah's ex-girlfriend
- **Jerry and Elva Canos** – Talya's parents who have now taken over Martin Castillo's operation

ONE

PAUL

"Stonewall One to Raven One, what's your position?" I hovered behind some greenery that shielded me from the bastards who were closing in and asked again for Cole to check in. "Raven One, I've requested your position. Do you copy?"

"Stonewall One. I'm coming up on your six." I could tell by the strain in Cole's voice he was hurt. "Got clipped in the arm."

"Copy that." I whirled and saw him coming

toward me, then I spotted Ty with Moore. "Dark Water One, assist Raven One." I was careful not to use our names. I knew the Cartel would be alerted to our presence the moment we crossed the border into Mexico.

"Copy that." Ty didn't miss a beat as he slid across the dirt and ripped Cole's shirt open to check the damage. He dumped hemostatic powder over the wound to help clot the blood.

"It's just a graze." Cole's voice was raspy with pain. "I'm good."

"We're good here. He's right. It's just a graze," Ty assured me, "but Dark Water Two just checked in. Says the next checkpoint is surrounded, and we should move to the next."

"I'll take a look." I headed in the direction he indicated. I just had to follow the path of dead bodies. It didn't take long for me to gain ground on Mark, Mike, and Keith, who were in a full sprint toward the compromised checkpoint. My infrared camera told me we were about to have company. "Raven Two, you have three men coming up on your ten."

"Copy that," Mark huffed into the radio. "You have eyes on Raven One?"

I smiled at that. I'd almost forgotten the feeling. The closeness we had. The way we could almost feel what our brothers were going through. "Clipped in the arm. He'll be fine. Beta Seven, your left!" I let two bullets go as I yelled and nailed the man about to fire at Keith.

I swung around and reassessed the situation. Our cover was blown the moment Moore walked up on one of the child scouts who had radioed in our location before he could stop him. In seconds, we were under fire and forced to head south when we needed to go southeast. Time was running out, and we didn't even know if our mark was still alive.

This rescue was incredibly important, not due to who it was, but what they did for a living.

"We have a Hummer approaching from the west side, boys," Mike said, "packed full of men and even more weapons. Shit," he paused, "is that—"

"Yeah, 'fraid so," John chimed in. "Shit, boys, they've got some sort of homemade RPG."

"Stonewall," Cole's voice broke through the radio, "I think we could use some code forty right now."

I grinned and got into position. "Copy that." I lined up my scope, flicked the top of the button open, and steadied my breath. I made sure I had eyes on who my target was as I cleared my head, ready to end this. "Code forty in three, two, one." I squeezed the trigger and felt my body come alive as each one of the canisters shot into the air and burst above the enemy, releasing a million little bullets straight down on top of them. It was one of my finest creations. It was a quick and quiet kill. Unlike what the Cartel offered us. But that was what separated the men from the monsters.

I scanned the area with the infrared. "Clear!"

We rushed past our next checkpoint with no need to stop and regained the time we lost. We moved like knights on a chess board. Each move was thought-out, but there were constant pawns at every turn. Endless bullets fired into the sunset, and our window to save our mark closed at a rapid rate.

"Check in," I called into my radio, "Blackstone start." I took note of all who spoke, and none missed a beat. That was a crucial part of being on a special operations team. Once Cole's team checked in, Ty's Dark Water team did the same. All ten were accounted for.

I was ahead of the pack and again used my camera to see what we were up against. "We have two doves, four chickens, and at least eight wolves between you and the mark." Which meant we had two snipers on the roof, four men walking the perimeter, and eight men around the only entrance.

"Copy that," Cole and Ty said one after the other.

I spotted Moore and Gear from team Dark Water sneak up and grab two of the chickens. They snapped their necks and moved on to the others.

My mind went back to all those years ago, when I was on Team Blackstone. The way we moved through the night as shadowy figures, people would second guess if they even saw anything, but before they could make a move, we made ours. That was our time to shine, and we were the best.

I could practically feel the men's adrenaline

surround me as I watched. My breathing evened out to an eerie calmness, my heartbeat slowed, and everything became very still. I'd waited a long time for that moment, and I was excited to show the men what I still had to offer.

I watched as Cole's team took the lead, with Mark, Keith, John, and Mike all hand to shoulder as they moved through the small hallway of the packaging building. Their bodies glowed through the infrared screen. "Left," I whispered to help keep their focus as I guided them. "Door on your right." Cole made a move, and they were with him. "Reach out and feel the rail for the stairs." We couldn't risk the guys using night vision goggles; they had to trust me to guide them. The Cartel was stronger and wiser than they were only a year ago. They'd come up with new ways to hurt us like never before. Our last mission, they were ready for the guys and momentarily blinded them when they used their NODs. It was a constant battle to keep up with their newest tactics, and we had to consistently revise our strategy.

"He should be behind that door." I tried to study a strange object that was reading as cold as ice. "Hold." I needed a moment. *What the hell are you?* I moved around the best I could, but whatever it was, it didn't seem to have a heartbeat. "Fuck it, whatever it is, just bang it. I have eyes and will eliminate if necessary."

"Copy that." Cole gave the signal, and gunshots and shouts echoed through the night air. "Your three,

Raven Two!" Cole shouted as Mark got pistol-whipped in the head by a Cartel rat.

"Move, move, move!" Ty yelled at his team as they freed the mark from the chains on the wall, covered his head for protection so he wouldn't panic, and bent him over at the waist to keep him low as they headed out into the hallway.

A strange feeling crept up my spine as something odd came over me. I swung the camera around and saw the building had suddenly emptied, the exits were clear of Cartel, and the two on lookout on the roof were no longer there. That little prickle intensified as it moved up my neck and into my hair. My sixth sense screamed as I slowly turned and scanned every inch I could see, and that's when it –

"Fuck!" I started to radio what I'd seen but stopped myself. I decided to make the call without the team leaders weighing in. After all, that was why I was there.

"Stonewall One to Stonewall Three, do you copy?"

"I copy." Cole's father, Daniel, the original Blackstone team leader, was all business.

I couldn't even count how many men were in a line and closing in on the west side. "We have a code red."

The radio went quiet. No doubt he'd switched from the teams' camera to mine.

"Permission to—?"

"Do whatever you need to," he interrupted, and I knew he could see what I did.

"Copy that." I switched channels then and gave an order to the pilot to move his pickup spot to a closer location. There was no way we could fight off that many Cartel with only ten men. I moved a few feet from where I was protected and got a better look at why the house was suddenly evacuated. The blood drained from my head when I saw a Cartel soldier run with a roll of wire from the building to where they all had taken cover in the shrubs.

"Fuck!" I switched the channel back to the teams. "Get out of there now!" I screamed, and all eleven men burst out the door as the first bomb went off. My camera blinded me for a moment, but I was ready and had closed my eyes a second before the place went up in a fireball. "Head east!" I headed down the hill as a second explosion went off then switched from my camera to night vision. The NODs weren't great, and it was a risk, but I needed to see better.

"Raven Two, on your left!" Ty shouted as bullets zipped in the darkness. I aimed my weapon toward where they'd come from and fired at will. The teams all wore watch trackers, and once the mark was found, one was put on him as well in case we got separated. "Two, four, six, ten, plus the mark," I quickly counted out loud. "All right, fuckers." I swung around, locked in an RPG launcher, and fired one of my own homemade creations.

"Holy shit!" Mark cried out. "I think you took my nuts with that blast."

"Nice to hear you're still with us." I chuckled and swung my weapon to pop three men coming up on John's ass.

The sound of the chopper was bliss, and I moved into position as he hovered to do the dangerous task of lowering to the ground.

"What the hell did I miss?" Keith shouted at me as he carried the mark over his shoulder. "You better tip the pilot for this one."

"Go! Go! Go!" Cole shouted once the chopper door closed. As it started to lift, the enemy fired with all they had. The chopper dipped to the side, and our mark went flying into the side of the beast before we could get him strapped in. He rubbed his shoulder in pain and his mouth gaped open at the impact as Cole quickly went to his aid.

I dug my feet in, flexed my hands, and waited as the fuckers raced toward me. It was like a battle scene in *Game of Thrones*. "A little closer." I listened as the chopper got higher in the sky. "Come on, come on." My head lived for this shit. "Bye-bye." I hit the button, and fifty little metal bubbles shot into the air, and as soon as they were over the enemy, I fired them all off at the same time. The sound would have been chilling if I were the target, but we were fighting good versus evil, and all bets were off.

"Fuck yeah!" Mark called into the radio. "It's like the Fourth of July!"

Then silence took over, and I struggled to check for any Cartel that might have been spared. I felt nothing for their pain, only that these monsters were stopped, and my teams would come home in one piece with their mission complete.

Once I got word that they'd crossed the border, I dropped my head back and allowed myself to suck in a deep breath.

"Paul?" West, my second in command, said from behind me. "Would you like me to take over?"

"Yeah, I would." I happily let go of the drone's controllers and stepped out of the pod to stretch my back.

"Great job, sir."

"Thanks, West. Let's get her home." I nodded toward the screen. The drone had been pre-programed to return to a post in Texas, and he would monitor it until it was safely back there.

It was my biggest accomplishment since I returned to Shadows over a year ago. I spent countless hours making sure the drone was small enough to fly with our teams but large enough that it had incredible firing power. It was silent, sleek, a real beauty. It would take an RPG to bring it down. There were six cameras that covered all the angles, and each could rotate three hundred and sixty degrees. The best part was the real-time communication I had with the teams while I flew it. It allowed me to be with them where I belonged without exposing my identity to the enemy. Basically, I conducted security from the sky.

I rubbed my tired eyes and looked at the time. I had been in the pod for nearly thirteen hours. I might not be able to show my face in Mexico anymore, as I'd been compromised, but I sure as hell had found a way to continue to fight alongside my brothers. People might think my story ended, but really, it had just begun.

It was nearly five p.m. when I went upstairs to the main living room of the safehouse. I spotted Doc Roberts talking to his new hire, Dr. Bash Barella, as they were exiting the kitchen.

"Good evening, Paul, how was the mission?" Doc Roberts fixed his glasses on his nose.

"All good, everyone's fine." I looked at Dr. Bash and changed the subject. "I hear you're adjusting pretty well."

"Slowly but surely, I am."

Bash was born and raised in Italy and had come to the US to attend medical college then made his way to Washington. Frank highly recommended him to Daniel, and Cole soon approved him to come work at Shadows. For the most part, he seemed nice, but he was careful to keep his personal life far from us. That might work in a different situation, but at Shadows, if you wanted people to trust you, you needed to get to know us on a personal level. That would mean sharing, and it was something Doc Roberts did very well. New guy still had a way to go before he'd find his place here.

"The guys and I will be doing a run up the

mountain tomorrow. Would you like to join us?" I knew the answer before I asked, but I figured I had to show I was willing to try for the sake of the house.

Bash pushed his long, thick, shaggy, black hair behind his ear as my words sank in. He always waited a beat before he'd speak. "I don't think I'm available, but perhaps another time."

"Perhaps." I shot Doc Roberts a look, and he seemed to read my mind. "Well, I need to find some-one. The offer's still there if you change your mind."

"Thank you, Paul." He shoved the sleeves of his black sweater up, and I hid my smile as I remembered what Cat had said about him. *'He's what I'd imagine Elio Capri's therapist would look like.'* She was right. He had a darkness to his eyes that I couldn't quite place, but he'd been cleared to be here, so that counted for something.

"I'll find you later," Doc Roberts assured me before they left.

I spotted who I was looking for. Savannah was in her favorite spot by the fireplace with Scoot, the moody house cat. He seemed to have love only for her. She often sat there whenever Cole was due to return from a mission. Over the years, she'd found that a good book and a spot by the fireplace helped calm her nerves, but I knew she rarely read. She secretly watched the window for headlights or news of the chopper. We all had our ways of coping; that was hers.

"Oh, hi." She perked up when she spotted me. "How was it?"

I rubbed my head as I sat down on the warm stones of the hearth. "Everyone's fine," I assured her. "Cole got clipped in the arm, but nothing too serious." Her face slipped, but she caught herself and looked away. "They should be back any minute."

"Uncle Paul!" Olivia came running into the room and sat down next to me, her big chocolate brown eyes beaming with excitement. "I made some revisions to that tactical vest problem you were having. What about something like this?" She turned her notebook around, and I studied the drawing she'd made with colored pencil. "It's okay, Mom." She held out a hand to Savannah. "Dad gave me permission to help out Uncle Paul."

"I didn't say anything." Savannah nodded, but I knew deep down inside she was nervous about how interested Livi had become in all things Blackstone. She had an inventive mind and loved nothing better than to come up with ideas.

"See, if we rotate this," she pointed to a piece of the vest that protected the underarm, "that frees this little notch right there."

I held the notebook closer to my face and looked at Savannah. "She's good."

"She is." Savannah jumped to her feet when the headlights from the SUV lit up the room. "They're here."

As usual, when the teams arrived home from a

mission, the families would all head outside to meet them. It was such a warm moment and one I'd always remember.

Shit, times like this, I remember how much I missed this place.

"Dad!" Reagan jumped in Keith's arms while Cole's youngest, Easton, wiggled his way through the crowd and body slammed into his stomach.

"Hey, big guy." Cole winced and tousled his floppy hair. "We're all here, safe and sound."

I felt someone stand next to me. I would soon start to debrief the mission with the guys, but this had priority.

John's wife Sloane chuckled. "I'll step back if you want to hug John."

I elbowed her in the side then playfully pushed by her and made a point to pull John in for a long hug.

"Miss me, did ya, big guy?" He laughed.

"So much." I stroked his back and made Mike laugh.

"And now the hug is over." He shoved me away and grabbed Sloane to pull her to him. "I got a stroke from Paul, so what do you have for me?"

She whispered something, and before anyone could remind him of the debrief in fifteen, they were gone.

"He'll only need five." Mark winked with a twin dangling from each of his arms. "Abby's showing our guest his room. Would you mind…"

"No worries. I got you." I pressed my fingers into

one of the boys' sides, making him buck with laughter.

"Uncle Paul!" Liam shrieked.

I dropped the little bugger upside down onto a stuffed chair next to the door.

I chuckled as I took two stairs at a time up the grand staircase to the top floor. I could hear Abigail's voice, and her words became clear when she opened the door. "I know this is a lot, Benjamin, but I promise you're safe now."

"Yeah." The man jumped back when I came in the room. "Sorry, and this isn't my first time," his hand landed on his chest. "Guess it doesn't matter that I'm still a little rattled." His eyes closed as he rubbed his shoulder and winced. "My body sure ain't what it once was."

"My apologies. I should've known better." I tried to put him at ease as I mentally kicked myself for not remembering how to behave around a house guest. "It's been a while since," I stumbled, "since I've been on house duty." This was a safe house, after all, and most of our 'guests' had been through a lot by the time they were brought here. I gave him an apologetic smile and stayed a little back from him.

Abby gave me a warm smile and squeezed my arm. "You were missed, and boy, it's great to have you home," she whispered as she gave me a hug. She turned back to look at the man who had already seen too much. "Benjamin Bale, this is Paul. He's special ops and one of the men who helped you out in the field." She moved toward the door. "Benjamin, whatever you need, just let me or anyone know, and we'll be happy to help."

"Wi-Fi?" he asked with a weak smile.

"Anything but that." Abby chuckled. "NDA, remember."

"You mean the encyclopedia I had to read and sign when we stopped over in Texas? The one that had the world's biggest consequence if you breach the contact? Yeah," he tried another smile, "I remember. I'm fine. I just needed that shower, and thanks to you, these clean clothes. I could do with a hot meal." He looked hopeful.

"That, I can help you with. There's food on, and when you're ready, I can bring it up here, or you can eat downstairs with the others."

He didn't miss a beat. "With people. I can't take the silence anymore."

I folded my arms and grinned at him. "Silence sure isn't something you'll find in this house."

"Certainly not." Abby laughed and rolled her eyes. "All right, then, I'll be downstairs when you're ready."

"Thank you." Benjamin sat on the wooden chest at the end of the bed and rubbed his eyes. I knew from his posture his body hurt. He'd refused treatment on his shoulder, which I respected, and I knew his head would be scrambling to catch up. The last twelve hours would have been a whirlwind. "Mr. Paul?"

"Just Paul."

"No first name, or is that your last?"

"Just Paul," I repeated then felt like an ass for my sharp tone. "It's complicated." I felt I needed to explain a bit. "I had sort of a family once, but the people in this house are all the family I need now, and here there's no need to have any name other than Paul." I felt the lump that came when I thought of my biological family and my shitty father. I'd never really had anyone who loved me, not like here. Then Talya's gorgeous face popped up, and I slammed that door closed so fast I swore I felt a breeze.

"Understood." He let it go. "Ah," he tilted his head, "any word on Nicole?"

"Nicole?"

"Nicole Winter. She's the war correspondent I was working with over there."

I mentally flipped through his file and couldn't recall that name. "I thought you were working with Kimberly Ann?"

He jammed the pad of his thumb into his eye and shook his head. "Kim was a mess. One explosion, and she was out. I've worked with Nicole on and off for years. The woman chews through cameramen like Skittles." He gave a huff. "Anyway, after Kimberly left, I ran into Nicole, and I worked with her until we were separated, and I was taken. I'd hoped you guys got her out too."

"Sorry, man. Her name's not been mentioned, at least not to me."

"No worries. Knowing her, she's sittin' in some Cartel's back yard sipping tequila." He chuckled while my brows pinched together. That was an odd comment to make. He must have caught my confusion and closed his eyes with a head shake. "Ah, of course, most likely her reputation isn't known here. They keep her pretty quiet." He stood. "Let me get my head on straight, and I'll fill you in."

I wanted to push, but I remembered my house training and didn't ask anything else. "I'm glad you're all right, Benjamin."

"Ben, please," he looked around, "and thank you. I promise I'll be better tomorrow."

"You've been through a lot. Give yourself some grace." I nodded and checked the time; it was time to gather my team in the conference room. "See you down there when you're ready.

The families only had a few more moments together, so I hurried downstairs to round up my team. They jumped up from the table and carried their dishes to the kitchen. I continued to the conference room. Daniel and Frank were already there. They were looking around at the new command center I had finished building six months ago.

Frank grinned as I stepped inside. "Impressive. I know I saw it when it was first finished, but now after seeing it live…" He pursed his lips and whistled. "I mean, what you were able to pull off this last mission was truly remarkable."

"I don't have to tell you the enemy is better,

smarter, and stronger than only a year ago. We need to match that and be ten steps ahead."

"Agreed." Daniel added, "The protection you offered the teams was invaluable. If we hadn't known that wall of Cartel was almost on us, I don't think the teams would be here at all. They made it home and in one piece, because of you."

I didn't like the attention, so I changed topics. "Does the name Nicole Winter mean anything to you guys?"

Frank set down the controller he was admiring and threw a quick glance at Daniel. "Why do you ask?"

"Apparently, Ben Bale, our new house guest, was working with her before he was captured."

Frank shook his head. "He supposedly worked with Kimberly Ann Smith, but I did hear she'd been deployed home for mental health reasons. After Ben's military team was killed and he was taken, you were sent in to get him."

"According to him," I pointed to the ceiling, "he hoped she was brought out as well."

Daniel moved over to one of the keyboards and typed her name into our database. A flicker of the screen later, and a stunning woman with fierce green eyes and brown hair to just below the collarbone stared intensely from the other side of the camera. Her brows were perfectly manicured into a slight arch that accentuated her slender nose, smooth cheekbones, and pretty, pink lips.

I huffed at how gorgeous she was, but I saw a look in her eyes that told me she didn't take shit from anyone. My gut feeling, this woman would be a handful, especially to those she worked with. I silently thanked God that Cole had never made us work with the press. We had bigger fish to fry than babysitting the media.

"Nicole Winter, born and raised in Billings, thirty-five years old, actively worked as a war correspondent for the past fifteen years." Daniel scanned the screen. "She's got quite the bio."

"Where?" I stepped closer to the screen.

"Southern Mexico and a little time in El Salvador." Daniel scoffed at something. "Seems she's worked with several cameramen over that time. She's had at least twenty so far."

"Damn." I knew a WC and their cameramen had to be in sync to do their job, so the fact she didn't get along well with others was interesting.

Daniel whistled. "Seems she's provided some seriously impressive information to the government over the years."

I noticed Frank was quiet, so I turned to look at him. "What do you know?"

"Not much, but I know she's under Bruce's umbrella." General Bruce had his own reputation for bending the rules, so it didn't surprise me someone with her impressive track record would get her orders from him. My guess would be she was told to get in, do whatever was necessary, and get out. "Which means I don't know much. Bruce keeps a tight lid on things. But I know she's one of the best if not *the* best WC out there," Frank continued. "She's obviously gained the trust of a few major players down there." He studied the screen.

"Like who?"

"Santiago Garcia, Mateo Tomas, Matias Lucas, to name a few." A cold shiver raced down my back at the mention of those names. I had to sit down. He was right; they were all major players in the Cartel.

Daniel leaned in to read something. "Look who she's with here."

He brought up a photo, and I nearly fell off my chair when I saw her shaking hands with my ex-lover Talya's father. The very man I'd helped to take out another major kingpin, Martin Castillo. Talya's parents wanted to move up and needed Castillo out of the way so they could take his place. I shook my head. That was a whole other life for me, and things were different now.

"So, Paul, have you ever run into her?" Daniel pointed at her press picture he brought back up.

"I don't think so. I'd remember those eyes." Again, I glanced at Frank and wondered what other secrets he knew, because surely, at some point, we could have or would have crossed paths.

"Who's the hottie?" Mark commented as he filed in with the others.

Daniel switched off the screen. We needed to debrief before we jumped into that one.

"We'll get there," he assured him.

"First, let's start from the beginning."

After we dissected and logged our mission, some of us decided to head to Zack's for some celebratory drinks. It was one of the traditions we'd started years ago to help blow off some steam. It gave the wives some much-needed time with their husbands and without their kids. It was wonderful that everyone lived together, kids and all, but it was also incredibly important to carve out alone time for the adults. We needed time to bond and keep our heads on straight.

I was happy that Keith's date, Liza, headed toward the table. She was a kick-ass weapons finder at Camp Green and had proved to be a huge asset to our organization. The wives did their best not to pry too much into what was going on with the two of them. The loss of Keith's wife, Lexi, had left him and his two kids stunned and grieving. He'd been through the wringer over the past year, and it was important for him to find some happiness. At least that was how Dr. Ivy explained it when she was trying to make the point that I should be doing the same.

"Sorry for being late." Liza smiled at Keith and then the rest of us. "Juliet flaked on me again, and I had to cover most of her shift at camp. I have no idea what's going on with her, but something's not right." She took the chair next to Keith.

"No problem." Keith poured her a beer. "Hopefully, whatever it is clears up soon."

"Cheers to that." She tapped his glass and took a deep breath.

I couldn't mentally pull up who her friend might be, and I knew mostly everyone at Camp Green. "Who's Juliet? Is she new?" I took a swallow of my own brew.

"New? No, not really," Liza ran her finger down a drip on the side of the glass. "She's been there way longer than me. She worked in soldier placements for quite a while, then was moved to my position to give me some much-needed time off, but so far all I've done is work more."

Keith leaned back slightly to stretch his shoulder. "I'll speak to Frank."

"You don't have to do that, Keith. I was only complaining. I don't want to get anyone in trouble."

"You won't," he assured her and smiled. Then we all glanced up as a blur of color whisked up to the table.

"There she is!" Ty grabbed Ivy and kissed her hard. "How's our houseguest doing?" Ivy, Shadow's second to newest therapist to work with team Blackstone, smiled indulgently at her husband. Their son, Hudson, had just started to stand and was on the go from the time he woke until he was down for the night. It was nice she was able to take a little break. Her uncle, Doc Roberts, had been with Blackstone for a long time and had moved over to Team Dark Water when Ivy came.

Ivy was a hit with everyone, an amazing woman

who had worked wonders with Keith after his terrible loss. I stopped that memory dead in its tracks and forced it down. That had been a hard time for all of us, and this was our night to relax.

"He's good." She nodded. "This was the second time for him, being captured, I mean, so he already knew the steps to help his head and that definitely was a factor. I think he's rattled, sore, and just needs a few days to get himself together and he'll be fine. He's been well trained and did everything by the book."

"That's huge," Ty agreed as he hugged her, and we all took a breath and digested that. It wasn't often the house took in someone who could handle what they'd just been through. It was one of the main reasons we needed Ivy and Doc Roberts and, I guess, Dr. Bash. Of course, they also worked with our own.

"Frank says he'll transfer him back to Washington and work with him there." Ivy took her drink from the waitress. "Thank you. Oops." She licked her finger after she sloshed her drink on her hand. "No need for him to stay more than a few weeks. I get the feeling he might stay in the States for a while, though. He's not in a hurry to go back at it."

"Good plan. Being taken once would be enough for a lifetime, but twice—" I put my hands out. "Phew."

Mark looked around then back to us. "No Dr. Bash?"

"No," Ivy gave a small shrug, "Roberts said he just isn't comfortable yet."

"That's not sitting well with me," Mike piped in. "I'm not asking him to be our best friend, but there was a reason you and Doc Roberts can get past our walls so well."

"Agreed," she sighed. "I'll see about reminding him of that, but he does like to stick to his office, so…"

We all stopped talking when two women maybe in their mid-twenties approached. One held out a pool cue. "We need two more. Any takers?" I glanced at John, who eased lower on his stool and pulled Sloane into him as a barrier. He smirked at me as if he enjoyed the moment.

"What about you?" The girl holding the cue locked eyes with me. "You've got this officer kind of SWAT look that says 'I've seen a lot in my day, so don't screw with me.' I kinda like it. So, you wanna play?"

"Hey, who's Janet's favorite player?" she called to a girl behind her. "You know, the hottie who plays for the 49ers?"

"Nick Bosa," her friend replied with a giggle.

"Yes, that's who you remind me of." Her eyes flared with interest. "You have his sexy jawbone, strong build, and those eyes that look like they could swallow me up in one bite." She mimicked chomping. *Gross.*

I hated that kind of flirting. Girls who are just on the prowl. I had to remember they were young, but I'd always been turned off by that approach. It stemmed from when I was undercover and saw how women fell at the feet of various Cartels just because they had power and authority. Sadly, we called them Crimson Hunters because nine times out of ten they'd end up covered in blood, often left for dead when the men were finished with them.

"Thanks, but I'm good." I forced a smile and glanced at Keith where he stood expressionless behind Cole and Mark. I knew they were all thoroughly enjoying this.

"Lucky for you, I don't take no very easily." The girl stuck out a hip.

"But tonight, you will." I smiled. Her expression flinched, but she tilted her head as if in thought. She either liked the challenge or she wasn't told no very often.

"Or I buy you a drink and you tell me what all of this means." She ran her hand up my tattooed sleeve. I put my hand over hers and gently but firmly pushed it off my arm as I stepped closer to her.

"I'm flattered, truly." I tried to drive my point home. "You're a pretty girl, but I've seen way too much shit, and one night with me would dull that light in your eyes. I promise you I'm not the man you want to be with tonight."

"Yeah, okay." Her eyes lowered, and I knew I finally got through to her. "Sorry for bothering you."

I nodded once, stepped back, and she grabbed her friend's arm, and they walked back to the pool table.

"So, cute, bubbly, doe-eyed girls are not your

type. Got it." Mark, who always seemed to be around for those moments, broke the tension and made the others laugh. "Just so I'm clear," he went on, "ugly, dominant, dead-eyed girls are your jam?"

"Women are my game, not girls. Especially ones who probably have Daddy's credit card and more hair product than you," I poked back, and Keith laughed loudly behind him.

"He does take more time than me in the bathroom." Mia laughed into her beer bottle but jumped when Mark swiped out and tickled her side. "It's true, and we all know it."

"I've said it once, and I'll say it again. It takes a special, well-thought-out grooming process to look this good all the time." Mark mocked flipping his hair over his shoulder, which again made us all laugh. "Don't hate because I care about how I look."

I stared at him, deadpan, then turned my expression to Mia. "I have so much respect for you."

"Yeah," she joined in on my sarcasm, "I appreciate that."

Mark reached for the pitcher of beer. "It's terribly unfair that you all pick on the prettiest one."

"Ohhh!" Mike laughed and rubbed his fully tattooed bald head. "You are far from the prettiest one, my friend."

We went back to playing darts and continued to give each other shit because that was how we bonded and shared the darkness we all carried on our shoulders.

That night, when we returned home from Zack's, I was met by Frank and Daniel on the front porch. I glanced at the time and saw it was well past two a.m.

"This can't be good." Cole kissed Savi. "I'll be home soon." She left to walk down to their cabin where they lived with their kids, and Cole joined my side.

Our generation of Blackstone had changed the way Shadows was run. Daniel had wanted the best for his safe house and for his son, and that meant he had to change the way things were run here. He had since built cabins for each of the families as needed, relatively close to the main house but far enough for privacy. As the men fell in love and had kids, it filled a hole that the house had been missing.

Living here gave them a sense of real life without having to give up what we were here to do. All of us were made for this life. The children were a plus, and some of the kids were going to be kickass special ops soldiers one day. Cole's daughter Olivia already left no doubt that she planned to take over Shadows when she was old enough. It was clear as day that it was what she intended to do with her life.

"Who do you need to see?" Mike asked with a yawn.

"Paul and Cole." Frank looked at the two of us.

Mike high-fived Mark, and the rest of the group headed for bed while I internally groaned and followed Cole inside and downstairs to the command center.

Abigail popped out of nowhere and set a canister of coffee and some homemade burgers on a side table. "Have fun tonight, boys?"

"Better now." I snagged a burger and polished it off in two bites. "Thanks, Abby."

"Anything for my boys." Her sweet face that now showed a few signs of aging smoothed out when she smiled warmly at us. "Good luck."

"Sorry for cutting into your night, guys, but something came up." Daniel pointed the remote at the TV. "Frank." He waited for Frank to take over.

"At zero-one-hundred, I got a call from Chili." Instantly, I sat straighter. "He's fine," he assured me, "but something's happening in Rosarito." Drone footage showed Martin Castillo's old property. We had destroyed the place a year or so back, but it had been slowly rebuilt by Jerry and Elva Canos since they'd taken over. The really messed up thing was that Jerry had been Martin's half-brother, and a long time back, they'd been building their Cartel empire together. I wondered what happened. Obviously, Jerry had other plans.

It was weird to see Castillo's property rebuilt. A place I had spent nearly a decade visiting looked so different. I watched as dozens of Cartel soldiers scattered in all directions, and I recognized Jorje, their head of security, as he jumped into a truck and tore off down the driveway.

Frank eased onto the side of the table. "We

followed the truck to Mexico City but lost them when the drone was fired on."

"Was Talya spotted?" I had to ask. It was her parents' house, after all, and she did work for them. Maybe I wasn't sure if she still did, but I knew she'd always hated it.

"Truth, Paul, we haven't seen her for almost a year."

Really? I had purposely avoided the drones we had around Rosarito. I couldn't take it if there was footage of her with someone else.

"Any idea what could have caused the chaos?" Cole studied the screen. "Because whatever it was, it was enough to have more than half their security team leave the property. I've only seen that a few times."

"Agreed." I pointed. "I know how Jerry operates, and he would never let that many of his men leave. Not without good reason, anyway. He was always beyond paranoid, and after the attack on Grim's hotel, he'd be even more so."

I shook my head and remembered the fire that had almost taken Grim Gates' Vegas hotel. I hesitated to describe Grim as a close friend, but after his help a year ago when I was on the run, I consider myself lucky to be able to call him one. The fire that almost destroyed his hotel was thanks to Jerry. He'd been upset that Grim had left Mexico when he did. Grim retaliated, but in the end, Jerry came out of it all with his skin intact.

"Whatever it is, it's big," Frank commented. We watched as the drone followed the trucks and flew down the road and into the thick of the city.

"Well, check this out." Daniel moved closer to the screen. "They stop here, then something spooks them," he squinted, "shots are fired, two fell to the ground, and the rest race off in a different direction."

"Wait," something caught my eye, and a cold sensation settled on the back of my neck, "back that up, please. Okay, right there, can you zoom in on that car?" I pointed to the Infiniti SUV.

"Yeah, I can do that." Daniel played with the controllers and was able to give me a better view of the driver. The face was blurry, but I could make out the twenty-thousand-dollar watch and pompous pinky ring. "What are you seeing, Paul?"

Frank slowly stood, and I knew he saw it too. "Fuck me."

I leaned my head into my hand and felt my stomach drop to the seat. "He's alive."

"Who?" Cole looked confused.

"Bruno Perez." Everyone went silent as the realization that Martin Castillo's nephew was still fucking alive.

Frank turned to look at me straight on. "That's impossible. You killed him. I saw you do it."

"Apparently, he pulled a me and returned from the dead."

"That doesn't look like Bruno." Cole tried to catch up while his face drained of color.

I puffed up my cheeks then slowly let out the air while my own head tried to connect the dots. I studied the footage again. "It's his driver for sure, and I thought he'd been killed in that explosion as well. If his driver's alive, then you can sure as hell bet Bruno is too. The shots from that SUV," I pointed at the footage again, "they were trying to take out Jerry's men."

"Paul." Frank didn't have to say it.

"Yeah," I shook my head, "we need confirmation that's really Bruno, because if it is, we're fucked."

PRESS

TWO

NICOLE WINTER

"Come on, you piece of shit." I smacked the side of the satellite phone. I'd snagged it from a police chief a while back and felt zero remorse for taking it. These people were so messed up they'd raid some poor person's business on the pretense of looking for someone they knew friggin' well wasn't even there. The raids were just a means to help themselves to whatever they wanted.

I loved Mexico, and I'd spent more time there than anywhere else, but the country was horribly corrupt, and the people were at the mercy of those who called themselves police. Of course, like everywhere, not all of them were bad, and I'd made a few good friends. It was just such a shame that the few spoiled it for the rest. Sadly, the bad way outnumbered the good. Money was the driving force in Mexico—money and violence.

I twisted the dial and tried a different channel, but I got the same static as before. I jammed it back into my bag and flopped my head back against the wall. This wasn't how things were supposed to go.

Suddenly, a child's brown, tear-filled eyes blinked up at me as his mouth moved but I was thrown back into a memory and remembered Justin's face before I left.

"Who was that on the phone?"

"Work." I zipped my knapsack.

"Why can't you tell me who it is?"

I shook my head. "You know I can't do that."

"If you leave this time, Nicole, that's it. I'm not going to wait around anymore for you to leave your job for me. It's been four years. It's me or Mexico." Justin leaned forward over the arm of the couch and nodded toward the engagement ring he wanted me to have. I stared at the diamond, and the noose around my neck tightened and the walls started to close in. Marriage was something I wanted someday but not right then. I needed to be free to do my job and help people. In my mind, it was more than a job, it was a calling, and Justin would never understand that. His was a nine to five corporate type. He loved his nice clothes, cappuccinos, and weekends he knew were his.

"You know I love my job, and what I do does make a difference."

"It doesn't to me. All I see is you leaving, and then I

hold my breath until you come home. Why can't you just stay here, be here, with me? Start a life, kids, you know, the whole white picket fence thing. Don't you want a house in a safe suburban town where we can make something good happen? That would make a difference." His brown eyes teared up as he pleaded. I pulled up the handle of my suitcase and gripped the handle for something to hold me in place.

"I'm sorry, Justin, but this was what I was made to do. It's what I need right now."

He snagged the ring off the table and snapped the box closed as if to mimic my action. "I'm sorry too." His eyes turned angry. "I'm sorry for you, Nicole. You can't see that you're going to spend the rest of your life alone or," he made a face, "dead in a hole somewhere." He brushed by me and headed down the hall. "And you wonder why no one sticks around in your life."

"Justin," his words lashed at a deep, raw wound, "that's too far."

He stopped and rubbed his face with a heavy huff. "You know what? No. It's time you hear this. Nicole, you're impossible to love." My chest heaved at his words. "You're unlovable because you don't give anything of yourself to anyone who might care for you even a little bit. Your own family trauma has spilled over into mine, and I can't do it anymore."

My anger over such a hurtful statement rushed to the surface. "All right, you want to toss all the blame at me for leaving. Let's be honest, shall we? Two months ago, when I called home, and I heard a woman on the other end of the phone, was that Pam? Did you sleep with your co-worker?" He looked away, and I knew it was true. Tommy the doorman had warned me, but I didn't want to believe it. "Be a man and answer me."

"Yes."

I let go of the air I held as my chest hurt. "Was that the first time?"

He dropped his hands with a defeated shrug. "No."

"Right," I sniffed. I didn't want him to see how much he'd just hurt me. "So, you want to marry me, make me leave my job, give up everything I worked so hard for and what? So you can have Pam on the side?"

"A least she's capable of loving me."

"Wow." His hits just kept coming. "So, if she loves you like you claim, then why marry me? Admit it, Justin. You just like my connections to Washington." He didn't even deny it; he just shrugged like I should have known all along. "Got it. Well, that's that."

He snickered, and I knew he'd need to have the last word. "Good luck being alone, Nicole, because that's all you have left." He glared like I was the only guilty one here. "I'll be gone by tonight. You can get someone else to water your damn plant."

I eyed the sad little plant that looked to be on its last leg. I curled it into my arm and awkwardly rolled my suitcase out the door. I knew that would be the last time I'd see Justin.

"You're off again," Tommy my doorman commented as the car rolled up to the curb.

"Yes, sir." I held out my pathetic looking plant.

"Seems I can't keep a companion in my life. So, for the sake of this little guy, will you take him?" He smiled warmly and nodded. He knew I referred to Justin too.

"Sure thing, Ms. Winter. He'll be bright and happy by the time my wife is finished with him." He eyed the wilted, brown-edged leaves. "You make sure you come back in one piece so you can take this guy back home."

"I will, Tommy." I leaned in for a hug. "Thanks." I waved but stopped myself when Pam's face popped up in my head. "Tommy?"

"Yes, Ms. Winter?

"Justin is moving out, so I'd appreciate it if this was the last time he or anyone else is here."

"You got it." He gave me a reassuring smile as I slipped into the back seat of the car and didn't look back.

I blinked the memory away, and my brain tried to catch up with what was going on in the here and now.

"You need to calm down. I can't help you if I don't know what's going on." I tried to get through to the little boy who was now screaming at me to help him.

"*Necesito ayuda*," he cried again and pointed over his shoulder down an alleyway. I could hear a woman crying.

"Okay." I looked around. I knew I had to move on, but I was a sucker for a kid in trouble. This part of town was crawling with Cartel. I generally worked the southern part of Mexico and sometimes El Salvador if the story was there. I knew I only had about ten minutes to spare before I had to make the next checkpoint. I had to hook back up with the military team that looked out for my safety. I'd been separated from them, and my cameraman Ben Bale had been taken. Now I had no idea if he was alive or dead. I pushed his sister's face out of my head. Now wasn't the time to let my mind go anywhere else. He had to be okay.

"*Prisa!*" the little boy screamed as he ran down the alley. He spoke Spanish so fast I missed most of it as I chased him. His beaten-up shoes twisted and slipped on the mashed-up asphalt, and he had to use the wall to stop his fall a few times. He finally stopped and pointed through a door to show me where she was. I stepped into the poorly lit house and saw his mother propped up against the wall, sweaty, her hands held to her bloody stomach. I did a quick scan to make sure no one was going to jump out at me, and thankfully the place was clear. I noticed they had very little, just a tiny table, three chairs, and a torn couch in front of a super old TV. So, then, why shoot her? They had nothing to offer. When it came to a Cartel killing, nothing made sense. She was simply in the wrong spot at the wrong time.

"*Ayuda!*" he cried.

Shit.

I patted his shoulder then dropped to my knees in front of her. I huffed. A wound like that couldn't be fixed. I pulled out some narcotics I had hidden away for myself in case I ever needed them. I hated to give them up, but no one should die in that much pain.

"*Agua?*" I asked the boy for water, and he raced out of the room. I packed her stomach the best I could, but I could see her intestines. "*Inglesa?*"

"A little." She shifted in pain, and her face paled even more.

"What's your name?"

"Clara." I swore her eyes started to dim.

"Who did this?" I grabbed the cup from the little boy, pushed the pill into her mouth, and held the glass to her lips. She wasted no time taking the pill. It was probably silly to waste it, but I had to try to ease her pain.

"Cartel," she sputtered.

"Do you have a husband?"

"*Sí.*" She closed her eyes, but I shook her shoulders to bring her back. "He's at work."

"No sleep," I said to her then barked at the boy to go get his father. He hesitated with a look at his mother but then left. No child should see their parent die this way. "I know it hurts, and I know you're scared, but you must fight. Do you understand? Don't let them win."

"*Soy luchadora,*" she whispered in Spanish.

I pushed on her wound but knew I had to get out of here. "That's right, you're a fighter." I pushed a smile past my lips and hoped the boy would return soon with his father.

I jumped as tires squealed outside the door and the woman grabbed my hand.

"Run," she wheezed.

Zip, zip! Two bullets drilled into her skull. A cloth was whipped over my head, and I was hauled to my feet and dragged outside. I spared a brief thought for the boy who would come back to see his mother dead. Life was a cruel bitch at times.

"Stop!" I kicked at whoever I could reach and was rewarded with a clip to my head. I went limp as black spots threatened to drag me down. I fought through it and tried to focus. I was thrown into a vehicle and shoved from side to side as they climbed in next to me. The vehicle took off so fast my neck snapped. I found that strange. Normally, they had the local police so well paid off that they could move through the streets without a care. So, why were we in such a hurry? A glimmer of hope was that my military team might be on their heels. Of course, hope was just a dream in these situations. Hope was reserved for me to save myself.

I settled my mind and focused. The bag over my head was thin, and I could somewhat make out the two men in the front and one on either side of me. I couldn't see the road, only the bright sunlight.

I was trained for these kinds of situations, and it wasn't the first time I'd been taken. This somehow felt different.

One of the men put his hand on my knee, and a million nasty thoughts pushed through my mind on how I was going to kill him, but I knew better than to react. They wanted a reason to hit me. The Cartel were savages, and it was my duty to show the world just how savage they were.

A trickle of warmth went down my temple, and I knew I had a cut from the punch. Great, just what I needed, an open wound to get infected. I wondered if I could negotiate a doctor's visit with whoever had taken me. I practically laughed at the thought.

I finally lost track of how many turns we'd taken and how far we drove. I could only tell the sun was lower, my head was tired, but I knew I couldn't risk falling asleep with *Touchy Toucherson* next to me.

Just as sleep began to win, my head snapped back as we headed up a steep hill then stopped with a jerk. I was yanked like a rag doll from the vehicle and dragged inside what I assumed was a house. The grooves in the tile floor tripped me more than once as I fought to find footing. Then I was tossed down on my knees. The painful impact vibrated through my bones.

"Ouch!" I shouted and ripped my arm from the hold of whoever had it in a tight grip. "Get your nasty-ass hands off of me!" My temper often showed itself at the worst of times. It could be a blessing and a curse, according to my mother before she left. She carried the same trait.

"Tsk, tsk," someone said from in front of me. I tried to balance on my throbbing knees as I peered at a shadowy figure through the thin fabric. "If she can't walk, what good is she to me?"

His accent was heavy and pulled at a terrifying memory. I knew that voice, and my first instinct was to run. He had disappeared for quite some time but sadly was back. I was so screwed. At least if I'd been brought here for him, I figured I wouldn't be killed right away, and that only made it scarier somehow. I hoped he wanted me as a tool he could use. It wouldn't be the first time, and I could work with that.

"Bring her to the chair." Of course, Bruno spoke in English. He wanted to be an American so badly. He saw himself as different from everyone else here. Then something hit me. Maybe Sully Sanchez needed my help with something and had sent this worthless piece of shit to grab me. Sully should have known better.

Sully wasn't the best human being in the world, but he was still one of them. I'd put in a lot of effort to win that man over, and I felt he trusted me, and it gave me a little leverage within this tier of the Cartel. That was, after all, an important part of my job, to work my way into their lives and report back whatever I could. He seemed open to helping me, and I had long ago planned to use him in any way I could.

Stay calm and see what he wants.

I was lifted off my feet and dropped onto a chair, then the bag was ripped off and I fought to fast-blink my way to a clear focus. Once my eyes adjusted, it was like a bomb ignited inside me. Though I already knew it was him, he was the last person I *ever* wanted to see again.

"Ms. Winter, I've been waiting for this day. It's been a while."

"Bruno Perez." I hated to even say his name. My insides still reeled from the psychological blow at the sight of him. "I wish I could say the same."

"Do you still wear that perfume that smells like lavender?" His eyes danced as if from the memory of the first time we met. My skin shivered over my bones and tried desperately to slither away.

"I believe I smashed the bottle when I was finally free from your claws." My words dripped with venom. Bruno was a sick narcissist who had too much power at too young an age. He shoved up his sleeves, and I saw his left arm had been badly burned. The skin was rough and wrinkly. I wondered who got close enough to do that to him and if they were still alive.

"Lucky for you, I have some more." He snapped his fingers, and a man handed him the same brand that I used to wear. He squeezed the pump, and a spray of that haunting scent burst into the air. He closed his eyes and inhaled like some psychotic bastard while I fought the memory it brought.

He pulled back my hair and sprayed the perfume on my neck and shoulders. The tiny droplets clung to my skin. It felt like tiny pinpricks as it absorbed into my body.

"It's sad, really," my anger was at full throttle, "that you hung on to someone who despised every single part of you." He then grabbed a fistful of my hair and yanked my head back. His eyes widened, but I refused to show fear. Not with him; he fed off it.

"When people don't submit to me, I enforce it, Nicole, or did you forget?" I shoved his hand away as he muttered something I didn't care to hear. He moved over to a table and fixed himself a drink. Then he turned, leaned on the table, and sipped the amber liquid. I fantasized about smashing the glass and ramming it into his neck. I would be doing Mexico a favor.

"You have a reputation for finding people. No?" His anger dissolved from his voice.

"Do I?" I pushed my shaky hands between my thighs to hide my nerves. Bruno was undoubtably the most ruthless and youngest Cartel member ever to climb the ranks of their world. I knew it was all thanks to his mother and who her older brother, Martin Castillo, once was. He'd grown even worse after his uncle's empire was torn down by an elite group of soldiers. I'd never met the famous Team Blackstone or Team Dark Water, but everyone knew who they were and what they'd done to Castillo. I'd also heard rumors that they dabbled in some dark stuff to get the job done. As someone who had once had to do the same, I fully respected them for it.

"Apparently, you found Sully Sanchez, and he had

been, how do you say, *underground* for a long time. I hear you are," he thought for a moment, "*amigos*."

"Ha! Friends isn't what I'd call it." I scoffed and tried to settle the tremors I felt in my legs. "We have an understanding and a mutual agreement about some things, but that's where it ends. That's where the line is drawn." I didn't need him getting any ideas. My luck, Bruno would get jealous and kill off Sully, and then I'd really be screwed. I'd worked so long to gain Sully's trust.

"*Sí*, lines were drawn…" He huffed and waved me off like he thought I was lying about how close I was to Sanchez. "Regardless, Sully says I can trust you, so I trust you. I want your help."

My fear turned to anger, and my temper picked up as I caught his drift. "You've never had to ask anyone for help before, have you?" His brows pinched together at my outburst. "I'm just trying to understand the way you went about this." Why was it my brain screamed at me to shut up, but my mouth just kept going?

"If your men had just said you wanted to talk to me, I would've come." That was a bold-ass lie, but I'd fake it 'til I made it. "Instead, you shot a child's mother, bagged me, and dragged my ass here, without so much as an explanation. Now you stand here and ask for my help? Seriously? Let's try this again, shall we?" I clamped my jaw shut and died a little inside. *Christ, Nicole, you're asking to be killed.*

So many emotions ran over his face, but to my

surprise, he flung his head back and laughed. "Sully said you had a temper and a mouth on you. It's a shame you never showed that side of you before. I'd never have let you leave." Christ, he was crazy. "I had no idea you were this entertaining." *Great, I just caught his attention for the second time in my life.* "*Tienes cojones.*" He laughed then stepped forward and handed me a photo of a pretty woman with brown eyes and a big scar across her chin. She held a baby.

"They are?" I raised my eyebrows at him.

He pushed his hands into his pockets as he walked over to the window and looked out. "The two people you're going to find for me."

"Why are you looking for them? Are they your family?"

"No." He shook his head. "*Hay una recompensa por su cabeza. Entiendes?* You understand?"

"A bounty." I repeated what he said. I felt I must have gotten something wrong in translation, he said a bounty on *his* head. Meaning the baby?

"*Señorita?*"

"There's a bounty on them?" I repeated to get clarification. He didn't answer, so I changed the direction of the conversation. "Something tells me you don't need the money." I snickered, then reined it in when he looked over his shoulder at me. "Why would Sully recommend me, anyway? I don't do that kind of work. I'm a reporter, not a bounty hunter."

He rubbed his chin as he turned. "You have a way

to find people." He slitted his eyes. "If you want Ben Bale to live, you'll do this."

That stopped my mouth from firing off again. He knew where Ben was. My cameraman wasn't just anyone. He was a friend, a fellow man in the fight for truth, one who always had my back, and I his. I studied the photo and hated that Bruno had just won.

A fellow war correspondent who had joined the *Washington Post* when I did and arrived three months after me flashed in front of my eyes and spiked my temper. "Like how you dangled Elise Manny in my face all those years ago and she still ended up dead?"

"Let's not get into semantics," he grunted. "She could have avoided her fate but chose not to."

I cleared my throat and pulled my temper back. "I say again, this isn't what I do."

"You will find a way." He smiled down at me.

I licked my lips as my brain flew in all directions. I didn't have much choice, especially if I could help Ben. "If I'm doing this, I need to fully understand what this is about," I pointed at the photo, "and who they are."

"I will tell you what I know."

"And you will let me leave when this is over." I needed him to say it.

"As you Americans say, we will cross that bridge when we get to it." I started to protest, but he stopped me. "*Señorita*, you will listen, as time is not on my side." He sat down and started to fill me in.

By the time it was over, I had a totally new mindset on what needed to happen. More than anything, I needed to get to this woman before anyone else did.

THREE

BRUNO PEREZ

I hugged the bottle of tequila between my legs and leaned my head against the headrest. The party was in full swing, and my cousins had brought in every female within a fifty-mile radius. They were only a few years younger than me, but they made twenty-three look like the new fifteen. They were here because I needed their reckless souls to do my dirty work, and they were too damn stupid to see I was using them. If one of them should make me angry, I wouldn't hesitate to take their life. I smiled to myself, as I knew I had my mother's savage business sense, unlike these one-track pussy-ridden minds.

My phone vibrated next to me, and I swiped it up to read the text.

J: Everything and everyone in place, just waiting for the green light.

I closed my eyes, pleased with how things were shaping up. This would be the ace in my back pocket. Mama may take some of the credit, but it was mine to play. It had to run smoothly, and I knew the timing would have to be just right. It was going to be huge. I thought carefully about my words then responded.

Bruno: Hold tight and keep your head up.

Armondo lowered his phone and glanced at me from the rear-view mirror. "She's ready."

"Any word on the cameraman?"

"No." Armondo made an unhappy sound as he cleared his throat. "I'm sure something will show itself soon."

"Try to reboot it if nothing pops up in the morning."

"*Sí.*"

I pushed the mouth of the bottle between my lips and downed a few shots of the amber liquid. My eyes watered at the taste, but I was rewarded with a warm stomach and a lighter head space.

I spun the cap back on, tossed it aside, and hopped out. I was met with a wave of stifling hot air. September was brutal, but I'd grown up here and was used to the heat. I'd take it any day over the cold. I hated the cold.

"Perez." Armando, who was right behind me, handed me a cold beer. I didn't break stride as I wove through the trashy girls and horny guys.

A woman blocked my path. "*Hola*, Bruno. Want to have a little fun?" She held up a baggie of Ecstasy. "My mouth has a reputation, you know?" I remained unamused when she ran a hand down my chest to my belt. I grabbed her wrist and squeezed as a warning to back off.

"I find that hard to believe, Concha. You have that large nose to deal with." Her face fell. "Don't get me started with your teeth. Go find someone who can look past your face."

"*Chota,*" she spat, and I kept moving.

I walked around the side of the house where a table and a few chairs were in a horseshoe.

"You're late," Mama barked in English as her security parted for me to move through. "I told Armando to get you here twenty minutes ago."

"Well, I'm here now, Mama." I snagged a chip out of the bowl and squeezed some lime juice over it. "What can I do for you?"

Esmeralda Perez was a force to be reckoned with. One bad look from her, and you were as good as marked for death. She ran a hand down her long brown hair, and her rings glittered in the evening sun. Many underestimated my mama and her ability to get a job done. They were fooled by her rather pretty face.

Little did they know, she was more ruthless than her beloved brother, Martin Castillo. "Did you do what I asked?"

"*Sí.*"

"*En inglés, cariño*," she reminded me. Mama insisted that we all learn English since it was the language of our enemy. But I also knew she thought it was safer to speak English rather than Spanish with the kind of people who often surrounded us. A bunch of idiots who weren't to be trusted.

"English," I repeated with a nod. "Everything went as planned."

"And the photographer?"

"Same." I reached for another chip but instead decided on the salsa.

"And?"

I shrugged and pushed back how much I hated when she questioned me. "And I'm waiting to hear back."

"Look at how tiny they are!" One of my cousin's friends had ripped off a girl's shirt and laughed at her small tits. He tried to stand, but he was so drunk he toppled forward, hit the table, and sent drinks flying. Everyone nearby shouted obscenities and jumped to their feet.

"He's out or he's dead," Mama snapped, and everyone went quiet. I filled my bottom lip with chew. No one fucked with my mother.

Our family was powerful, and we controlled most of Mexico City. When my Uncle Martin was killed by those American fuckers, his empire in Rosarito was flattened, and we knew we could be in for a hell of a war. Mama was smart and had us lay low after the attack on Armondo and me. We let the people think my uncle's reign was over and that I was dead. We had waited long enough, and it was time to show the world we were back and to reclaim all that was ours.

"Where is Sully now? He needs to know…"

"*Agáchate*!" The man who had fallen and knocked over the drinks was on his feet again. He stood over the half-naked girl. I pulled out my gun and shot the fucker in the head. Mama merely took a sip of her drink and waved at my cousin to handle it. As the girl jumped up and raced away from the dead body, my cousin didn't move, and I saw his drunken face. I yelled at him, but he just shrugged and went back to his booze.

"Idiot." I signaled to Armondo to deal with the body.

"No problem." He grabbed the guy by his shoulders and hauled him away. We had pre-dug holes around back for such situations.

I glanced at my older brother, who sat far back from us but watched intently. He had a chance to be a part of this, but he refused to give up his current girlfriend, and it infuriated Mama that he put her before family and now as an outcast he's basically dead to us.

"Sully is doing what he needs to do. He's fine," I assured her.

"I don't have to remind you about how serious this whole thing is."

"No, Mama, you don't." *You remind me every damn time I see you.* "I have everything under control. We'll win this battle and then the next. They have no idea what's coming, and I intend to keep it that way." I spat some chew in a cup and leaned back into the chair. "Unlike the others," I glared around the property, "I know my role, and when we win, I will take my place at the top of the family and control both Rosarito and Mexico City the way it should be."

"Very good." She lit the tip of her cigarette and drew the embers back into the tobacco. "I'm tired of losing my family to those northern *cucarachas.*" Her eyes watered for her brother, and I knew his death sat heavily on her heart. "I don't care what else you do in this world after, but you climb this family to the top and destroy every last one of those Americans."

I leaned forward and took her hand. "I promise you, Mama, I'll cut out their hearts, their families' hearts, and jam them on posts around the perimeter of our property for all to see. We will take back our land once it's stained in their blood."

She blew smoke out of her mouth as she studied me with her dark eyes. "Make it rain blood, son."

FOUR

PAUL

"Uncle Paul?" Easton tugged at my shirt, and I moved my attention from Olivia's soccer game to where her brother peered up at me. "I need to pee." He shifted from foot to foot.

"Hey, buddy, I can take you." Savi started to stand, but I held up a hand. "I got it." I lifted Easton up like he was a football and tickled him as we raced off.

"Uncle Paul," his laughter rang out, and it made me laugh harder, "I'm going to pee!"

I spun him around before I set him on his feet and watched as his body dipped to the side. "You need to lay off the juice, my friend. You're starting to walk like your mama after a few glasses of wine."

"Huh?" He looked confused, and I shook my head.

"Never mind." I chuckled and opened the door to the diner across the street from the field. I tugged off my ball hat when a hostess greeted us with a friendly smile.

"Well, hello, there. Table for two?"

"We need to use the restroom please." I placed both hands on Easton's shoulders to show it was for him.

She scrunched up her nose. "Sorry, it's only for customers, but there are restrooms just down the street." I looked out the window and wondered how far down they were. I wasn't familiar with this town. It wasn't often Cole let Olivia participate in the away games, but he figured since we traveled to North Dakota so often and Mark had a shipment to pick up that we could attend this one. The fact that Olivia was beside herself excited made it doubly worth it.

I bent down to Easton's ear and pointed to the picture of the chocolate milkshake. "I won't tell Mom if you don't."

"Tell mom what?" He grinned, and I nodded for the hostess to seat us.

Once Easton saw where our table was, we hurried off to the restroom. I checked to make sure the coast was clear and gave him a fist bump as I left. He was old enough that I didn't feel he needed me to wait. The kid was at that age where he wanted to do things himself, and I fully embraced that as an uncle. Still, I kept one eye on the entrance and another on the side exit.

I picked up the menu and eyed the cheeseburger. It looked good in the picture, and I was suddenly hungry. I wondered if I should eat something, since we were to head straight home after this.

"What can I get for you, darlin'?" The waitress held up her notebook.

"Chocolate shake, cheeseburger and extra fries, please." I knew the little bugger would home in on my fries, so I made a defensive move.

"Coming up." She left, and I pulled out my phone to check in on my team. They were keeping an eye on Jerry Canos' compound in case some new activity started. There was a lot of unrest in that area of Mexico, and now that we pretty much knew Bruno was alive, I was damn nervous about what that might mean for us.

The waitress set the food in front of me, and I smiled, unsure I wanted to eat something made that quickly. I didn't think much more of it and went back to my phone. So many emails had come in from Frank. He wanted me to show off my new drone at a conference next month. My answer was always the same. No. I wasn't about to share my technology just so some government department geek could make their own version and cash in on it. My stuff was strictly for our teams to help save innocent people, and no one else.

Easton slid into the booth. "Feel better, little man?"

"Yup." He grinned and reached for my fries.

"Whoa, you wash those mitts?" I eyed his hands. At his enthusiastic nod I let him go at them. I heard the door of the diner open.

"No, thank you, miss. I'm meeting someone." That voice made my head shoot up and I instantly scanned the room. *What the...*

"Mr. Gates? What on Earth brings you here?" Something was seriously off. How the hell did he find me?

"Relax. Mike told me you were here."

"Why would he do that? How would he even know I was here?" He didn't answer that but glanced at Easton and head pointed for him to move over in the booth so he could join us. The look on Easton's face almost made me laugh.

Grim Gates was covered nearly head to toe in tattoos. Not like his Uncle Mike's, whose were all colorful. No, Grim's were black, gray, and white. Plus, Grim had this whole mafia feel going on and carried himself with a level of power that would make most people uncomfortable, let alone a child.

"It's okay," I assured Easton as he crawled under the table to sit next to me. His hand clamped down on mine, and I gave him a light squeeze to show it was okay.

"Hello, there." Grim, to my surprise, gave Easton his attention. I knew he'd recently become a new father himself. "I'm Grim." He held out a hand, and Easton looked at me. I gave a nod to shake it.

"Your hand's like a drawing." Easton admired it as they shook. "Uncle Mike has color in his. Why don't you?"

Grim gave him a lopsided smile. "I don't have a lot of room for color."

"Hmm." Easton shrugged and instantly relaxed. He dipped one of *my* fries into the whipped cream on top of his milkshake and became absorbed in the food. Grim turned back to me.

"I have my contacts, and I used them because I needed to speak with you. It's not something I wanted to talk about over the phone, and I've no idea where you live, so it was my only option." He paused, and his upper lip curled a little with distaste as he glanced around. "So here I am in Sunny Ridge, North Dakota." He lifted the edge of the sticky menu with the tip of his finger and then nudged the napkin wrapped fork and knife slightly toward the middle of the table. "Lucky me."

I'd run into Grim Gates off and on over the years, and we had a little history, but I'd never been able to get a good read on the man. However, he'd helped me out of a very difficult situation once back in Mexico, and I knew I could trust him. The fact Mike, one of my brothers, had told him where I was spoke volumes. I still had a lot of questions, but curiosity as to why he wanted to talk to me made me put my concern of how he found me aside.

I handed Easton my phone with a wink and opened it to a game I knew he loved but knew his dad didn't approve of. He grinned and began to play.

"All right, Grim, what's so important that you came all the way here from your fancy hotel in Vegas to tell me?" He glanced at Easton then back at me. I nodded and knew the boy would be checked out for the most part.

He reached into his breast pocket, pulled out a white envelope, and slid it across the table to me. "I was asked to give you this. You can read it later." He shifted in the booth and unbuttoned his vest. "Look, Paul, I know you thought Talya and I dated back then, but like I explained to you before, we were merely friends with a common goal, that of deceiving her parents." I was instantly uncomfortable with the mention of her name. "She needed me as a buffer, and I needed the in with Jerry and Elva. She was in love with you."

"That was a different life, Grim." I hated that her name pricked at my armor. "She's not a part of my life now. It's easier to pretend she's gone."

"Yes, well, that's why I'm here." He cleared his throat as if what he was about to share was hard for him too. "The night my brother was killed in New Orleans, Talya came to see me." He gave a glance at my face, and my skin grew cold. "She told me that she needed to get away from her parents."

"That shouldn't surprise you, Grim. We both

know she didn't agree with the business they were in." He nodded and tilted his head at me.

"Shall I continue?"

"Okay, sorry."

"She went to stay with her cousin, then her best friend in Mexico City, but later they moved to Campeche. They had to keep their whereabouts quiet, given..." His voice trailed off as someone came into the diner. We waited a beat, but it was just a mom and child, so we both relaxed.

"Why was she keeping her whereabouts hidden?" I prompted Grim to go on.

"Because she was pregnant." His face was neutral as I stared into his dark eyes. "She was pregnant with your baby, Paul." He used my real name, and that got my attention.

"Ahh." I couldn't speak. I was too busy doing the math on how that could be. Fuck, the last time I saw her...Oh, my God. I covered my mouth as everything hit me. "I need to see her."

"You can't."

"Who the hell are you to tell me I can't see her?" Anger pushed through my shock. "Give me her address."

"Uncle Paul, is everything okay?" Easton looked concerned.

"It's okay, son." Grim smiled at him. "Your uncle just doesn't understand something." Easton looked at me again, and I pulled myself together and gave him a reassuring look.

"Paul," Grim said quietly as he pointed to the letter, "I had made a promise that night I saw her in New Orleans, that if anything happened to her, I'd give you this." He pushed the letter closer to me. "All I know is that she was keeping the baby hidden from her family, because she didn't want it raised in the Cartel life. She did it so someday you could be part of the child's life, and not as enemies."

"Wait a minute." I looked at him hard as something he said clicked. "You said if anything ever happened to her. Is Talya in some kind of trouble?" He puffed out his cheeks and slowly let out a breath.

"Talya's dead, Paul," he said with a quick glance at Easton, who was busy with the game. The blood from my head drained into my stomach and threatened to make me pass out. "I don't know much, but I can tell you what I heard from Chili when I called him this morning." I blinked a few times and couldn't believe what was happening or that he and Chili, my old undercover friend, had spoken. "Jerry knows about the baby, but so do some other very powerful people. That child is going to be used as a bargaining chip for power, and then..." He looked away but continued. "Talya was a dear friend, so if you need anything," he dropped his card on the envelope, "call me."

"I, ahh—" I couldn't form a sentence.

"Just so the lines are clear, I'm not doing it for you. I'm doing it for her." He stood and looked down at me as my world spun off its axis. "Her father's desperate to find his grandson, so much, in fact," he ran his thumb along his bottom lip with a small hiss, "he had the nerve to ask me for help, and Jerry Canos never asks anyone for help. He even tried to push a million-dollar reward at me."

I pulled in my chin and thought how crazy that was when you considered it was Jerry Canos who tried to burn down Grim's hotel not long ago.

"Disgraceful," Grim muttered, more to himself, then looked at me. "They have a two-day head start on you. I suggest you read the letter then haul ass."

I looked down at the letter then back at him as he turned to walk away. "Grim," I called, and he looked back at me, "boy or girl?"

He cut his eyes to Easton then back at me, and I nodded. "Be careful."

I have a son.

In a foggy state of mind, I tucked the letter in my pocket, paid the bill, and Easton and I left to find the others.

Cole was packing up the SUV, and I could see his sore arm still slowed him down some. Savannah handed out snacks to the players. "We won, three to one. Where were you guys?"

"We got milkshakes and fries," Easton called as he raced to tell his mother.

"Cole," my voice was low and cold, "I, ah, I think I may need your help with something."

He immediately called Mark to take over. "Let's go chat over there." He pointed to a bench just off the playground. We walked in silence while I tried to pull my head together then took a seat on the snot-infested wooden bench.

"I'm not one for beating around the bush, so I'm going to lay it all out for you." I pulled out the unopened letter. "Grim Gates just found me." I pointed in the direction we'd just come from.

"As in here, here?"

"Yes."

"Shit, I guess that's what Mike was calling about. I missed the call."

I took a deep breath. "I think I know what Jerry Canos' men were freaking out over."

"Really?"

"Talya went to see Grim a while back because she was leaving her parents' business to go raise her child away from the Cartel life."

"Talya Canos has a child?" He seemed just as confused as I was.

"Did. I guess she was killed." I blinked away how much that hurt. "And, well, it turns out that baby is mine." I watched as he absorbed the information. "Yeah, that was my face too."

"Holy shit, Paul." He shook his head. "I'm sorry about Talya, but holy shit."

I nodded repeatedly. "So, as you're digesting that, here's something else. The word is out about him, and now my son is most likely the youngest child ever to be at the top of the Cartel's most wanted list. They'll use my kid as a bargaining chip." I wiped the sweat off my forehead. "Cole, if those monsters get their hands on him… Oh, my God. And if Jerry and Elva get him, I'll never have a relationship with him."

Cole rubbed his face and let out a long breath. "How old is he?"

"One and a half, maybe two? My head's too foggy to work out the math."

"Young enough not to be swayed in any direction." Thankfully, Cole's brain was already working out details. "All right, we've been under the clock before. We can do it again. Let's get back to the house and figure this all out."

"Cole," I knew it was a big favor to ask, but he knew I'd go there, "when we do this, I want to be part of it, and I don't mean the drone."

He saw Savannah watching us. "Let's talk at home and work everything out with the others."

"Yeah." It was all I could manage to say. We stood, and he turned to look at me straight on and put his hands on my shoulders.

"For just a second, clear your head of everything and really hear me when I say this." I nodded. "You're a father, Paul."

"Seems that way."

"You're one of us now." He laughed and clapped me on the back. "Listen, man, we're gonna get your son home safe and sound so you can raise him on the right side. It's really amazing that Talya did that for both of you."

He was right. I could fall apart over Talya later. Right now, I needed to get to my son.

PAUL

I paced by the door for the third time, and for the third time I chickened out and kept walking. I'd get to the end of the living room and turn back. I was never good at the whole "sharing my feelings" thing. Maybe that was because I never had anyone to share them with growing up. I never knew how close family could be until I met John, and then Blackstone, and then Shadows.

Keith appeared with his phone to his ear. I listened and used him as a temporary distraction. "I'm not sure what's going on, Frank, but this Juliet woman seems to be flaking on her shifts, leaving Liza to hold down the fort." He paused. "I've only met her once. I didn't get a bad feeling, but she asked a lot of questions—" He stopped mid-sentence to listen. "Just about me and the kids. I think she was trying to be

friendly, but…" I tuned him out. The distraction wasn't working, so I headed back toward her office.

"You're going to have to replace those floorboards if you don't come inside. Come on and join me already!" Ivy peered at me from behind her glasses. She lifted her son Hudson off the floor as Olivia appeared.

"I'm ready to take him for a walk," she announced to Ivy

"That's wonderful. I can't thank you enough, Olivia." Ivy smiled. "Do your best to wear him out."

"I will. Have a good session, Uncle Paul." She took the little guy's hand. "Hudson, I spotted some bunnies near the horses! Want to go see?" He shrieked with excitement as Ivy kissed his chubby cheek.

Ivy chuckled. "If he needs changing, take him to his dad."

"Copy that." Olivia waved as they left.

I cleared my throat and stepped inside her office. It was white and modern, but it oddly put me at ease right away. "Take a seat."

"Yeah." I sat on the edge of the sofa and flexed my palms together, hoping to relieve a little tension.

"Is this about your son?" She always dove right in. Ivy was brilliant at being blunt and straight to the point. That was how we operated here, and that was why she was such a great fit for the house.

"It is, yes." The heel of my shoe tapped the floor as I sat there and eyed up the moody housecat. He basked in the long fibers of the shag rug. His legs were flung open, and his manliness was on full display. I was still unsure if he was trying to impress but had to admit the cat had something to show off. *You do you, little guy.*

"I'm so sorry, Paul." Her comment drew me back to her. "I didn't know Talya, of course, but I wish I had. Losing her must be hard on you. If you loved her, then she was a very special person."

"She was." I rubbed my nose as a wave of emotion ran through me. "But even if she was alive, it wouldn't make a difference for either of us. We come from two very different worlds."

"You do," she agreed. "But that's never stopped a heart from wanting what it wants." She inched her glasses up her nose as she leaned back to study me. "You and Keith have a lot in common. How goes the dating pool?"

I laughed at that. "Shit, at my age, I'm lucky if a woman even looks in my direction."

"You're in your early forties," she drawled sarcastically, "and don't make me remind you I'm not that far off." I grinned, and she joined me. "Seems to me you were approached at Zack's the other night."

"Those were girls, not women."

"Fair." She scribbled on her tablet.

"Talya wrote me a letter," I blurted as I tossed it on the table between us. "I haven't had the balls to break the seal on it yet. It's crazy because we leave tonight, and there could be something crucial in there, but I just don't know if I can open that door again."

"Your head must be reeling over all this." She shook her head in sympathy.

"Yeah, she was so important to me, but the circumstances made it impossible. I had to push her away countless times, and that last time—" I let out a breath. "We still crossed paths now and then, and I couldn't help myself. I'd give in, and now look." I stood and dug the heels of my palms into my aching eyes as I paced. "I mean, this entire thing is fucking crazy. I never even knew I had a son, and now he's just lost his mother. He's God knows where in Mexico and apparently being hunted by the Cartel. I've been thrown into a race to get back someone who is half me before something terrible happens to him. I have to get my son." Just to say the word *son* felt strange in my mouth, but I knew deep inside I wanted him with me.

"Yeah," she nodded, "this entire thing is fucking crazy. And you're right. You, Cole, John, and Keith all have to keep your heads on straight. This is a deeply personal mission for all of you. In saying that, Paul, if you had more information to help with your game plan, wouldn't you use it?" She eyed the letter.

"Of course." I chewed the inside of my cheek as I looked at it.

She leaned forward and slid the envelope toward me. "Read the letter. Let Talya help you save your son. That was, after all, why she sent it. She knew you'd save him from the life she never wanted for him."

I still hesitated to reach for the envelope.

"Let me tell you, after the things I've heard about Grim Gates from our friends, Tess and Kenna, he's not a man who would stick his neck out and track you down if he didn't believe Talya had something important to tell you. I hate to spin it this way, but you're a father now. So, man up, grab your balls, and read the damn thing."

"Grab my balls?" I laughed, happy to shake off some of the stress. "Did they teach you that in school, Doc?"

"Nah, that was all Doc Roberts." She beamed as she stood. "I'm going to go get some coffee, and you're going to read."

"Actually," I moved to block her path, "could you stay? I mean, I'm not trying to make it awkward for you, but I really don't want to read this alone." I picked it up and handed it to her.

"Are you sure?"

"Yeah, I spent a decade living a lie down in Mexico, I couldn't share any of my real thoughts or show who I really was. All those, ah, vulnerable moments and the like. I had no one I could trust. I missed my brothers here, and it wrecked me to know they thought I was dead. Since I've been back among my family—" I cleared the lump from my throat. "Well, let's just say, now that I've got a son, I need to start opening myself up to people, and I want to start with this."

"All right, then." She sat back down, and I eased myself onto the sofa. "But if you want me to stop, just say the word."

"Yeah." I waved at her to begin. She ripped the side, blew a breath to separate the paper, and slid it out.

"Bear with me. It's a mix of English and Spanish." I knew Ty had been helping teach her some Spanish. She was quite good at it already. She had this.

"Eric, not to sound cliché, but if you're reading this letter, it means something has happened to me. It also means I can tell you the truth. I have entrusted Grim with this letter, and I know he will do as I asked. First and foremost, I'm sure he told you that he and I were never anything but good friends. He helped build a barrier between me and my family. My parents are not who they were when I was young. The vast corruption that blankets our beloved home has its claws in them now. I barely recognize them anymore.

"I had planned on leaving and forging my own path, but my heart was always with you. I always knew there was something different about you, but I could never put my finger on it. Maybe that was what drew me to you in the first place. I could see a goodness inside that heart you so desperately hid from others. I know now you pushed me away to protect me from whatever it was you were hiding.

"Which brings me to this. That night in the bar, on our last night together, we created something incredibly special. We will have a child, Eric. I don't know what sex it is, but our baby should be here sometime in April.

"If something has truly happened to me, please, Eric, you must save our child from the Cartel life. I beg you with all my heart to do this. I'm going to believe that the man I knew would die to save his own child from such a path. So, here is what you need to know. A copy of the baby's birth records will be left here." Ivy turned the handwritten letter around to show me there was an address. "Up until the baby is born, I'll be living with my cousin from grade school, then my best friend, Selena, in Mexico City, but after I deliver, we're moving to Tabasco. But if I think we're in danger, I'll head to my favorite place. Remember that trip we took when we first met, and we stayed with the one-winged dragon? That's where I'll go."

I saw Ivy glance over at me, but I shrugged as I desperately tried to pull up that old memory. It just didn't want to show itself.

"Eric, it is my heart's wish that our child will be kept out of the Cartel world. The baby will have a much better life with you. You need to get to our child before my parents do. This baby will be the first and only grandchild for them, so you know what that means. It also means there will be others who would take pleasure in getting hold of our child for their own terrible reasons. You must get there first!

"I'm so sorry we could never be together, you and me. How sad life allowed us to meet, only to continually rip us apart. At least something wonderful came from our love. Give our baby a life full of adventure, love, and safety. It's up to you now.

"Forever yours, Talya."

Ivy reached for a tissue and dabbed her eyes while my panic for time started to set in.

"Oh, Paul. She really loved you and sacrificed so much so that someday you could have a relationship with your child. If that isn't love, I don't know what is."

I sniffed and quickly dried my own tears with the back of my hand. I grieved the loss of Talya all over again. My heart wanted to slam that door shut, but I couldn't because I had a son to save.

"I think Cole should see this." Ivy pointed a soft pink painted fingernail to the addresses scribbled on the bottom of the letter.

"Yes, he does need to see it." Filled with a sense of urgency, I jumped to my feet and took the letter she held out. "Thanks, Ivy."

"Thank you, Paul, for letting me in to share this with you. It's a big step."

"I've gotta go."

"Yes, you do." She laughed as I ran out of the room and down the long hallway.

"Abby?" I called as I entered the kitchen.

"It's June." June was Abby's sister and just as loved as anyone else here.

"Hey, June," I kissed her cheek as I snagged a chocolate square from the cooling rack, "have you seen Cole?"

"He's downstairs with Frank and Daniel."

"Thanks." I handed off the chocolatey goodness to Olivia as she came through the door with Hudson then raced by them.

"Yes! Another!" I heard her squeal as I disappeared down the stairs.

Savannah stepped in my path, and her big brown eyes twinkled. "I know now isn't the time," she held up her hands, "so I'll say it really quick, then tuck it away for later when everything sets in that you have a son."

"Okay." I glanced around her shoulder, knowing every second counted.

"You will not be raising this child alone. He'll have endless family who will love him with all our hearts. We'll take the lead from you on how you want to do it, and if you'll allow it someday, we'll speak very highly of his mother, even though we never met her. Because," she stepped closer as her words smoothed my panic slightly, "if you loved Talya that much and she gave up so much, even her own family, just to keep your child away from a life of crime, she must have been an amazing woman."

"She was." I smiled. "Ruthless and stubborn but —" I shrugged, and Savannah's eyes lit up even more.

"I'm so sorry I never got to meet her. Something tells me she'd have fit in here."

"If only she wasn't part of a Cartel," I joked darkly. She looked down, and I knew something else was bothering her. "Out with it."

"You sure it's wise stepping over that border again? I mean, the last time you did that, you died." She made a face as if to say *you know what I mean.* "I'm still shocked Cole agreed to this."

"He didn't really have a choice because he knows I'll go with or without the guys. I wouldn't risk it if it wasn't for my son." *Son.* That was so strange to say. "Anyway, my appearance has changed a lot since I lived in Mexico. I've bulked up, I'm cleanshaven, I even had some tattoos removed and cut my long hair into this crew cut." I grinned at her as I pointed to my head.

She laughed. "It's definitely an improvement."

"Besides, Savi, most of the men who knew me are dead, and I had very few encounters with the ones who are left. I know the risks. I know they'll kill me if given the chance, but I also know that if they get to him first, it's over."

"I understand. Just promise me you'll come home safe, both of you."

"You have my word." I leaned in for a hug. "Thanks, Savi, for getting ahead of the storm, and when that moment hits me, I'll remember your words." I pointed to my head.

"Okay, one more thing." She handed me a small

black bag. "It's a few things you might need when you find him. Diapers, clean outfit, stuff like that…you never know."

I looked inside and thought how helpful and thoughtful she was. "Thanks, Savi."

"Of course." She smiled. "That's all. Now, off you get," she teased and let me continue toward the main conference room.

"Sorry, Paul?" Tommy Gear, Ty's team member from Dark Water, stopped me on the steps. "I can tell you're busy, but can I just…" He hesitated then put out his hand for a shake. "I'm leaving for Washington soon, and I wanted to say it was a real pleasure to work alongside you."

I shook his hand to clear the current situation from my head and granted him a warm smile. Gear's sister, who sadly spent her life in a wheelchair, had taken a turn for the worse. Frank offered to refer her to a doctor in Washington and helped move her and his mother there. After much consideration, Gear decided to join Eagle Eye's team and move to their new safe house that just finished being built. As much as Ty didn't want to see him leave, he needed to go. No soldier could do his job to its full potential when his head was worried about his family. I sidestepped that thought.

"The pleasure's all mine, Gear. You're a hell of a soldier, and you'll do great under Frank."

"I appreciate that." He waved. "I'll let you get back."

I hurried down the stairs and avoided a Nerf gun for the third time that day.

"Holy shit, dude," Mark's stunned tone told me he just heard the news, "this is so crazy. Paul's got a son." I caught Mike's look toward Cole as he shook his head in shock.

"And he's how old?"

"One-ish," Cole answered.

"It explains a lot." Frank pointed to the muted TV that replayed Jerry Canos' video of everyone scattering into the city. "If Talya really is," he paused and glanced at me as I entered, "gone, and her parents didn't know until now they have a grandson, they'll fight tooth and nail to get to him before anyone else. He's the first-born son in a drug lord's family. He'd be worth everything to them, and to a lot of others."

"I know we ship out tonight and what we have to do, but we're going in blind here. I mean, do we even have a place to start looking?" Keith asked.

"Actually, we do." I held up the letter and made my way over to the computer that was projecting onto a massive screen. I wanted to leave immediately but I knew we couldn't jump in headfirst. This would be a very dangerous mission not only for me, but for my son, and I needed to keep a clear head. We had no idea how many people we were up against. "Talya wrote me a letter and told me her plans." I typed in the address in Mexico City. "She had planned to be here," I tapped the screen, "until the baby was born. Here is where a copy of his birth record is hidden." I dragged my finger across the screen.

"Really?" Cole squinted at the location. "Interesting."

I nodded. "So, then Talya planned on living with him here." I typed in another address. "But she did say that if she got into trouble they'd go to a place special to her."

"Which is?" Frank asked.

"I'm not sure yet. It was somewhere we went years ago. I can't quite remember, but I'll do a little digging, and I'm sure it'll come to me. At least it's a start. Talya was a smart woman. If she thought danger might come, she'd make sure she had options. I figure if she saw it coming, she'd go to the third location, but if she didn't—" I eyed him with a worried look, and John put a hand on my shoulder.

"Let's not go there yet, Paul."

I nodded at my friend and pushed back the fear.

"Damn," Mark whistled, "she sure was one determined lady to do all this to keep the little guy hidden."

"It's impressive." Cole studied the map. "Smart lady to give us a direction."

Movement at the door had Frank quickly blur the screen as it slid open, and Savi looked in. She glanced around and locked eyes with her husband. "Excuse the interruption, but Benjamin Bale is here and has something to share with you all. He thought it might be important, seeing as you're leaving tonight."

"Okay." Cole flipped the file in front of him closed while I switched off the screen.

Ben's walk looked painful, and the torture the Cartel had inflicted during his captivity was evident.

"Forgive me, but I wanted to share this." He held up a tiny chip, and Mark held out his hand to inspect it further. "It's from my camera. I hid it before they destroyed it. As you might know, the teams we're paired with train us to hide our footage in any way possible. Lucky for me, the monsters who searched me didn't check under my busted dead toenail."

Mark's face paled, and he dropped the chip on the table like it scalded his hand. "My bologna sandwich isn't agreeing with me, suddenly."

"Maybe it's because you eat bologna," Mike scoffed as he pulled out a small device to project the images into the computer.

"Have you guys gotten any word on Nicole Winter?" You could see by his expression he was worried about her. They'd have had each other's backs in the line of work.

"Not yet." Cole answered.

"Okay," he let out a small breath, "she's got a reputation of being a badass, and at the risk of her kicking the crap out of me later, it's important to know she's actually a big softy." His voice cracked at the end. "She runs with the big sharks but wears her heart on her sleeve. You have to gain her trust before she'll let you in. I'm only telling you this because when you're over there, if you see her, she might need a ride home."

Cole started to shift through the papers in the folder. "What about the team that was assigned to you? I don't see where they came home."

"They were executed." He rubbed his shoulder. "I believe I was the target, and that meant they had to be killed." His eyes glossed and he stared at the floor. Something passed through Cole and Frank. Apparently, that knowledge hadn't been reported to Washington yet. "One of them was only twenty-two and had a pregnant wife back in Kentucky. I don't believe Nicole knows that they were killed and might be trying to head to the next pick-up point."

"Excuse me." Frank raced out of the office with his phone to his ear.

"Ben," I pulled his attention over to me, "what can you tell me about the Cartel activity in Mexico City?" We had our intel, but insight from a war correspondent's photographer would be invaluable.

"It's riddled with Cartel, worse than before, thanks to Pedro Perez, who just resurfaced after a few years. There are rumors that his son Bruno is alive, but I haven't seen that firsthand." I gave a quick glance at Cole. "If Bruno Perez is alive, that's going to be a real big problem for Nicole."

"Why?"

"Because she just spent the last six years gaining the trust of Sully Sanchez, who I now know was in the pocket of Bruno Perez. And if you know anything about Bruno and the type of women he likes, well, Nicole has been at the top of that list." He looked pointedly at Cole. "Your wife, to give you an example, would be just his type of woman, Mr. Logan. I hope for her sake she doesn't go on your missions."

"She certainly does not." Cole didn't miss a beat to clear that up.

"Good, because his last few girlfriends were found at the bottom of the ocean but not before he crushed in their faces. He's a horrible human."

"Has he had a run-in with Nicole before?" I was curious to know how much trouble she might be in if we did cross paths.

"Yeah, once before, when she was still new at her job. She wouldn't talk much about it, but whatever happened, it left a mark. She barely slept for a week after that and had these crazy nightmares. I just pray he's gone."

"It's a good thing we're aware of all this." John glanced at Cole. "Thank you, Ben. We'll take a look at your footage and let you know if we have any questions for you."

"Of course." He moved slowly toward the door but stopped. "I'm sure whatever you're working on now doesn't have to do with finding Nicole, but if she's still missing in a few days, do you think they'll send someone out there to find her?"

"If she's as resourceful as you say, chances are she'll pop up soon." Cole gave him a reassuring smile.

"But of course. Frank's already on it." He pointed to Frank outside the unfrosted doors.

"Thank you." He disappeared through the door.

Daniel flipped the screen back on. "Nice to know correspondents and their videographers still have a good friendships like back in my day."

John opened and closed his mouth then decided to speak. "Going back to tonight's mission, and I totally agree it's of the highest priority." He nodded at me. "It's about family." The guys all hit the table with their fists to show their support, and the lump found its way back to my throat. "We all know that every one of the borders will be swimming with Cartel, the airspace will be on high alert, and Jerry Canos made our faces public after the Castillo hit. Now we could potentially be up against Bruno Perez, and he's a major problem. I just want to throw it out there that if we do get our hands on this boy first, how in the hell will we get him back here?"

I spoke up. "I have an idea. I'm just not sure you're going to like it."

PRESS

I closed the folder and felt sick. These men were the definition of a monster. Bruno made Martin Castillo look like a damn saint, and that man was no angel from above. He was where he deserved to be—in the dirt.

"Now, you know the plan, you know what to do, so there should be no problem, yeah? I can trust you?"

"No one said anything about trust, Bruno." I used his first name, as I knew how much he'd hate me being so informal. His eyes narrowed on me, but I kept my expression neutral. "I'll do what you ask, but on one condition. You guarantee you'll let my cameraman go."

"You think you can negotiate?" He laughed.

"You obviously need me, or I wouldn't be here

right now." I raised my chin at the men around me. "Clearly, they're not up for the job." I smiled when they looked pissed. "If I do this, I want assurance that you'll leave me alone and let him go."

Bruno walked up to me and rubbed the side of his nose as he leaned in. It was clear he was embarrassed that I spoke to him that way in front of his men. Why I insisted on poking the beast, I'd never know. You'd think I'd have learned something from last time, but apparently, I hadn't.

"Here is what is going to happen. First…" I didn't see it coming but sure felt it when he backhanded me across the face. The air shot from my lungs and a bright light flashed before my eyes. "Second." He did it again but harder. The pain increased by ten. "Third, no one negotiates with me. I say when you leave, when you come, and what will happen. Do you understand?"

I barely heard him as my ears rang from the impact. I tried hard not to show how much it hurt, but it was hard given that Bruno had a mean hit.

"Go." He waved at the men, and once again a bag was shoved over my head, and I was yanked outside and into the front seat of a truck. "Don't come back unless you have the kid."

We took off down the road, and I was left to stew over his words.

Hours later, my face still burned, but not as much as my insides. My anger grew with every mile.

"We're almost there, *señorita*." The driver hit my

thigh to get my attention, and I jumped at his touch. "You know what to do?"

"Am I to do it blind?" I snapped, then the bag was ripped from my head. It caught my chin on the way off, and I yelped.

I felt a hand slide over my stomach, and I froze as my temper flashed through me.

"You touch me again, and I'll twist your balls so hard your great grandfather will feel the pressure," I barked at the guy behind me. I didn't give a damn if he understood what I said; he'd get my drift. I drilled my elbow into his wrist. Bruno apparently didn't trust me as much as Sully because he put these two men with me. They had zero boundaries when it came to their hands.

How in the hell did I get in this situation? Why did he want that child so badly?

"A *chica* with fire," the man purred to his friend behind the wheel. "That only makes me harder."

"Says a man with a lifetime of plaque on his teeth." I scrunched my nose. "How lucky am I?" So, they understood English. I'd keep that in mind.

"Want a taste?" He ran his tongue along his teeth, and my stomach heaved.

"I would rather pour acid in my mouth." I leaned my elbow on the windowsill and took a frustrated breath. I wasn't sure what was worse, Bruno or these two dipshits. I touched my tender cheek and knew Bruno was worse.

Around two in the morning, we finally stopped

driving and pulled into a small truck stop. "Sleep." The driver ordered, and I curled into a ball and fell into a light sleep without much effort. I was exhausted and knew if I didn't sleep when I had the chance, I'd be a mess and not on my A-game later. So, I took the risk and let my guard down.

Later, I woke to the sun, and we were in a different place with nothing but desert road ahead of us. I glanced at the clock and saw it was well into the early afternoon.

"Concussion make you sleep." The driver pointed to his head, and I tried not to stare at his blackened and broken teeth. I rolled my neck and stretched out my sore muscles.

"How much farther?"

"A while."

I opened the window to get some fresh air and wondered how I was going to get away from these men without pissing off Bruno too much.

I let my mind wander. When he finally pulled over into an empty parking lot, I quickly engaged my brain and looked around.

A motel sign blinked that it had rooms available. Something told me it was a permanent fixture. No one in their right mind would stay at this replica of the Bates Hotel from *Psycho*. The driver put the truck in park then flicked his wrist at me.

"I'm not staying here." I shook my head. "I'd rather sleep in the sewer than risk getting whatever the hell your mother gave you when you slipped out of the gaping hole she calls a man trap."

The driver rubbed his mouth and muttered, "I could do so many creative things to you."

"But you won't." I looked over my shoulder at the man behind me. He looked to be passed out, his stupor probably brought on by the tequila bottle still clutched in his hand. I weighed my options with the driver. "Because your boss Bruno needs me to find that child. Thanks to my connections, I can, but if you so much as lay a hand on me, you can kiss your job goodbye."

"You think you have Bruno all figured out, don't you?"

"I don't give a flying fuck about Bruno." I looked away. "I just want to get my cameraman back so I can get back to my own job."

"Do you really think he'll let you leave after?" He laughed darkly. "None of us get to leave." That was an interesting comment. He seemed to catch what he just said and tossed his cigarette butt out the window. "Go in first, ask about the girl. *La madre* was seen here after she left Mexico City. It is possible they know something. Once you get the details, book us two rooms. I'll be watching, so don't try anything."

I bit my lip and wondered why the child's mother would stay at such an awful place. I figured it was a waste of time, but at least they had power here, and power meant a phone. I needed to play this correctly.

"You think some loser who spends most of his day

looking through a peephole in the rooms he rents is going to remember some woman and her baby from, what, a year ago?"

"It's a lead."

"It's a stupid lead. Bruno wants me to use my resources to find the kid. This," I pointed to the motel, "is a waste of our time."

"Maybe so," he leaned over me and opened the door, "but we start here, and we stay here."

"Whatever." I grabbed my bag, but he reached for it and pulled it back.

"You try anything, and I kill you."

I yanked my bag free and stepped out of the truck.

The smell of rotten food and cigarettes hit as I opened the door, which made my eyes water. The yellow-brown stains on the curtains confirmed the tobacco use, and the wood paneled walls were peeling at the top and bottom. I hit the bell on the desk and cringed as the soles of my boots stuck to the fibers of the rug.

"You're an American?" a man's voice barked. I looked up at the camera and nodded.

"We rent by the hour, *señorita*. Condoms are in the vending machine out back. Do you want the honeymoon package or the birthday package?"

"Do you have a *burn this place down to the ground* package?" My voice dripped with sarcasm, but I reined it in fast as a massive man stepped out of the office. His stomach peeked out of his t-shirt, and his belt held on for dear life.

"She might not be much, but it's all I got." He dropped a logbook on the counter.

"You speak very good English."

"My mother was an American. What can I say?" He shrugged. "Your pimp give you that?"

"No, the dipshits in the truck did." I touched my face then pulled out a twenty-dollar bill. "I'm looking for any information on her." I put the picture on the counter and felt a shred of sadness, knowing the baby's mother was dead. Not that I was about to share that. "She's a friend of mine, and I think she might be in trouble." I got good at lying over the years. It was part of the job and one of the things that helped keep me alive.

"I get a lot of women coming and going from this place." At my surprised expression, he shrugged again. "I don't ask questions as long as they pay and don't destroy the rooms."

"I can't imagine many would come to this place with a baby. No offense."

He picked the photo up and held it close to his face. "Yeah, sure, I remember her." He slid the twenty off the counter, and I knew he was lying. "She said something about heading to El Salvadore."

I leaned forward and dropped my head into my hands with a long sigh. "Look, man, I've been through the wringer with those two morons outside. Things went from good to absolute shit once I hooked up with them. You want to know why I'm in this country?"

He shrugged but then curiosity got the best of him. "Why?"

I pulled out my press badge and handed it to him. "Finding her isn't for my job. She's my friend, and I need to know they are both all right. They," I pointed over my shoulder at the truck, "have their own reasons for finding her. That's a problem I haven't figured out yet, but they have my cameraman hostage, and I've become a pawn in this entire shit storm." I gulped in a breath. "Right now, I just want to know my friend isn't dead with an infant in her arms. I also need a hot shower and a bed, so I beg you, please help me out."

He studied the photo again, then looked outside, then back at me. "They did that?" He pointed to my face, and I looked away to drive the point home that I wasn't in a good situation. "How anyone can hit a woman is," he squeezed his eyes shut and I saw some compassion I wasn't expecting, "sick." He then opened his logbook, flipped back a few pages, and turned his back to me. I quickly scanned the page and stopped at the letters, TC. I traced my finger along the line and read room 402.

"She was nice." He held out a key. "The baby was cute too. Never heard it cry the whole time." He reached under the counter and set a cold water bottle and a prepackaged gas station sandwich in front of me. "It's not much." He shrugged.

"Thank you." I felt my eyes water at how kind he was.

"Carlos." He smiled. "Not many people come in and talk to me." His posture stiffened, and I knew I was about to have company. "The pimps don't like phones in the room," he whispered, "but if you look in the closet in the back behind the towels, you'll find one that plugs into the wall."

"You're a good man, Carlos. Thank you." I snagged the key and stepped back as the driver of the truck walked through the door.

"Evening," Carlos greeted him. "Heard you're looking for some rooms."

"*Sí.*" He glared at me. Carlos handed him a key, and I noticed it was for room 408. I appreciated that he put them a few doors down from me. "We're looking for someone."

Carlos nodded. "Like I told the lady here, I know what room she was in, but that's about it. She paid cash for two nights but only stayed one. I'm not in this business to ask questions. I just rent the rooms."

The driver grunted and looked around. "You know what happens to people who lie to me?" He leaned forward and grabbed the front of Carlos' shirt.

"Hey!" I stepped in to try to diffuse the situation. "I'm the one sent to ask the questions, and I'm doing it." I glared at him and held up the key to the room. "Let me do my job. Stay out of it."

The man's face flashed with something evil, and I swallowed hard but kept my eyes glued on his. He let go of Carlos then reached out and grabbed my arm and dragged me outside. I caught a glimpse of Carlos' terrified expression as we went by the stained window toward room 402.

"Let go!" I tried to wiggle, but he was strong. He nearly broke my finger when he snagged the key out of my hand to open the door. He tossed it on the table in the corner of the room and pushed me down on the bed.

I cringed at the spores that would have shot up from my impact on the mattress. I'd probably get an STD from the comforter. I could be a germaphobe if I allowed myself, but that kind of thinking didn't work for someone in my profession.

He opened all the drawers, then the bathroom cabinet, but when he opened the closet I internally panicked. I needed that phone.

"I need to eat," I blurted just as he was about to pull the towels down. "If you want me to do this, I will need to eat."

He cursed and slammed the closet door. "Stay here." He headed outside, and a moment later returned with a half bottle of tequila. "Eat." He chucked it at my feet then slammed the door behind him. I rushed to the window and watched him pull a chair over to my door. Then he dragged his half-drunk partner out of the back seat, and I heard him curse at him and point to the chair. The guy stumbled over and sat in it. I continued to watch until the driver grabbed his bag and went inside the room

Carlos had given them. One look at the drunk in the chair with his head now slumped onto his chest and I knew it was safe to find that phone.

I raced over to the closet, pulled the towels down, and felt around for the phone. My fingers snagged a cord, and I pulled hard and caught both the base and the receiver before it hit the filthy carpet.

For safety precautions, I turned on the shower and sink faucet for some white noise. I plugged it into the wall and nearly sobbed when I heard the dial tone. It rang and rang until I finally heard the asshole's voice. I started the timer on my watch.

"Can you speak freely?"

"Not for long."

"Go."

"Bruno Perez is alive." I waited for a response, but nothing. "He found me and wants me to find some murdered woman's baby. Whatever the hell it's all about, I'm in the thick of it."

"Location?"

"Mexico City. I'm in some dive motel—"

"Who's the woman?" He hated when I gave too many details.

"Her name was Talya Canos. There's something about this baby that's got a lot of people interested."

"As in Jerry Canos' daughter?"

I shrugged like he could see me. "I don't know a lot about who's who in the Canos family. You know I work the southern part of Mexico." I wouldn't pretend I knew information that I didn't.

"I'll look into it. Check in when you can, and get a phone."

I rolled my eyes but knew we had only a couple of seconds left before we could be traced. "'Cause that's easy."

"Nicole?"

"Yeah?"

"Don't die." The line went dead before I could tell him about Ben. It would have to wait until my next call.

"I'll do my best." I sighed as I unplugged the phone and put it back where it had been. Just as I closed the closet door, I heard a voice coming from— the bathroom?

"Hey, miss?" Carlos tapped on the small paned window, and I rushed to open it. It slid over only a few inches, but it was enough that we could see each other. "I've got something for you. I found it in her room after she left. Not sure if it's anything, but she was obviously on the run from someone. Anyway, I kept it. Not sure why." He slid a piece of paper and a map through the opening. "The map's from me." I quickly unfolded the paper and read an address. He'd circled where it was on the map. This man was gold. "I hope you find her."

"Thanks Carlos. You just gave me another place to check out." He smiled then stepped back to leave. "Hey," I called, "I won't forget this. Thank you."

"Take care of yourself."

"You too." I closed the window and tucked the

address and map into my boot in case I got company. I desperately needed a shower and took care to jam a chair under the doorknob before I undressed.

I tossed my clothes in the tub with me and stood on them as I scrubbed myself. After a good ten minutes, I'd worn the bar of soap down to a nub as I got rid of the grime on my skin then did the same to my clothes. I felt the need for food as my stomach grumbled, and my mind went to that prepackaged sandwich that was still back in the office. I decided it wasn't worth the trouble.

Shouts drew me from a dead sleep, but as I got up to look, a huge explosion sent me into the wall. As I lay on the floor in a daze, I put my arms over my head to protect myself from the debris that fell from the ceiling. What the hell was going on?

Bang! Another explosion went off. It seemed to come from the room next door. I army crawled across the floor, grabbed my bag and my clothes that I'd hung on the chair to dry. Somehow, I wiggled into my damp shirt, jeans, and boots and shoved the rest into my bag. I pulled out the tiny GoPro, Jack, my contact at the *Washington Post*, had gifted me a few years back and managed to get it in place. His words came to me. *You never know what you might catch when you're not looking for it.*

I crawled to what was left of the door and peeked outside. It was like a war zone. Dust hung heavily in the air and began to affect my lungs. I held my shirt over my mouth and nose as a filter.

Zip! Zip! Two bullets whipped by my head, and I ducked back into the room. My heart beat furiously in my chest as everything inside me screamed at me to run. I knew from experience that it was the worst thing to do. I calmed myself and reassessed the situation. I needed an exit plan. A blast from behind the garage bins decided things for me, and I bolted out the door into the open. I stayed low as I raced across the parking lot, and just as I reached the truck, I was grabbed around the waist and flung to the ground.

"Pequeña serpiente!" my driver hissed in my ear. *"A dónde crees que vas?"*

My adrenaline was at full throttle, and I used it to elbow him in the stomach, but he was ready for it and whirled me around, so we were face to face. "You think you can fight me?"

Zip! A bullet came from somewhere, and his body jerked, then he fell next to me. I didn't waste a second and began to dig through his pockets for the keys.

"Fuck!" I shouted when I didn't find them. Where the hell were they?

"Agárrenla!" a man shouted, lunging for me, but I threw him off, and I half stood and raced around to the driver's side. The touchy drunk guy lay slumped over the steering wheel with a bloody head. I ripped open the door, tossed my bag over him, and pulled his lifeless body onto the ground. I used him as a step stool to get in and slammed the door closed. My heart leapt as I spotted the keys on the floor. I managed to slide them in the ignition and got it into

drive. A man's face appeared over the hood of the truck, and I froze as he pointed a gun at me.

"Drive!" Carlos jumped in the front seat and banged on the dash. My foot tramped hard on the gas pedal, and I felt the bump as the wheels ran over him. I spun the wheel and whipped the truck around. I didn't care who I came in contact with as long as I got the hell out of there. Once I hit the road, I kept my foot hard on the gas to see how fast that truck could go.

"Holy shit!" I cried. "Are you okay?" I dared a quick glance at him. "Yeah, you're okay." My eyes filled with tears as I looked back at the nightmare behind us.

"Yes," he nodded a bunch of times, "I'm okay."

"Shit, we just dodged death." I drove blindly until I calmed down and could think.

Carlos kept his eyes on the side mirror like he was watching something or someone I couldn't see. It dawned on me that I didn't know him at all, and with my luck, he was a Cartel member too.

"Do you know who those men were?" I cut him a side glance.

Carlos rubbed his temples then made an attempt to pull his shirt down over his belly. "Maybe, I mean…" He huffed as he tried to find the right words.

I didn't have time for games. "Who do you think it could be?"

"I just don't know if they'd be bold enough to

cross territory lines. Maybe this is the beginning of a turf war," he said more to himself. "Maybe this is so much bigger than I realized."

"What is?"

"And now my home is gone and—"

"Carlos!" I snapped. "We were almost blown up back there. Tell me what you know so I can be ready if we're about to get company."

"Okay, okay." He turned awkwardly in his seat to face me. "About three days after your friend and her baby rented a room, these men came in looking for her. Of course, this is all Cartel land, but these men were from a different family."

"What did their tag look like?" Since 2015, Cartel soldiers were branded with a tattoo or *tag,* as they called it to show loyalty to the family they worked for. It was often found on their wrist so they could flash it easily.

"Three lines inside a box." I may not know much about the Canos family, but I did know that was their tag. "I'm in Perez land, and they wear—"

"A snake with a gold ring around its neck," I finished for him. Part of my job was to know these things.

"Right." He seemed impressed I knew. "Well, those men wanted to know what direction she left and to see her room."

"Did you show them the address you showed me?"

"Yeah, I did." He tapped his thigh and looked

uneasy. "I'm not looking for trouble but if those men risked everything to cross enemy lines to find that woman, I wasn't going to get in their way."

"I would have done the same." I wasn't about to judge him for that choice. The Cartel were ruthless and had zero regard for anyone's life. They were only out for themselves. "Do you think it was the Canos' soldiers who blew up your motel?"

"I have no idea, but what I do know is I'm outta here. Could you drop me off at the nearest bus station?"

"I can do that." I thought about the address and map in my boot. I wiggled my toes and could feel them still in there. *Thank God!*

SEVEN

BRUNO

"**S**on of a bitch!" I tossed my crystal glass across the room and watched as it shattered against the massive stone fireplace.

"*Lo lament—*"

"Nando!" I spun around and glared at the man I had ordered to drive the reporter around. *"Hablas inglés?"*

"Sí. Yes." He seemed to struggle to switch to English and lowered his head. I had no sympathy for the pain he must have suffered. His face looked to be half melted from the explosion at the motel. "We did everything you asked. How could we know that Canos had his people follow us?"

"You should have been on watch," I snarled and thought if he hadn't been with me for so long, I'd snap his neck. I remembered what I told Nicole about

Talya Canos, that she was dead, and that I wanted to be the one to find her baby. Everything came down to that fucking baby. She'd better realize that if she didn't come back with that child, I'd hunt her down myself and kill her with my bare hands. "Where's the girl?"

"She stole my truck and headed south. She's with that fat motel owner."

"*Qué?*" I stepped around my desk in a need to put a barrier between us. "Why the hell is he with her?"

"I don't know." He jumped when I slammed my fist against the fine mahogany desk.

"Mr. Perez," my secretary buzzed in over the intercom, "Mr. Sanchez is here."

"Yeah," I grunted. "I don't care what you need to do, Nando, but don't come back until you fucking find her!"

"Yes, sir." He raced out the door as Sully came in.

"Does he know he's got a fucked up face? Because he's got a fucked up face." Sully Sanchez eased into a chair, and I raised a brow at his comfort level in my office. "I know things took a dark turn but, Bruno, everything will be fine."

I crossed my arms at his assurance and my temper grew. "How can you predict such an outcome?"

"Because of what we have in place." He reached over and poured himself a drink. "You can trust Nicole."

"How?"

"Because I've tested her more than once. I even set up a big operation where if she had told anyone, the *federales* would have been all over it." He shrugged. "Guess what? Nothing happened. She has been well paid and has shown me her loyalty more than once."

"She has shown me nothing but disrespect."

He squinted an eye at me. "Perhaps it's your approach, *mi amigo*. Kidnapping, violence, the way you talk to her, perhaps it isn't the best way to win over an American reporter. They conduct business very differently."

I rolled my eyes at his soft approach. That was where we were very different.

"Where is she now?"

"You tell me," I snapped at him. "She was in her room at the motel under watch, and then there is a huge explosion, and one of my men is killed, and the other," I pointed at the door, "is missing half his fucking face. Now, I'm told she drives one of my trucks and is with the owner of the motel!"

"All right," he raised his hands to calm me down, "so have your man track her down. I can promise you she's still looking for the child."

I shook my head. "And how do you know that?"

"Because you have her good friend, and one thing to know about Nicole Winter is that she'll do whatever is necessary to protect someone she cares about. I know. I've seen it firsthand." At his words, I dug my teeth into my bottom lip. "What is it?" He leaned forward when he sensed my mood change. "Did something happen with the cameraman?"

"Those *pinches gringos* from the north took him."
His face lit up, a wide grin stretching across his lips.

"Oh, really?"

"*Sí*." I tapped my fingers on the desk.

"That's a good thing, then, yeah?"

"*Quizás*. In time… we'll see."

My phone vibrated, and I turned it around for him to see.

J: I have something for you.

"See," Sully beamed, "things are looking up."
I hit the J and connected the call.

PRESS

EIGHT

NICOLE

Carlos knocked on my window, and I jerked awake. I couldn't believe I'd fallen asleep. He held up a small bag. He looked all around as I rolled down the glass. Two men stood a few feet back from him. Instantly, I was on high alert, and for a split second, I thought he'd brought Perez's men to me.

"Who are they?" I pointed with my chin.

He tried to put my mind at ease. "My cousin came with his friend. You need to get rid of this truck. It might be tracked, so you can take mine. The keys are inside." He pointed to a rusty old blue pickup truck. "When you get to wherever you're going, hide it somewhere. You can text me where and I'll come get it." He waited a beat. "Take this." He handed me a flip phone. "This has pre-paid minutes. I was able to get you twenty. Sorry there isn't more."

"No," I yawned as I felt the weight of the last few days crash down on me, "that's great. Thank you."

He passed me the bag. "Water, juice, nuts, and some strange looking protein bar, but it's something." He shrugged.

"I appreciate it." I dove into the water since I hadn't had any in too long. I glanced around the bus station that looked to be out of service. "Where are you off to?" I glanced at his friends. As much as Carlos was a stranger to me, he made me miss my team. My mind flashed to Ben, and I truly hoped he was okay. I wouldn't put it past Bruno to torture him just for the fun of it.

"We'll head north. I might even go visit some family in the US. It's time I left this place."

"Might not be a bad idea."

"Can you drive a stick?"

My stomach sank as I climbed out of the blood-stained driver's seat. "Of course," I lied. I had driven one before and almost died, but that was a problem I'd just have to deal with.

"Good. She's a bit sticky moving into third but she'll get you there." He opened the door, and I slowly slid behind the wheel. The seat felt bouncy as I moved around. I started the engine.

He leaned in the open window. "Listen, I put my cousin's number in that phone as well as mine. If you get into trouble, and I'm over the border, at least you have someone to call. Stay safe out there. It's not a place for someone like you." He shook his head.

"Don't I know it." I waved then quickly sent my contact at the *Washington Post* my new phone number. Jack was a good guy, and I knew he'd be sweating it out waiting for word from me. I put the truck into first, but as I tried to release the clutch, the truck jerked forward a few times and stalled. I didn't look back as I started it again. This time I managed to get it to move and ignored the grinding when I put it in second. I pulled out onto the dusty road and hit the gas. I remembered his comment and ignored third gear completely and put it in fourth. I was thrilled when the truck didn't stall. "We're gonna do just fine, Rusty. We're one with the road." I grinned happily and propped the map up between the speedometer and the wheel and headed toward God knew what.

A few hours later, I'd finished all the stuff from the bag, but my stomach soon grumbled and begged for some real food. I fought with the gears and managed to pull over at a gas station where Rusty promptly stalled. I took a huge breath and started it again and was pleased to get the truck into a parking spot. I dug around for the GoPro camera. I knew I looked like death had beaten me with a dead cat, but that would only help sell my story. I got out and held up the camera. I made sure that the background was of the brick wall with its peeling paint. I didn't want anything in view that could tie me to a specific location.

I arranged my face as I pressed record. "My name is Nicole Winter, and I'm a reporter with *The Washington Post*. At 4:29, while I was following another story and was asleep in a motel room just outside Mexico City, there was a massive explosion. As you can see on this footage, two Cartel families came together over what we think was a turf war. At this point, I am unaware of how many casualties there were, but I can confirm the deaths of two Perez soldiers.

"I am happy to say that I was able to escape unharmed, and that I fully intend to find those responsible for this attack and publicly out them myself." I stared directly into the camera and hoped Bruno would see it. "I would say I'm sorry for those who were killed and their Cartel families, but that would be a lie. These people are monsters, and monsters deserve to rot in the ground."

I turned off the camera, used my little contraption to upload the video to the phone, and sent it off to Jack. Almost immediately, I got a response saying it would air within the next thirty minutes once it was approved. I leaned over the truck and let the pain caused by Bruno, his men, and the explosion flow over me. I let it remind me why I was there. I packed away the camera and knew I needed sleep, but that wasn't in the cards. I squinted into the sun as I made my way inside the gas station to get some food.

It took me a few hours and some testy moments with Rusty before I finally reached the town where I'd find the address Talya Canos had written. To say my head was on a swivel was an understatement, and by the time I got there, my shoulders were killing me from the tension I carried.

I'd made my career from chasing stories about the Cartel. I became an expert in forging fake relationships to get intel, and I wasn't above using whatever was necessary to get what I needed. Minus my body—that was never on the table. There had been victories, perhaps small ones, but victories, nonetheless. Somehow, this time it felt different, like there was a level of darkness headed my way, and I only hoped I'd see it in time.

I checked the address twice as I parked and got out. I looked up at the massive church that towered above me. It was stunning, with its fifteen-foot stained glass window that depicted angels and doves in bright sunlight, long, golden pieces of glass like the sun's rays looked to almost touch the Earth.

As magnificent as it was, something nagged at me as I walked up the steps toward the wooden doors. As I reached for the brass handle, I let my hand fall. It didn't feel right.

I turned and looked around. If Talya was on the run and worried she might be followed, why would she leave the address in the room? She would burn it, or flush it, or take it with her. Why did she book the room for two nights yet stayed only one? My mind spun as I rehashed it all. Had there been someone on her tail? Did she plan on staying only one night but made it look like two? What if she'd planned on leaving after the first night and had the room booked for someone else for the second, and was that someone supposed to find this address and would know what it meant?

"All right, all right, all right." I stopped my crazy spinning and looked around from the top of the church steps. "Why would I send someone here? Come on, Talya, talk to me." I scanned the area. "If I had a baby, what would I need?" I spotted a market. "That would be handy for diapers and food and such." I moved on to a taco truck. "That would be good for mom, quick food that took cash. Okay, so far, all that made sense to me. But what else? There needed to be a bigger reason. "Why bring someone here? If I were running from something or someone, I'd want to blend in…" My words trailed off as I spotted a sign held up by two concrete angels. Roughly translated, it read *Hope Heaven Orphanage*.

I hurried down the stairs and made my way toward the place. It took a few moments to find the door, as it was camouflaged by large shrubs. There were no handles, just a little intercom with a broken button at the bottom that dangled from some wires. I pushed the button back into place and hoped the wires were all still connected. I pressed it and waited, as I heard no bell sound come from inside.

"*Sí?*"

"English?" I knew many of the sisters who worked in Catholic orphanages spoke English.

"Name."

"Nicole Winter. I'm looking for a friend. She might be in trouble, and I think I might be too. Can I please come in?" I hated that I had to lie to a sister of the church, but I needed to find that baby before Bruno or someone else. No child should be used as a poker chip in some Cartel power game.

The door creaked open, and a nun peered down at me. "Are you alone?"

"I am," I promised. She stepped back and opened the door just wide enough for me to pass through.

"I'm Sister Margaret," she said as she slid a big bar across the door. "Forgive the judgement, but we need to be careful. We often have unwanted visitors. These children are vulnerable, and it keeps us on our toes. Please follow me."

"I understand, and thank you for letting me in." I followed her down a long hallway to a comfortable sitting room where two sisters sat bottle feeding infants. My heart warmed at the sight, and I fought to keep back my own tears. So many children were born full of love and hope and had no idea what kind of a world they were about to grow up in.

"Sister Clara, Sister Maria, this is Nicole Winter. She is looking for a friend who may be in trouble."

"Oh, dear." The wrinkles around Sister Maria's mouth deepened as she frowned. "What was her name? Perhaps we could help you."

"She would have come by about a year ago, and her name was Talya Canos." I noted a slight change in her expression. "She had her baby with her. I know she was running from someone."

"That name doesn't ring a bell." Sister Margaret didn't miss a beat when she answered, which instantly told me they knew something. "I'm sorry. We can't help you."

"Please," I held up my hands, "I know her last name brings fear. Normally, it would put mine through the roof too, but you have my word I have no affiliation with the Cartels other than it's my job to report to the world how horrendous they are. In spite of her last name, she's my friend and is a good person, and I'm only trying to help. She's in trouble, and the last time I spoke to her was just before she came this way. Please, you have to trust me. I'm scared for the baby."

"Trust is something earned here, my child. We have many under our care." Sister Margaret seemed to have made up her mind not to help me. "We don't know this woman."

"I've earned the trust of many." I pointed to their television. "May I?" The three of them hesitated, but Sister Margaret finally nodded. I turned on the small set and switched the channel to CNN. *Please work.* "I'm her friend, but I also work for the press." I nearly cried with glee when my video popped up. "See? I was there." I pointed to myself and then pulled at my shirt to show that I was still wearing it. "I was there when that happened at the motel this morning. It's about the Cartel. They are the ones who are looking for her."

"Then you understand our position." Sister Margaret's eyes found mine. "The Cartel often send people here. We have never seen this woman."

"Sister, please, I understand your fear. My job is to document the fighting between the Cartel families to help shine light on this never-ending war. I'm here to find my friend, yes, but also to help the locals get back a country that's rightfully theirs."

Sister Clara hugged the baby she now rocked close to her chest. "How did you know to look here?"

I reached back into my pocket and pulled out the address of the church. "Because she left this for me. I just didn't get it until yesterday."

"That address is across the street." Sister Margaret stood and waved for me to follow her back to the front door. "Thank you, for what you do. Please, Lord, watch over this child." She prayed, but I could see I wasn't getting through to her. "Now, Ms. Winter, it's time for you to leave."

I closed my eyes and dropped my head and pulled my oval pendant of Saint Jerome Emiliani out of my shirt. I knew what I had to do. I needed them to truly trust and hear me, so I recited the prayer. "Lord, I pray for your protection over my child. Send your angels to guard them and keep them safe from harm." I kissed the pendant of the patron saint of orphans and looked at the wings that were spread protectively around a baby.

Sister Margaret took a step closer to study the necklace, and then her eyes softened and her mouth turned into a sad smile. "Oh, child," she cupped my face and whispered, "amen."

"Amen." I repeated.

"Come, dear, not here." She looked at the other ladies. "Sisters, it's all right. It's time." They dispersed and a moment later joined us baby free in an office that looked to be little more than a storage room. Sister Margaret and Sister Clara pushed a cabinet along the wall to reveal a hidden door.

"The Cartel likes to keep tabs on our financial records. They want to know how many children, particularly boys, we have and their ages," Sister Maria explained as the other two ladies unlocked the door. "They're always looking to expand their army." She clucked her tongue. "We don't work for them. We work for the Lord, and he blessed us with this room to secure our valuables. The Sunday collections from the church next door, any valuables the children may have brought with them, also the identities of the children, and any other important documents we need to keep from prying eyes."

"Please come in." Sister Margaret pointed to a chair. "Forgive our mistrust, but you're the second person to ask about Talya Canos and her baby this day."

A heavy weight dropped into my stomach, and I fought to stop the panic that washed over me. Were the Cartels a step ahead of me already?

"Who else was here?"

"We have a rule here. If you're male and want to speak to someone, you must wait until the father can join us." Sister Margaret dug through some documents in her desk. "We've had too many close calls to handle the opposite sex alone. We simply explained that Father Antonio would be at the church tonight, and they can ask their questions then."

"Fair enough." I was happy whoever it was had accepted her explanation. Maybe I still had time.

Sister Margaret seemed to have found what she was looking for and put a file on the desk. She leaned back in her chair. "Talya was frightened." She put a hand to her chest. "She thought she was being followed and begged us for help. She said she might need to leave the child in our care."

"Did she say who was after her?"

"No, but in our experience, when a woman runs from her home with an infant, it generally means she's afraid of the father." I nodded. It made sense, statistically. "Talya asked to spend a few nights here, then one night she left her son with Sister Clara and left. We weren't sure if she was coming back, but the next morning she returned, thanked us, took the child, and left. That was the last time we saw them."

"Did she ever say anything that might lead to where she went? Or mention anyone she was meeting?"

Sister Margaret glanced at the others, and I knew there had to be more. Sister Clara gave a slight nod, and then the others followed suit as if in silent agreement. "She did ask us to hold on to this." Sister Margaret placed a hand flat on the file she had pulled out of the drawer. "And this." She picked up a tiny stuffed rabbit with floppy ears and handed it to me.

"She left his stuffed animal?" She really must have left in a hurry.

"I think she was more interested in making sure this," she pointed to the file, "ended up in the right hands."

"All right, what is that?"

"Her instructions were that someday someone might come for it."

"Who?"

"I'm not sure, but you, Ms. Winter, might be that person." She seemed to weigh her decision then slid the file and bunny over to me. I set the tiny stuffy on my lap and flipped open the file.

"Holy shit." My eyes popped open. "Sorry." I gave an apologetic smile then went back to reading the document. "Wait," I studied the birth certificate, "the child's father is listed as Eric Noah?"

The sisters looked at one another, and Sister Clara nodded.

"Yes, we looked into the man," Sister Margaret added. "He apparently held a position in the Cartel to the north."

"Yes. I definitely know him. He was Martin Castillo's right-hand man." I sure as shit had heard about that hit. Wow, the infamous human trafficker

Eric 'the Tunnel to Hell' Noah was the boy's father. That said a lot.

"I believe they are both deceased," Sister Clara chimed in.

"Eric Noah's body was never found," I mumbled as I absorbed the information then gave an involuntary shiver. "I'm shocked you know as much as you do." I looked at Sister Margaret.

"We may live in an orphanage, my child, but in these times, we keep ourselves educated about the Cartel. It has served us well." Sister Margaret put a hand on my knee. "These are dangerous men."

"No doubt. The only thing is if he's the one she was running from and I'm correct on my timeline, maybe Eric Noah didn't die in that explosion, and..."

"He could be still alive," Sister Maria finished my sentence, "and is looking for his son."

"Sister, you're absolutely sure Talya never said anything that might point to who this birth certificate was left for?"

"No, she just asked us to hold it and that someday someone might come looking for it." Sister Margaret rubbed the cross that hung from her neck. "If I've learned anything from being a nun all these years, it's that evil never truly dies. I won't believe this man is dead," she pointed to Eric Noah's name, "until I see the body." Her eyes narrowed on mine, and I felt she was warning me that evil was near. "There will always be a place here for you, my child," her eyes softened, "for you and for baby Eric."

"I bet she went to Campeche," Sister Maria blurted. "One night she told me that she wished little Eric could see where it all began. She said it had been a place where she'd felt happy and safe. There was something about a dragon who flew with one wing." She looked thoughtful.

"Dragon?" I repeated as Sister Margaret huffed.

"Fanciful dreams of a young mother. Don't confuse those with reality, Sister."

"She's only trying to help." I smiled at the younger nun. "Who knows, it could be a metaphor for something." I tucked the information away and stood. "Thank you." I smiled warmly and hugged them. "It's a place to start, and maybe I'll be able to find them after all." I said my goodbyes and headed back to the truck.

"Campeche is known for its historic fortifications, colonial architecture, and Mayan ruins." I kicked my feet up on the dash as I studied the tiny fact sheet. I'd taken it from the shelf at the gas station when I arrived in the city. "There's no mention of dragons, though."

I flopped my head back with a sigh and caught a glimpse of myself in the rearview mirror. I cringed at how swollen my face was. Makeup had helped, but nothing could hide the fact I was at the mercy of Bruno fucking Perez. I could only imagine how many men he had on the hunt for me.

Sure, I could call my contacts and have them get me out of Mexico, but that would mean my time here as a correspondent would be over. I could handle this and still do my job. I just needed to find the kid and hand him over to whomever then lie to Bruno that he'd been found by someone else.

A sudden memory flooded my nostrils of that Godawful perfume he wanted me to wear. It made my stomach roll violently. "Stop." I snapped, and the memory fizzled away. That was years ago, and I wasn't in that position anymore.

I glanced at the pre-paid phone and knew I needed to check in, but every call was risky, and I was afraid to waste my minutes. I looked at the time and waited for the second hand to reach the eleven then pushed the number. On the second ring, *he* picked up, and I mentally started to count.

"You're alive."

"Barely."

"You alone?"

"I think so." I looked around. "I'm in Campeche. If someone said they saw a dragon here, where might that be?"

Silence. "Let me see what I can find." The call ended. I eyed the bag of things I'd bought in a different city and pulled out a touristy outfit. I needed to blend. I wiggled into it then tossed the phone, truck keys, disposable camera, and paper map in a cheap wicker purse and set out to see what I could discover.

The air was chilly but not too cold, and my outfit of jeans, boots, and a white, off-the-shoulder sweater seemed perfect as I looked at the people around me. I inched the blue ball hat a little farther down to help hide my beaten face and put on a pair of dark sunglasses.

I walked slowly and stopped at a couple of vendors for some fresh fruit and nuts. While I paid, I casually asked each person about one-winged dragon pictures or statues in the area but was met with confused shrugs. No one had any idea what I was asking about. Perhaps the one-winged dragon Talya spoke of was just a personal fantasy of hers.

I walked for hours and showed Talya's photo to several people who looked like they might work there and weren't just tourists. Finally, when my feet refused to go any farther, I stopped at an outdoor café along the beach.

This was a difficult hunt unlike any I'd ever done, and I'd located more than one wanted Cartel member when no one else could. I prided myself on my success record. But this was different; I had almost zero to go on. I knew very little about this particular Cartel family. Talya was dead, and she was the only person who could be remotely recognizable if she'd ever even come to this place. Even the baby would look different now. I sipped my coffee and wondered what to do.

Part of me wanted to call in and say I was done here and head back to the States, but there was a baby involved. A baby without a family to protect him. God only knew what would happen if any one of these people got their hands on him. I wondered where Talya would have hidden the child if she'd been running from the father or someone else. I couldn't walk away.

I watched a diving instructor check his tanks and gear as he marked on a clipboard, then I smiled as a young couple kissed under a beach umbrella. It was a lovely place, and I could imagine spending time here. I sipped my drink and thought about ordering something to eat, but as I picked up the menu, something pulled my attention. I put my drink down and looked back at the diving instructor, who was in conversation with a rather handsome man. When I glanced at the man, he turned and walked away.

I gathered my things and decided to look for a hotel for the night. I made my way back to the truck and started down the coast highway. I rather liked this part of Mexico and made a promise to myself that someday I'd come back here. *Ha! Give your head a shake, Nicole.* I laughed out loud and opened the window. The sea air helped my head feel better. With all the shit I'd been through in the last forty-eight hours, I decided I would treat myself to an upscale hotel. I saw a place I liked and pulled into the Ocean View Hotel. They had some rooms free, the perks of it being off season.

As I headed to the stairs, I noticed the man from the beach again. He talked to one of the staff by the pool. *Coincidence?* In my job, I noticed things. Something cold washed over me, and I wondered if he'd been following me. I watched them as they began to laugh, then the man slapped the pool guy on the shoulder as he pointed at a far set of stairs. I relaxed a bit, as it was obviously a nice place. I'd chosen it, so why not him?

Once I got my things up to my room and checked out the place, I touched base with General Bruce in Washington. I needed to fill him in on where I was and what I was working on. He let me finish then told me about my team and that they'd been murdered. I hung up on him as he apologized and let the horrible news sink in. Once I got a handle on myself, I headed to the bathroom.

I skipped the shower and went for a hot soak in the tub that looked out over the ocean. I opened the large windows and invited the salty breeze in. With far too many bubbles, I sank into the hot water and gave a small cry at how wonderful it felt. The cuts on my skin stung, but I didn't care. I needed some pampering. I hadn't relaxed in what felt like eight months, and given the news I just got, I needed it. I pumped a nice amount of delicious-smelling shampoo into my hand then took a deep breath and slid under the water. I scrubbed my hair clean of dust and debris from the attack on the motel. The silence was almost too much for my thoughts to handle, so I popped up, leaned back, closed my eyes, and pretended this was my vacation, not my everyday life. Soon, I drifted off to sleep.

At some point, I woke with a jolt, and my

pounding heart reminded me of how stupid it was to fall asleep in a tub. I blinked away the fog and felt around the cool water for the plug. The bubbles were all dissolved now, and the little tea candle I had lit was down to the bottom of the wick. How long had I slept?

My stomach growled as I got dressed and dried my hair. Satisfied with the little makeup I'd applied, I headed down to the restaurant and hoped they were still open.

"Table for one," I told the waiter and followed him outside to a table under a heater. "*Gracias*." As he handed me a menu, I spotted the man again. He was talking to someone in Spanish by the large chiminea. I studied him carefully. He was tall, fit, and lean, and by the way he held himself, I wondered if he was law enforcement. He kept one tattooed arm folded low over his chest, while he rested the other on top and rubbed his chin as he listened. I recognized the stance. It was a tactical move, so they had their arms up, ready to fight if someone made a move. When he turned and looked my way, I quickly glanced down at the menu. A moment later, I looked back, and he was gone.

"*Buenas noches, señorita.* What can I get for you?" The waiter smiled.

"Shrimp taco and a margarita, please." His smile widened as if happy with my choice, then he disappeared and left me with one hell of an ocean view. I let out a deep sigh.

I remembered when I was a child how much I wanted to see the ocean, but I was twenty-one before I did. I'd never forget how cold the Pacific Ocean was, then a short time after that, I experienced the warmth of the Atlantic. TV shows had me screwed on that one.

"Want to tell me why you're following me?"

The man was suddenly sitting across the table from me. His strong jaw ticked as his gorgeous, dark green eyes narrowed in on mine. I swallowed and leaned back. He didn't seem threatening, but my stomach fluttered, and I thought about my words carefully before I opened my mouth. His chest and shoulders were quite broad, and his arm muscles gently stretched the sleeves of the t-shirt he wore, but not to a point where I thought it was intentional. He was intense, but I knew he was no member of a Cartel. He was far too American-looking. It put me at ease, and it came to me that I shouldn't let my guard down with this man. My danger radar was off.

"Funny, I was going to ask you the same question," I finally answered him. "You were, after all, digging around where I was having lunch."

He leaned back and showed he was as comfortable as I pretended to be. "Lunch would mean you ate something. You didn't eat. You sipped your drink, watched me, and left."

"So, you were watching me?"

"I watch everyone, Nicole." I quickly pulled in

my chin and sat back as I adjusted to his use of my name.

"If you're trying to intimidate me by using my name, it won't work. I'm on the news. I'm in people's living rooms, phones, and airports weekly. I'm used to others pretending they know me."

The corner of his mouth rose like he found what I said entertaining. "I was warned you were spicy."

I tried not to shift in my seat, but he caught it. Who did he know who thought they knew me? "Better you know now." I pursed my lips and tilted my head in a challenge.

"So, you admit I do know something about you."

"June 4th, Oaxaca City, New Year's Eve, three years ago. Could have told you that," I shot back, referring to the time I got into a fight with a local Cartel member live on air. "I got a raise after that."

"Or last year when you were in Mexico City covering the story on those kidnapped children from El Salvadore and you tore a strip off the police chief."

"That was a good one." I smiled at the memory of his red face when I told him he was live on air.

"But that's not how I know you, Nicole."

I leaned back as my food arrived. "Then how?"

"Tell me why you're here, in this town, and I'll tell you how."

I shook my head as I dipped my shrimp taco into a heavenly avocado dip. "A job."

His smile slowly faded, and I wondered what just went through his head. "Who hired you?"

"I'm press. I get my orders from Washington." I shrugged because I did work for the military.

"No one hired you to work this location."

"And you know that how?"

"Because you're supposed to be in Tapachula, not Campeche."

Everything in me bottomed out as his words sank in. Who the hell was this man? He got up and left with me more confused than when he arrived.

NINE

PAUL

“Excuse me.” I stepped away from a member of the hotel staff to answer Cole's call. I hadn't heard from him since the previous day and had been worried something might have happened. Daniel's reassurance that all was well had eased my mind only a little. “Tell me you got it.”

“Someone already picked it up.”

“The birth certificate?” My stomach dropped. “What? How?” I fought to remember my training and took a couple of slow, even breaths. This was on a whole different level than anything I'd been involved with before. I already felt the pull of what it would be like to be a parent. Fuck, I *was* a parent. *Breathe, in and out, in and out.* “Start from the beginning.”

“Talya didn't go to the church. You were right about that. She went to an orphanage across the street. The sisters wouldn't give us much other than confirming she'd stayed there for a few days. They told us we could wait around and speak with Father Antonio, but he didn't show up until this morning. They must have called him because he knew why we were there. We explained who we were and why we were in Mexico. Plus, we showed him the letter from Talya, and that seemed to soften him up a little."

"Good." I nodded like they could see me.

"Turns out someone came by yesterday, after us—"

"Who?"

"Some woman. The priest said she seemed to know Talya. I guess she left a mark on the sisters, enough to convince them to give her the birth certificate."

I rubbed my head. "My guess would be Talya's friend."

"That's ours too. I asked them to describe her. They just said she was slim with dark hair. Not much, but it might give us a clue."

I had no idea what her friend looked like, but Cole was right. Even the smallest detail could help. "At least we know Talya and the baby were there, and that's something."

The sound of an engine as it fought to change gears ground through the speakers. I wondered what the hell they were driving. "Damn this thing," I heard John complain.

"You have to baby her, John, go easy." Cole

chuckled. "So, tell me you found the place Talya talked about in the letter."

"Yeah, I'm here now. I spent the night and dug around a little. I haven't gotten much from the locals yet, but I will."

"All right, text me the address. We're on our way."

"Pastels, fedoras, and boat shoes," Mark hooted, and it made Cole laugh. I shook my head. You never knew what went on inside Mark's brain.

"Hold on, Cole." I spotted Nicole by the front desk. "You know that war correspondent Ben Bale was worried about? She's here."

"Nicole Winter. Really?"

"Mmm." I watched her show something to a guy, who shrugged at her then waved her off.

"I suppose it's not surprising. Frank said she's working in that area. She had a clip on the news about that Cartel hit on the motel. Ben was relieved when we told him. She's probably working leads."

"Hey, man," John's voice came through, "ask her if she's heard if Bruno Perez is alive. It would be good to have confirmation on that."

"Yeah, good idea." He had a point. She'd have a lot of connections, probably more than I even realized.

"Handing you back to Cole."

"Okay. See you soon, buddy."

"John's right. That's not a bad idea. Have you talked to her yet?" Cole was back.

I turned my back on Nicole in case she read lips.

"Yes, but not much, a bit of a closed book. She's a pro. I gotta respect that."

"Me too, but give her ten minutes with Mark and we'll see how true your theory is." He chuckled, and I grinned at how true that statement was.

"Did you give her much?"

"She was watching me, so I let her know I knew her. Just enough to bait the hook, nothing more."

"Good. Okay, I'll see you in a few hours."

"Copy that." I hung up.

I looked back at Nicole. She seemed to be studying something. Curious, I walked toward her. She stood next to the front desk and stared at the wall above the attendant's head as he answered phones and tended to guests.

She must have sensed me next to her because she pointed with her chin toward the emblem on the wall. "That's a strange looking shell, isn't it?"

I studied the oddly shaped shell for a moment and remembered Talya's words. She said she wanted a special way to remember this place. Our special spot, she called it. I remembered her smile as she told me what it looked like to her.

"Yeah," I said without thinking, "looks more like a dragon wing to me." Her eyes widened, and she turned to look at me.

"What did you say?"

"Well, it does, doesn't it?" I shrugged. She tapped her lips while I studied the bruises on her face. I was about to ask about them when she seemed to snap out of whatever trance she was in. The puzzled expression faded, and the intense gaze from her photo settled on her face. "Aren't you going to accuse me of stalking you?" I grinned, and she raised her eyebrow as she recalled our earlier conversation. "Or are you stalking me?" I raised my own brows.

"I'd have to know who you are in order to stalk you." She seemed at ease with me. "Or at least know your damn name."

"I've stalked people with less information," I teased, but there was a level of seriousness to my words.

"Good to know." She shifted her bag over her shoulder. She flinched, and I wondered if she was in pain.

"You take anything for that?"

She looked away with a huff then shifted her bag again, but more gently this time. "If you must know, the last pain pill I had, I gave to a woman who'd been shot in the stomach, then a few minutes later she was dead with a bullet in her head."

"Guess our worlds aren't all that different." I gave her a sad smile.

"Not the first punch I've taken and probably won't be the last. It's all part of the job."

Punch? I wanted to dig, but one of the workers I'd been trying to track down appeared, and I didn't want to lose him. I pulled out my stash of pills in their tin container. She gave it an odd look before she looked up at me again. "This'll help." I handed her two. "Take one now and one later."

"So you say." She made a face. "The last time I was given a white pill, I ended up in a drug lord's house in the middle of nowhere. Thank you, but no thanks." She stepped back.

"Do I look like I'm trying to drug you?"

"Well, you apparently think you know me."

"Oh, I do."

She rolled her eyes, and I found myself rather amused that I got under her skin. "You accuse me of stalking you, and now you're handing out pain meds from your pocket."

"It's just a gesture." I kept my eye on the guy I wanted to talk to. "Take them."

She shook her head. "Hot coffee and a walk on the beach are more my speed." She turned to walk away, but something ate at me.

"Nicole?"

"Yeah?" she answered as she turned back.

"You gave away your last pain pill to a woman shot in the gut. She'd never make it anyway. You must have known that."

Her mouth drooped and her eyes went from sad to vulnerable. "I had to do what I could. She had a ten-year-old son."

A rush of emotions went through me when I saw how much she cared about the local people. "I'm sorry she died."

"Me too, but it's why I'm here." She looked down then headed for the door.

Before Shadows, I'd met my fair share of war correspondents, and most were detached and more focused on filming everything they saw rather than on what was actually happening to the people around them. I understood it. It hurt less that way, but when we lost our empathy, I thought it made things even more dangerous. That was when tunnel vision presented itself.

"*Disculpe*." The man held out his hand. "The front desk told me you wanted to see me?" he finished in English.

"Yes," I smiled warmly, "I'm looking for my girl-friend. She went missing a while back with our son." I went with the family angle to pull at the heart strings. "The woman at the desk said you might know her." I pulled out a photo of Talya and the baby. He leaned down and studied it for a moment, but then his eyes went to slits as he studied me.

"How do I know she isn't running from you, *señor*?" His face hardened.

"No, no, she was here for a holiday, then she disappeared. Please, I really love them. I need to find them. I'd never hurt her or our son."

"Okay, *si*," he seemed to accept my story, "she was here for a time, but I have not seen her for a long while. Leonardo, who cares for our pool, he really liked the little one. He will be here," he glanced at his watch, "at two for work." He pointed out the French doors toward the ocean. "Pool is that way. You should speak with him."

"If you think of anything at all…"

"Of course." He nodded. "I think about it."

I spent a few hours in my room on my laptop talking to Chili about where Talya could have hidden our son.

"I have some calls out, to my boys in the south." Chili's presence over the video call was oddly comforting. He was my only link to my past life here, but the only part of that life I missed was Talya. "Something happened about a week and a half ago in Mexico City that sparked this whole witch hunt."

"Mexico City?" I asked, and he grunted his confirmation. "Any idea what that was?"

"No, call it a sixth sense, but something happened. Mark my words. It's ugly, too."

"Yeah," I dropped my head in my hand, "I feel that, too."

"Let me dig. If there's something to be found, I'll find it."

"I appreciate it."

"You know I got you. Always have."

"I know." I gave a quick wave and closed my laptop. I glanced at myself in the mirror across the room. I looked worn out. The creases around my eyes seemed to have deepened overnight. I lost the woman I loved for the second time in my life. But now I knew we have a son, and I would move Heaven and Earth to find him. I just needed to do it before his *grand-cartels* did.

My phone buzzed.

C: ETA two mins

I grabbed my room key and headed downstairs to the lobby to meet the team.

Holy Spirit Parish was sprawled across the side of the white van that looked to be on its last legs. I swore it wheezed as it came to a stop in front of the hotel. Mark jumped out first, and I pressed my lips together as the rest followed. They looked like a group from a Florida senior citizen home out on a day trip.

I eyed Mark's white boat shoes, pastel pink shorts, green button-up shirt, and cream fedora and had to squeeze my eyes shut so I wouldn't laugh out loud.

"Paul!" Mark slapped me on the shoulder, looked around, then took a deep breath of sea air. "If I start talking about early bird specials in front of the staff, I'm pretty sure I'll get a free dessert." Mark lived for his tummy. It was just another scar from his past which we all understood.

John, who looked exhausted in his equally awful pastel outfit, shook his head at me. "Four hours in a cramped van, that's a lot of Mark." I chuckled and nodded in sympathy.

"A church van, hey?" I asked as Cole came around to join us. "Forget I asked."

"We need to blend," he grunted as Mark ran his finger along the brim of his fedora, feeling every inch of his new look. "For the record, the outfits were not my idea."

"You sure about that?" I teased and mentally made a note. Savannah was going to get a kick out of that one. Cole's white cotton pants and green palm tree shirt were finished off with a shell necklace. *Nice touch.*

"I'm pretty sure I'm one confession away from a sainthood endorsement." Mark grinned, owning everything about his outfit.

Mike tossed his bag over his shoulder while he puffed away on a fat cigar. "Not too shabby." He nodded at the hotel.

"You guys'll certainly liven it up." I smirked at how his tattoos clashed with his matching yellow pants, shirt, and shoes. I looked around for Keith. He was still inside the van's open door. He seemed to hesitate to step out, and I soon saw why.

"Oh, shit." I covered my mouth as he eased out in a pair of green cotton capri pants that showed his lily-white ankles above canvas sneakers. His pink polo had white alligators all over it, and he wore a rope bracelet.

"Not one fucking word." He pointed at me. "Not one."

"Some of us embraced the undercover look, and some of us did not." Mark pointed at Keith and made a face.

"Watch your back, Lopez," Keith snarled as he rushed past.

Mark grinned at me, clearly enjoying every damn second of it. "He's just grumpy he didn't get your outfit." He handed me a bag, and I dropped it in horror like it might bite me. "The colors will compliment your skin tone." He winked and tossed his head then joined the others at the front desk.

There was no fucking way I was wearing whatever was in there. I glanced at Cole for help, but he signed for me to go change. I flipped him the bird but did what he said.

"Welcome to the holy party!" Mark cheered as I joined them at the pool a few minutes later, dressed in what the little shit brought me. At least I appeared the complete opposite of how I looked when I played the part of Eric Noah for ten years undercover with the Cartel.

I had caught my reflection in the windows as I strolled toward them. Keith rolled his eyes as jealousy radiated off him.

"I call it hot nights in Miami." Mark grinned at my blue loafers, white cotton pants, and blue shirt that buttoned only halfway up. My exposed chest was decorated with a massive cross that had fake crystals down the center. The pants left nothing to the imagination. I let out a huff. I'd gone from a Cartel badass, to Agent Paul, to Mike Lowrey in *Bad Boys*. Fuck me, I missed Montana.

Keith glared at Mark. "Explain to me why he gets

to look like Mike Lowrey, and I have to look like Captain Pantoliano."

"You have great ankles," Mark tried to explain with a straight face but dodged behind John when Keith went to punch him. He stuck his head out. "We're all jealous of your ankles."

"I'll get us a round." I turned on my heel and headed for the bar. "Four pitchers of whatever you have on tap, *por favor*," I ordered and jotted down my room number to be billed. I felt a sense of ease settle over me now that the guys had arrived, minus the ridiculous outfits. I'd never admit it out loud, but Mark always brought much-needed humor to otherwise dark situations. He was needed in a world like ours, and after the life he'd been dealt in the start, it always gave me hope that no matter what we had to endure, we'd be fine when we came out the other end.

"Damn." Nicole stepped up next to me and dropped her purse and duffle bag at her feet. I wondered where she was off to next. "When did Boca Breeze Retirement Home recruit you?"

"Funny." I laughed into the glass the bartender handed me as he poured beer into the pitchers. "It's a long story."

"And I bet it's a good one." She waited for the bartender to look over at her. "Mai Tai, please."

On cue, Mark arrived with his shit eating grin. I looked at John for help, but he shrugged. I knew he'd enjoy a Lopez shitstorm.

"Ah, yes, the famous Nicole Winter," Mark

purred and batted his long lashes like a teenager in heat. "I heard you met my buddy."

"Met would imply I knew his name." Nicole tossed me a scowl but then smiled warmly at Mark. "Nice to meet you…?" She waited for his name.

"Mark." I glanced at Cole, who gave me a nod that it was all right that she knew our real names.

"I must say, Mark, your outfit is rather fetching," she teased, and he gave me a proud smile.

"Don't encourage," I muttered.

"Did you like my nifty fanny pack?" He dragged the zipper along the tropical print pouch and pulled out a ChapStick.

"So help me, God, if you put that on…" I warned, and he rolled his eyes and zipped it closed.

She stuck her straw between her lips and drew the orange liquid into her mouth. "Is he always this grumpy?"

"Nah, it's just an act." I laughed, and Mark waved. "Get a few drinks in him and he'll ease up."

"I find that hard to believe." She smirked around her straw.

Mark grabbed two pitchers off the bar. "Come join us."

She hesitated. "I'm not sure if I should."

"Don't you want to know how we know you?"

"Let me guess," she chuckled, "from TV?"

"Nope." He walked backward with a grin toward the guys' table. She bit her lip and suddenly looked a bit uneasy.

I shook my head as Mark put the beer on the table for the guys. I knew he wanted to know what she knew, if anything. I was equally interested, and I still wasn't convinced she hadn't been following me.

PRESS

TEN

NICOLE

"**Y**ou don't seem like someone who'd be nervous to join a group of Floridians for a drink," he teased. This guy had an intensity about him, and I could feel his stress. He intrigued me. Who was he, and what did he want from me? I was almost positive he'd been following me.

"Tell me why you're here." I needed some kind of answer before I'd consider letting my guard down.

"Bible study." He didn't miss a beat, and I rolled my eyes.

"Forget it." I dropped some money on top of my bill and swung my bags over my shoulder.

"Fine, we're engineers for various construction companies, and we're here for a conference."

I pushed my sunglasses through my hair and shaded my eyes. "Wow, you're such a bad liar."

"Think what you want," he shrugged, "but don't tell me you aren't a little curious to find out how we know you."

"You're persistent, I'll give you that. Fine, but the least you can do is give me your name."

"Paul."

"Paul." I waited for his last name, but he just stared at me. "All right, Paul." I waved for him to lead the way. He grabbed the rest of his order, and I followed him to the table. The guys all stood while Mark pulled me over to a seat next to him, then Paul joined us.

"Everyone, Nicole," Mark jumped right in, "Nicole, this is Mike, John, Keith, Cole, and of course you've met Paul."

I repeated their names in my head a few times to make it stick. Then something hit me. I turned to Paul and chuckled.

"What?"

"I see why you went to the Bible cover story. You all have biblical names. Well, with the exception of yours."

"We get that a lot." Cole chuckled, and I took a moment to admire how handsome and fit they all were.

"Well, you got me here. Let's hear it." I leaned back in my chair and looked around the table. "Spill your secrets."

"Before we do anything like that," Paul said, "what were you doing at that motel?"

"At what motel?" That got my back up.

"Come on, Nicole, we saw the clip on the news channel."

"So, you do know me from TV." I raised my brows at him.

"Not only from there." Mark raised his chin at me and wiggled his brows.

"So, you want to pick my brain first before you'll tell me." I shook my head, annoyed, but not a single one of them looked about to budge. "Wow." So that was how they wanted to play this. Well, two could play at that game. "I see trust isn't easy for any of us, but I'm outnumbered here, so screw it. I was following a lead." I chose my words carefully and kept that part vague. "And it took me to the motel. Carlos, the owner, shared with me that he was working with the DSA about the struggles he was having with the GMP. I didn't think much of it at the time, but later that night, we were attacked." I waited to see if they'd get it. I tilted my head at Paul. At his blank expression, I looked around at the others. They all tried to hide their blank expressions and began to shift in their seats.

"So, it wasn't DSA or GPM?" Mike, whose name I'd never forget given his head-to-toe tattoos, tried to play off their confusion but screwed up the abbreviation.

"No," I laughed. I knew I had them. "Why would any of that have to do with an attack on some sleazy motel?"

"Any of what?" Cole tapped his finger on the table, and it drew my eyes to Mike, who sat next to him. Mike stretched his arms over his head. *Would you look at that tattoo.*

"Really?" I set my glass down harder than I meant to. "You guys are supposed to be the best, and to be honest, I'm a bit let down." Mark filled a glass of beer and slid it over to me. "Thanks." I smiled and then gave a dramatic sigh. "I guess you shouldn't meet your idols."

"Well, now I'm fucking lost." Mark tossed a hand in the air.

"All right, all right." I leaned forward and rested my elbows on the table and made no attempt to hide my smugness. "Let's start from the beginning now that I see what this is. So, Paul here accused me of following him, and I must be honest, he did catch my eye."

"Good to know," John chuckled, but I didn't look amused.

"I wasn't following you," I looked at Paul, "but you just happened to show up in two different places where I was. I found it odd but decided it could be a coincidence."

"Right," Paul huffed, and I glared at him. Christ, he was annoying.

"Later, Paul offers me some pain medication, which he carries in a GI spec matchbox holder. He also mentioned that our worlds were very similar, and add to that the fact you all look like a real-life version of Team America. And Keith," I smirked, "you're one strange look away from shedding that Godawful outfit."

"I take offense to that," Mark muttered, and John bit back a grin.

"Your point?" Paul cleared his throat.

"My point, Paul, is you lied to me. Engineers for construction companies, my ass." I held up a hand and used my fingers as I spoke. "DSA means Division of the State Architect and GMP means Guaranteed Maximum Price. Common construction terms, which you'd know if you were actually working for a construction company."

"Well, damn," Mark chuckled, "you're good."

"I'm not good," I sipped the beer, "I'm great. Just like you guys are supposed to be. Isn't that right, Blackstone?" All six men went still. You could hear a pin drop they were so silent. "And Mike," I figured I'd give one more example of just how good I was at my job, "when you flexed your arm, I spotted an angel, half black and half white. The black side has clipped wings and the white side doesn't." I held up my hands as he went to speak. "Please let me finish because this is good."

He looked around the table and shrugged. "Fine, have at it."

"I also remember the story of the famous Cartel family that got taken down by Blackstone. And how Salvador's daughter went missing. She had a distinctive tattoo on her back, a black angel. There was a rumor that she fell in love with one of her Blackstone rescuers, and now that I see your tattoo and connect the dots, here we are." I chuckled, proud of my discovery.

"Most people wouldn't know that information." Mike studied me carefully, and I backed off a bit.

"Most people don't study facts like I do. Plus, I was asked to do a story on her family." The tension in his huge shoulders loosened a little. I decided it would be in my best interest to lighten the mood. I needed them to see I wasn't a threat. "And now, here I am, sitting by a pool with a bunch of men dressed in pastels who resemble a box of saltwater taffy."

"Did she just call us taffy?" Mark leaned over and asked Keith, who just glared at him. "Well, color me impressed." He dragged his hand down his outfit. "I really like her."

"You'd like a skinless cat if it complemented your outfit," Mike grunted and made John crack up.

"I'm impressed but also concerned with how much you know," Cole said. It was clear he was the leader of the group, and his intense expression was focused on me.

"I'm very good at my job. I'm constantly research-ing, analyzing, and finding any back door, neighbor, or ex-girlfriend who can get me deeper inside the Cartel life. I've given up a lot to do this job, and I don't take it lightly."

"I respect that." Cole nodded and seemed to relax

a little, which in turn made me relax. "How did you get separated from your team?"

I let out a deep sigh, one I'd been holding forever. "I went to meet with someone I'd been working hard to develop a relationship with. When I got back to where we were supposed to meet, everyone was gone, along with my cameraman. I found out later, one of the soldiers had been killed and my cameraman taken hostage." I took a breath. "I was trying to get back to the rest, but..." I trailed off.

"And?" he prompted.

"Well, usually, when something like that happens, I'd lay low and wait to hear from them. Just this morning, I was able to check with my people in Washington and assured them I was all right, and I got the green light to keep going. That's when I discovered the rest of the team was killed." They were my friends, and their death screwed with my head and sleep. "Now I'm just worried about Ben."

"Ben's fine," Paul said, and I blinked at him. "We extracted him a few days ago."

Though I was beyond relieved to hear that, I closed my eyes and fought back the urge to go back to Bruno's place and drive a bullet through his heart. How dare he use Ben like that?

"Prick," I muttered, and Paul drew in his chin at me. "Oh, I didn't mean Ben." My head spun in circles about how Bruno had played me, again.

"Your injuries, are they from the explosion?" Keith's voice barely pushed through my rage.

"Ha!" I tapped my fingers on the table and tried to calm myself. "This would be the handiwork of Bruno Perez."

A cold chill settled over the table, and I wondered which Pandora's Box I'd just opened.

"Hang on." Paul's jaw ticked as he drew in a deep breath. "Bruno Perez did that?" He pointed to my face.

"Well, him and his friggin' waste of space men he calls soldiers."

"Fuck," John muttered.

"Yeah." Mark looked at Cole, who jumped up and put a phone to his ear.

I looked at the others as I tried to follow what was happening. "So, you thought he was dead?"

"Considering I blew up him and his driver last year, yeah, I thought he was." Paul snickered.

I dropped my head and connected the dots. "That explains the burn scars on his arm." My phone vibrated in my pocket, and I gave it a quick glance. It was Jack. "It's my contact at the *Post*." I shrugged and put the phone away. "I'll call back." I figured something must be up, but I didn't want to call in earshot of the guys.

"We should let Beckett and Moore know," Mike said, two names I didn't know, then jumped up with his phone in his hand. He stopped short when Cole rushed back to the table.

"Frank said there's some action four miles from here. John, grab our bags. We gotta go."

I quickly picked up my own bag. In my world, plans often changed like the wind, and if something big was about to happen, who knew if I'd be back? I stood when they did. I itched to see Jack's texts, but this was happening now.

"No," Paul shook his head and held up a hand, "this isn't press related."

"Says you," I huffed and didn't back down.

"We're an American special ops team, Nicole. We don't take tagalongs."

"Tagalongs?" I hissed at him. He made me feel like I was six, following a sibling to the movies.

"Stay here and stay out of trouble," he ordered as I fumed.

"Nice meeting you in person, Nicole." Mark, the nice one, stole a piece of bread off another table as he raced off. Paul was right on his heels.

"Jackass." I flipped him the bird then looked at my phone as I headed out the side gate.

> Jack: Major activity near Santa Clara. Sources say Jerry Canos was spotted.

I called him as I wiggled into my GoPro harness. Any Cartel presence needed to be filmed. I'd learned early that a missed shot was someone else's gain.

"Damn, girl, what do you see?" He jumped right in, which I loved. There was no room for small talk in our world.

"Nothing yet, but I'm getting a ride there now." I

waved, and a taxi's tires squealed as the driver pulled over. "Jack, I need an address."

"Yeah, umm," I could hear the clicking of the keyboard, "head south to Santa Clara, and keep along the coast. You can't miss them."

"Got it. I'll call you back."

"Stay alive." The line went dead.

I gave the driver the address and urged him to hurry. *"Apúrate!"* My excitement grew as we flew down the coast, the blur of the ocean from the corner of my eye a constant stripe of tropical blue. It was heartbreaking that such a beautiful country had such evil woven through it. Though the same could easily be said about America.

The car skidded to a stop, and I was barely able to brace myself against the seat in front of me.

The driver screamed at me to get out. *"Bájate!"* My stomach was still in my throat from his sudden stop. *"Bájate!"* he repeated and hit the steering wheel to get my attention. I followed his line of sight and saw why he wanted me out.

Nando, Armondo, the man I left for dead back at the hotel, had a gun pointed at the driver. His face was torn up with cuts that seemed to shimmer in the sunlight like some sort of demon.

"Muévete!" Nando waved his gun for me to get out, and when I hesitated, he pointed his weapon at the driver and drilled one into his chest.

"No!" I lurched forward and used both hands to press against the hole in his chest. "No! No! No!" I pleaded with any one of the gods above to save the poor man. "Just hold on," I begged, but then I was hauled out of the car by my ankle. I managed to grab my purse before my back slammed down on the bottom of the doorframe, then the wind was knocked out of me as I smacked down on the pavement.

"Nando!" someone yelled and got his attention. I took the opportunity to flip onto my stomach and try to get up, but he grabbed me by my hair and lifted me to my feet. The pain was intense, but I blocked it out thanks to the adrenaline rush that filled me.

"You think I wouldn't find you?" he yelled then pushed me forward, but I struggled to get my footing. His nasty hand clamped down on my arm, and he dragged me behind him. "I'm smarter than you!" He hauled me past his men who were in the middle of a gun battle. We were caught in a full-blown shootout, but Nando didn't seem to care whether we got hit by a bullet or not. "Why did you come here? Did you find *el niño*?"

"No, I didn't. I have nothing," I pleaded. The soles of my boots fought to grip the chewed-up cobblestones.

"Liar!" He shook me like I weighed nothing. "Those are Canos' men." He pushed me up against a wall and stood pressed against my front. His nasty face was inches from mine, and I had to turn my head to avoid his breath. He reached up and squeezed my cheeks then allowed one hand to drop down to painfully pinch my thigh. I yelped, and it dropped away. "They followed you here, yes?"

"I don't know!" I was as confused as he was as to how everyone came to be there. "I followed my gut, okay? You understand? *Mi instinto*, and—and—" I couldn't think straight, "and maybe they did too."

He suddenly turned and raised his gun and shot a man who ran toward us. "What do you know?" he tried again, and I squeezed the bag on my shoulder a little tighter. It was one of those times I wished I had a weapon in it. "You were at the orphanage. What did you find there?"

Holy shit. How did he know I'd been there?

"N-nothing."

"Liar!" he yelled again and spat at me, and I cringed at the spray. Then, without warning, we were both blown off our feet when an explosion went off close by. I hit the ground with a cry and felt debris cut into my side. I couldn't waste a second to feel what damage had been done. I forced my eyes open in the massive dust cloud that surrounded me and tried to see what was going on. I locked eyes with Paul, who stood across the way with a stunned expression on his face. My guess was it had been him who threw the grenade.

With a mouth full of sand, I coughed to catch my breath, picked up my purse, and stood on shaky legs. Instinctively, I looked down at the camera on my chest and saw the little red light was still on. Thank God. People would never understand how far the

Cartel would go to get what they wanted unless you had physical proof. Laws meant nothing to them.

I looked around for Nando, but he was gone. I hoped his body parts were spread in the street. Although I didn't think I would be so lucky.

I dashed across the street, the bottom of my shirt up to my mouth to act as a filter. Everything burned, my eyes, my lungs, my muscles.

"Stop!" Paul grabbed me around the waist and tackled me to the ground. "Grenade!" he growled into my ear, and a second later we were both rocked by another explosion. His heavy body shielded me from the worst of the blast. "You good?" he asked. His voice seemed far away, but I could still feel him on top of me. I nodded, and he jumped to his feet and kept low as he scanned the area.

I managed to sit up as my ears and vision fought to clear. He began to gather my belongings that were strewn about and shoved them back in my purse. I made it to my feet, and as he handed me my purse, he gave me a strange look, but before I could ask, he seemed to shake it off. "Come on. Stay low." He took my hand and pulled me to follow.

Bullets flew over my shoulder, and I cringed when one hit the wall above me. As we arrived at the main road, I pointed to the open door of the taxi. "I need my stuff from the cab." Before he could stop me, I pulled my hand from his and veered toward the taxi.

"I'm so sorry," I whispered to the dead driver as I pulled my duffle off the seat.

"Are you trying to get yourself killed!" Paul grabbed my arm and pulled me toward the road. Then, with a screech of tires, the church van stopped in front of us. The door was tossed open, and Paul pushed me roughly inside.

"Go!" he screamed, and the van groaned and wheezed as it did its best to speed away from the mayhem.

Paul's hands were all over me as I lay on the floor. He pulled up my shirt and checked my bloody side. I'd been through many battlefield situations, but never without a team of soldiers having my back. If I was honest with myself, I'd admit it had been a reckless move to show up without backup or a plan, and I knew better. I tried to rationalize it with my excitement of meeting Blackstone and the high of maybe discovering more about the child, but I knew I could have gotten myself killed.

Paul broke my thoughts. "She's good. Nothing that can't heal." His hands left my body.

"Copy that," Cole said.

"Nicole," Paul made me look at him, "give it to me."

I shook my head, confused. "Give you what?" My voice outed my nerves.

His expression had changed from concern to anger. "The birth certificate."

ELEVEN

PAUL

Nicole didn't answer and didn't move, so I grabbed her purse from her and dumped the contents on the seat. I had to steady myself as Cole swerved by a car and the engine struggled to regain speed.

"Hey!" She tried to reach for it, but I slapped her arm away and held up the redacted paper.

"Where did you get this?"

Mark leaned over in his seat and reached out to her to help her sit up. "You all right?" She gave a small nod then glared at me.

"I'm not going to ask again," I warned.

"Cole," she called, "please pull over. I want to get out."

"I will as soon as it's safe," he shouted and continued to fight the wheel. She braced herself as

Cole passed another car then managed to get on her knees and gather the rest of her things. She refused to look at me as she put her stuff back in her purse.

Cole slowed and took a big turn then pulled up behind a building. It didn't surprise me that he did as Nicole asked. He would never hold anyone against their will. None of us would, unless we had a good reason, as it went against everything we believed in and worked for. After Cole rescued Savannah all those years ago, he was particularly careful to make sure women felt at ease around us. In that moment, however, I didn't care how she felt. I needed answers, and she apparently had them.

I reached over and locked the sliding door, but she slipped through to the front seat and slid over and out the passenger side like water.

I ripped open the door and went after her. "Hey! I'm not done with you."

"Yeah, you are." She picked up the pace.

I broke into a jog and grabbed her arm and spun her around to face me dead on. I held the paper inches from her face. "Why do you have this? Why are you following me? Do you know?"

"Know what?" She tried to step back, but I increased my grip. "Let me go!"

"Answer me!" I shouted, and her eyes went glossy with tears. Shit, I hardly recognized who I was in that moment, but every second that passed was a second they were getting closer to my son.

"Whoa." John appeared and placed his hand on

my arm. He gave it a gentle squeeze. "Brother, I know," he gave me an understanding look, "but she's not the enemy."

I dropped my head and released my hold on her. John turned to Nicole.

"Are you okay?" She nodded and cleared her throat like she was trying to hold it together. "Look, you two, I know you have stuff to talk about, but we can't be here right now. There are bad people only moments behind us." He smiled at Nicole. "We're all on edge right now. This mission has been trickier than most, and whatever else is going on, you being here just tripped us up."

"This is my job."

"I know that, and I respect that. We've never worked with the press before, so you'll have to forgive us if we don't know the protocols. We have our way of doing things, and you threw us for a loop back there. C'mon, let's get back to the van and we can talk this out."

We all looked up as we heard a vehicle.

"Okay," Nicole threw another glare at me, "I need my things, anyway." She pulled away from us and began to stomp toward the van. "You can take the front seat, Paul," she called over her shoulder, "and no more manhandling."

I never agreed to that.

"John."

"I know." He slapped my shoulder as we followed her. "We'll find out what she knows."

"We need to find a new place to stay. Mark, check the maps." Cole was all business as he pulled carefully back onto the road.

No one spoke a word after that. Cole drove like the wind, and we all remained alert for any unwanted visitors. I kept my sunglasses on and watched Nicole through the side mirror. Her eyes were huge, and she turned away and looked out the window more than once to hide her tears.

I felt like shit for how I'd treated her, but she knew stuff I needed to know.

We decided to stay at a larger hotel to blend in a little better. Cole parked behind some shrubs to help hide the van and turned off the engine. He turned around in his seat and looked back at us.

"Nicole, we need to have a conversation about what's going on. It seems to me that whatever it is you're into, it's got you into a lot of hot water."

"It's my job, Cole. I can take care of myself. Thanks for your help, but I can take it from here." She reached for her stuff and made a move for the door handle.

Cole tilted his head at me and threw me a look as I went to grab her. I quickly dropped my hand.

"Look, let's help each other out here. How about you stay here tonight, get something to eat, some sleep, and give us a few minutes to talk in the morning. I think you owe us that much."

She pursed her lips as she considered his words. "All right."

Cole nodded then held out a card. "In the meantime, if you need anything, call me."

She didn't miss a beat. "I need a laptop."

"On it." Mark pulled one of our extras from a pack. It was secure, and I knew we could retrace her movements on it later. *Good one, Mark.*

"Thanks." She slid it into her duffle bag. "But I want to make something clear." Her voice was low and emotionless. "I'm here to do a job. I never asked for your team's protection, though I am thankful for your help back there, and I don't have to play by your rules."

"I know," Cole nodded and wiggled his hand for her to take his card, "but remember we're not your enemy."

"Maybe you should remind him of that." She chin pointed at me and snatched the card and hopped out.

Cole turned to look at me. "Maybe John or Mark should talk to her later. You need to work on your approach."

"No. This is my fight. She's got a copy of my son's birth certificate, Cole. I need to know how she got it."

"This is *our* fight," he corrected me. "If you want to get the answers yourself, fine, but you'll need to figure out a softer way to approach the subject."

I nodded and huffed out a deep breath. I knew Cole was right. We were a team, but I still struggled to get my head back on right, especially here in the field. I had been on my own for so long. I handled situations very differently when I was Eric Noah.

"Old habits die hard," John mumbled behind me as if he could hear my thoughts. "Don't forget who you are and that you always have been Blackstone. Don't forget your roots, brother."

"Look at your pants." Mark scowled at Keith. "They're ripped. I can't take you anywhere."

I rolled my eyes, took a deep breath again, and headed inside. I needed a shower and time to think.

As a team, we mingled with the locals during the evening, carefully showing Talya's photo to people. We asked if anyone had seen her or the child, but we came up empty. Mike had stayed behind to follow up on some leads with friends of his wife. Catalina knew the area well and had given him some numbers to call. He also kept an eye on Nicole, who apparently never left the hotel.

I checked in with Chili and Frank, but still nothing. It was maddening. I paced the room so much I swore I wore out the carpet. When I couldn't take it anymore, I headed down to the restaurant. I was desperate for something to do. I was going out of mind without answers. The morning couldn't come soon enough. It felt as though the Cartel were closing in, and I prayed they were no closer to finding my son than we seemed to be.

"Table for one?" the waitress asked, and I nodded. Her sympathetic glance made me aware I was showing my exhaustion and lack of hope. I mentally kicked myself and smiled. I ordered a beer and glanced at the menu. I had to eat something.

"I know, Jack," Nicole's voice came from the booth in front of me, "but if he wants the

footage, he'll have to be fine with some of the faces being blurred." I strained to hear her better. "I can't tell you who they are." She paused. "It's confidential. Look, I was almost killed today, my body hurts like hell, I've pissed off one scary-ass man, Bruno wants me…" Her voice cracked, and I heard her sniff. "Look, if he wants this footage, then he gets blurred faces." I heard the phone hit the table with a thud. "Shit," she huffed.

"You look like you could use a drink." A man with a heavy French accent stood from the table next to her booth. Clearly, he didn't pick up on her social cues, because even I could hear she was way past the point of being friendly.

"Thanks, but I still have some wine."

He didn't seem to be fazed by her rejection. "Maybe you'd like some company."

I heard the clicking of a keypad. "My boyfriend will be here any moment, but thanks anyway."

"Here's how I see it." The man eased into the seat across from her, and I lost sight of him. "You're a beautiful woman, and you've clearly had a bad day on your vacation, so I will do you the favor and wait with you until your *boyfriend* arrives."

"Wow," I mouthed as I sipped my beer. I had to

hand it to him; he was ballsy. My waitress started to come over, but I caught her eye and held up the menu then shook my head with a smile to let her know I wasn't ready yet.

"Tell me, ahh…" He fished for her name but continued when she didn't offer it. "Why are you here tonight? I hope it is for pleasure and not for business."

She let out a heavy sigh. "I'm really not interested in company."

"That's not what I asked."

"I know, but this is me declining your flirting. Like I said, I'm waiting for—"

"Your boyfriend. Yes, I heard you the first time. I'm simply asking what you're here for."

"There's a difference between being confident and being cocky when one approaches the opposite sex. One is intriguing, and the other is a turn-off. Can you guess which one you are?"

"Answer my question, and maybe I'll leave." His tone made my hand tighten around my glass. I spotted two men watching them. Everything clicked then. He probably didn't want them to see he was being rejected.

"Work. I'm here for work."

"What do you do?"

"You want to know what I do?" I could hear the fire crackle through her voice. "I find very bad people and make friends with them to get information. Then I use it against them later. I do very dangerous things at my own expense for other people's gain. I'm wrapped up in something so big and so ugly I don't see a way out, and now a lot of people are going to get killed."

The man laughed loudly, and I could only imagine the murderous rage Nicole felt. "I love how American women are so dramatic."

I pushed my beer away, stood, and loomed over the man.

"Sorry I'm late, honey." I tried to control my own temper as I rested a hand on her bare shoulder. "There was a problem, but we got it fixed." I stared at the man whose mouth was now twisted as he eyed his friends. *Do the smart thing and leave.*

"No problem." She looked up at me, relieved. "I'm glad you're here now."

When the man didn't move, I glared at him. Normally, I would be respectful, but he didn't deserve it. "Did you enjoy my girlfriend's company?"

"I did." He smirked, and my hand flexed on her shoulder. "She is a beautiful woman, but I feel her flair for the dramatic doesn't look good on her." He tried for an insult because he felt threatened and embarrassed. A sure sign of an insecure man.

"I never asked you to join me, and for the record," she leaned forward, and I let my hand drop away, "the next time a woman sends you a clear message that she's not interested, maybe you should listen instead of forcing yourself into her space."

He took a sip of his beer to drag out his moment

as if he thought he had some control over the situation.

I'd had enough. I knocked his beer out of his hand, grabbed his elbow, bent it outward, and slammed his head into the table. He yelped, and I leaned down so he could hear me.

"Leave before I break your arm in front of the men you're trying to impress." I nodded with my chin over my shoulder. I held on to him a beat longer to drive my point home. "You even so much as look in her direction again, and I'll show you exactly what *my* job is."

I roughly let go, and he snarled as he rubbed his neck. Thankfully, he was wise enough not to push me any further and rushed to leave the table.

The waitress came rushing over, and I handed her a bill for the broken glass. "My apologies for the mess."

"No problem." She looked over her shoulder at the asshole who now stood with his buddies, then she stepped back and motioned that she wanted to say something. I followed her a few steps from the table. Nicole threw me a confused glance. "That man is Gabriel Valentin, and he has been watching the *señora* since she arrived. He even asked my *amiga* about her. He works with those men."

Interesting.

"*Gracias.*" I headed back to the table, and Nicole gave me a worried look.

"What was that about?"

"Nothing I can't handle." She didn't need to know. I planned to keep an eye out for the guy.

To my surprise, she let it go. "Well, thank you." She looked exhausted and rubbed her head then flinched a bit. "How much did you hear?"

"Enough. May I?" I pointed to the seat the guy had vacated, and she nodded, so I slid into the booth. I remembered John and Cole's warning to be nice and that she wasn't who we were fighting against. "I think you and I got off on the wrong foot." I glanced at Gabriel Valentin, who was on his phone. He didn't take his eyes off us.

"Mm." She started to click away on her laptop.

"What are you working on?"

"I'm under a deadline to get today's footage edited and out to Jack, my contact at the *Washington Post*. CNN's reporter wasn't far from where I was, but they don't have what I do."

"Edited? Correct me if I'm wrong, but I always thought you correspondents sent in raw footage, and they handled it."

"Normally, yes, but," she turned the screen around, and I saw that she had blurred my and Cole's faces, "I'm meticulous, and I'm always afraid they'll miss one, and given who you are, I'm not taking any chances."

I liked that, and again I felt like shit for being so mean to someone who was making sure our identities were kept out of it.

"I appreciate that."

She closed the computer and slid her drink back in front of her. "It's my job."

I knew it wasn't all her job. She could have sent it and hoped her boss would do what he was paid to do and protect us.

"Paul, do you want to tell me the real reason you're here?"

The waitress came by and put some appetizers on our table. "On the house." She smiled. We thanked her, and once she left, I leaned toward Nicole and rested my elbows on the table.

"I think you and I might be after the same thing." She tilted her head at me and chewed the inside of her cheek as she waited for me to continue. "Trust is everything in our respective jobs, correct?"

"Yes."

"All right, this is me trusting you. I just hope you'll do the same." I went against my head and followed my gut. "Blackstone's been hired to find a missing toddler, one that if found by the Cartel will most likely end up dead in a matter of months. He's the grandson of the Canos family, but they only just learned about him a few days back." I waited and watched, but her face remained unreadable. She was good; I'd give her that. "Which brings me to you."

"Me," she repeated, not as a question but as statement.

"You've shown up in three places where I've been, and then today, when your purse spilled out, I saw a copy of a birth certificate. I realize now we might be searching for the same child. I need to know what you know, because at the end of the day, he's an innocent baby, and no baby deserves to be used as a pawn in a game of power." I held back my personal connection.

Her piercing eyes drilled into mine as she took a moment to think. Her slim fingers rubbed across her collarbone and drew my eyes to the delicate skin at her neck. A thin gold chain disappeared under her black tank top, and I found myself curious as to what might be on the end of it.

"If I share what I know," she said quietly, and I pulled my gaze back up to her eyes and gave myself a mental shake, "you have to promise me that you guys won't cut me out of this operation. You'll promise to share what you know, in real time, and let me continue to do my job along the way."

"I can't promise that." She grabbed her laptop and went to stand, but I swung up my leg to block her way out. "I've mentioned before that Blackstone doesn't work with the press, or anyone else, for that matter. Our training doesn't lend itself to that. We all know what we need to do, where we need to be at any given moment. It's how we get home to our families with a heartbeat. Babysitting someone as we go just isn't going to fly here."

"What's the difference between someone you've rescued verses someone you work with?" She had me there. "You're still doing your job while you protect them and get them out, right?" I hated that she had a point, but I didn't want to admit it. She let out a frustrated sigh. "You sure know how to be a gentleman one moment and insulting the next." She pushed my leg down and slid out of the booth.

Fuck. I dropped my head and wished I could shake the stress that sat heavily on my shoulders. I was a nice guy—at least I thought I was, once upon a time—but sometimes I didn't recognize myself in the mirror. Ivy said I would slip from time to time from being Paul to Eric. That I had to fight the urge to protect my real identity and remember I was me again. That was proving to be harder than ever since I discovered I had a son up for grabs with the Cartel.

My phone rang, and I dug it out of my pocket. "Hey."

"You in your room?" Cole asked.

"No, I was talking to Nicole."

"Good. I just got off the phone with Frank, and he wants us to let Nicole in."

I glanced at the door and thought how odd that was. It wasn't like Frank, unless he knew something we didn't.

"He didn't give me much." His tone told me he thought the same thing. "He said she's been cleared and that it would be wise to have her on our side. She's got some connections we could use through Sully Sanchez." I hated that asshole. "Should I send Mark down?"

"Everyone needs a little Mark in their lives," Mark chimed in.

"He never misses anything, does he?" I grunted.

"Nope, never." Cole chuckled. "So, do you want him?"

I looked up at the ceiling and knew I needed to make things right. "No, I got this."

"All right, check in later."

"Yeah." I hung up, swung out of the booth, and headed out of the restaurant.

The lobby wasn't too busy, but she wasn't there. I moved out to the pool area, but she wasn't there either. I headed to the front desk and brought up a photo of Nicole from the internet.

"*Disculpe*." I started to speak Spanish but stopped myself and remembered I needed to seem like a typical tourist. "Did you see this woman walk by just now?"

"*Si*," the man nodded, "she asked for directions to a clothing shop."

"Thanks. Which one?"

He gave me quick directions, and I headed outside. She was brave; I'd give her that. After what we'd just been through with the Cartel, she still had enough balls to leave the hotel to shop. I found the place easily and immediately spotted her as she stood in front of a mirror in a black halter dress. I suppressed my whistle as I studied her. The dress fit her body like a glove. There was a long, narrow cutout that ran from the neck down to her pelvis. When she moved, I saw her bare thigh peek out of a slit. It was sexy but elegant. Why the hell would she need a dress like that? I shook off the strange feeling that had come over me.

Her face fell as she saw me, and she whispered something to the woman helping her before she came toward me. She granted me one hell of a death glare as she approached.

"What are you doing here?"

"We weren't done talking." I couldn't help but think about how gorgeous she looked. "What are you doing in that?"

She looked down at the dress and shook her head. "Sully's having a party, and I need be there."

So, she really does have an in with Sully Sanchez.

"Wearing that?"

"Wow, thanks." She mistook what I meant. "A friend of mine gave me a tip and the guest list for a party Sully's having tomorrow night. Seems there'll be a guest my friend thought I might want to talk to, and if I'm going to find—" She stopped herself. "Let's just say I need to speak to him."

"What makes you think he'll speak to you?"

"Because," she purred and raised a brow, "he just so happens to enjoy American women." I could hear the disgust in her voice.

"When and where?"

She laughed darkly. "No, Paul. You made it perfectly clear where we stand. I work alone." She turned to leave, and I caught the back of the dress and saw it mirrored the front. The curve of her spine made my knees weak. Christ, I forgot what it was like to be around a single woman. I thought of the wives at Shadows. They were almost like sisters. Nicole was definitely not a sister. She was something else entirely.

"Shit." I turned away and hated the feelings her body drew to the surface. When I left Talya in Mexico, I promised myself I wouldn't look at another woman again because of what I did for a living. Life had proven to me over and over that I wasn't meant to find happiness that way because it always had to come to an end. Now more than ever, I needed to focus on anything but a woman. Especially one who would rather see me hit by a bus.

I watched from outside the shop as she bought a pair of shoes and earrings. She paid and headed out.

"You done?" I asked, and she rolled her eyes. "I figured we should get something to eat."

"I'm not hungry." She turned away, and I moved to block her path.

"Yes, you are." I didn't mean to sound knowing. "Everyone needs to eat, and we are not done talking."

She looked across the street when something caught her eye. "Let's go this way."

I wanted to ask what she'd seen but instinct told me to follow.

She seemed to relax and never said another word. We found a food truck a few blocks away and ordered some tacos. We sat at a table under some twinkle lights, and to my delight, she ate heartily. I hated girls who didn't eat; it wasn't real.

"I spoke with the team." I figured I should break

the silence since I shut her down last time. She kept eating. "It'll be an adjustment, but we'll work with you. More than anything, we need to be able to trust you and know you trust us."

"What's messed up is that you're an American soldier. You had my trust from the start. It was you who broke it. You accused me of following you, then you insulted me and yelled at me rather than just ask me about the birth certificate. I understand you're here to do a job, but so am I."

"Nicole, I—"

"Let me finish, Paul. I need you to respect my job and not belittle me because I don't wear camo and carry a rifle. We're all working toward the same goal, and until you can see that, I don't think we can do this."

I pressed my lips together and knew she had every right to call me out. I came at her in the wrong way, but she didn't know how personal this whole thing was. Not that I'd tell her.

"You're different than the other guys." She brushed her fingers free of cilantro. "You seem heavier, more uptight."

I nodded. "Maybe I've had more than my fair share of heavy."

"I can understand that statement." She sighed then reached into her bag and handed me an envelope. "One of us needs to start the trust train. I guess it'll have to be me."

I looked inside and saw my son's birth certificate.

It was the original. This copy wasn't redacted, and a million emotions ran through me as I read Tayla's name, then next to it, *Eric Noah*. I blinked away sudden tears before she could see them and swallowed hard. She'd named him after me. The old me.

"Thank you." I quickly tucked it in my pocket, worried that I would show how much it affected me. Suddenly, her eyes shifted over my shoulder and her expression fell.

"What?" I went to turn, but she grabbed my hand to stop me.

"We're, what, ten minutes from the hotel, nestled between two buildings next to a taco truck?"

"Right."

"So, what are the odds the man from the restaurant would be here?"

TWELVE

NICOLE

"Pretend to take a selfie and try and get a clear shot of his face." He handed me his phone. I smiled and pretended to pose and snapped a few in a row then handed it back to him.

"I'll send this to Cole to run through our database and see if anything comes up." I kept my eye on the sleazy French man and wondered how long he had followed me. "He still there?"

"Yes." I rolled up the checkered paper from my tacos.

"Tell me how you knew where to find the birth certificate," he urged. I didn't answer right away. I felt uneasy, and he reached under the table and put his hand on my thigh. My gaze went right up to his. "Relax. He's just watching."

"Right." I repeated his words in my head. "Bruno told me he took my videographer and would hold him hostage until I found that baby. It was obvious the child was someone pretty important. He also made damn sure I knew I needed to get to the child before anyone else did. He obviously wants him badly."

"And?"

"And two of his men took me to start searching. They had a possible lead on the mother. The guy with the cuts all over his face was the one in charge."

"The one who had his hands on you at the shootout?"

"Yes." I nodded.

"Give me the short version, Nicole." He wanted me to hurry my story along, but it was hard, as my head was everywhere else but where it should be.

"Then Carlos turned out to be really nice." I closed my eyes and got my mind to focus. "He's the owner of the motel. He bought my story that Talya and I were old friends, and I was looking for her. He shared that she had left an address in her room. After the explosion, I got separated from the others, so I headed that way."

"Seems odd she'd do that."

"Do what?" I focused on him again.

"Leave an address there. You think it was on purpose?"

"Maybe." I shrugged and sneaked a look at the

French man. "She did book that room for two nights and only stayed for one. If you're running from someone and you leave an address for someone else, you'd sure run the risk of the bad guy seeing it."

"Yeah." He looked thoughtful. "So, you keep it vague and give a landmark and hope that the person who you do want to find it can figure it out."

"Exactly." I raised my brows to show we were on the same wavelength. "So, when I got to the address she left, which was a church, I put myself in her shoes and thought where I would go with a newborn."

"The orphanage." He nodded like he was impressed. "We thought the same thing."

I drew in my chin at his comment. "You knew about the orphanage?"

He rubbed his lip like he was going to lie but changed his mind. "We had some intel too, but the guys couldn't get past the sisters. How did you?"

I didn't know why, but I felt like I might have missed something. I knew Blackstone had incredible resources, but there was something closed off about Paul, and it made me wonder. "Have you met Talya before?"

He shook his head. "No. How did you get past the sisters?"

I went to touch my pendant but rubbed the side of my neck instead. My past wasn't part of this. "I guess my story was good enough it played on their hearts. I think they could see I wasn't looking to hurt them, only to find them."

"The fact that you're a woman probably helped." He nodded. "I can't say I would blame them for that."

"Yeah," I had to agree, "and that's when one of them mentioned that Talya wanted her son to see where everything had begun or something and mentioned a one-winged dragon in Campeche. I just stumbled upon that hotel with the shell logo, and when you mentioned that it looked like the wing, I realized I'd found the place." I shook my head, still in disbelief at my luck. "How did you know to look there too?"

"Intel." He didn't offer more.

"For someone who wants me to share what I know, you're pretty guarded with your own details."

Before he could reply, I felt my heart jump into my throat when I saw the French man heading toward us. "He's coming."

"Grab your bags." He stood, and we hurried around the food truck and out into another street with more vendors. "This way," he said over his shoulder.

For such a big guy, he was quick on his feet. The street was busy with locals, so we stuck out as tourists. I wasn't familiar with the streets in Campeche, so I had to rely on Paul for direction. People called out as we went by to try to sell us something, and I tried my best to be polite as we hurried past them. Some were downright pushy, desperate to sell something. A man grabbed the edge of my shirt trying to sell me some shoes, and I tried to say no and pull away, but he wasn't having it.

"Paul!" I called, and he reached between us, took my hand, then pulled my shirt from the man's grasp. He pulled me close to his side and kept one hand on my hip and the other out straight to make a path for us.

"Here," he ordered, and we ducked into a fish market. He shielded me from view of the door as I fought to catch my breath. I was in shape and took pride in my endurance, but my breath came in nervous gasps and my stomach was in knots.

"Paul." I squeezed his arm when I spotted the French man step into the fish market.

"Impossible." Paul looked down at me, then his eyes narrowed in on my purse. He slipped it off my shoulder, bent down, and emptied it on top of a freezer.

"What are you doing?" He opened my makeup bag and fished around inside. I grabbed my mascara as it rolled off the top. "Hey! I don't have much, so —" He held up a small flat thing, the size of a quarter, with a lion's head engraved it in. "Is that a tracking device?"

He snapped a few photos of it then tucked it in his pocket and looked around while I grabbed all my stuff and shoved it back inside my purse. He grabbed my arm and whisked us back outside.

"Okay, let's get back to the hotel," he grunted.

"Paul, was that a tracking device?" I'd seen them

before, but none had looked quite like the one he'd found. He didn't answer, and I knew it wasn't time to argue.

"Cole," his phone was to his ear, "she was bugged." He paused as he listened. "All right." He hung up then he picked up speed, and I fought to keep up.

"What did Cole say?" Again, I got silence. I curbed my temper momentarily.

My legs and feet killed me by the time we made it back to the hotel, but I wasn't about to complain. I needed to show I could keep up. That I was one of them. I glanced down at the new dress still draped over my arm and felt bad the fabric was now a wrinkled clump. I didn't have many pretty things, because I basically lived out of a knapsack. I always tried to convince myself I didn't care about material things, but the truth was I did to a degree.

A group of seniors were loading a bus for the airport, and their luggage was all around them. Paul let go of my arm and offered to help a lady put her bag in the storage compartment. As he did, he slipped the tracker in her souvenir bag and smiled as he stood.

"Thank you, dear." She gave him a gummy smile, and Paul kindly patted her on the arm as she took the stairs with help from the driver. Seconds later, the bus engine started, and they pulled away.

Paul didn't miss a beat in his stride as he took my

arm and walked me back inside the hotel like I was a child in trouble. "That'll buy us a few hours."

He spoke more to himself than me. That made my back go up. *Enough.*

When he entered the elevator, I stayed back. "Nicole," he ordered, "get in."

"We had a deal."

His jaw flexed as he cursed under his breath. "I'll explain once we get inside a room."

I weighed my options and figured it was better to get out of the lobby than to fight out in the open. "I warned you to keep me in the loop." I stepped into the elevator. "You talk about trust, then you give me nothing," I muttered and hoped I'd made my point. The doors closed, and we stood in pissed off silence as the floors ticked by on the screen. Once they opened, he headed for his room, and I followed. He looked over his shoulder as he opened the door, and I stopped dead in my tracks when I took in what the team members were doing. It looked like a fully operational command center being stripped down at Mach speed. How did I miss all their equipment in the van before?

"You made it." Mark grinned at me with a hand full of wires. "Welcome to the dream team."

"I'd say thanks, but so far it's been interesting," My voice was full of sarcasm.

"In fairness, I did offer to be the one to ask you to join us, but Paul wanted to do it."

I draped my dress over the back of a chair and let

my bag fall on the floor. "I find that hard to believe." I tossed Paul a look, but his face was emotionless as he grabbed his own bag and started to root around inside it. "So, who was that French guy, anyway?"

"Gabriel Valentin," John said, "probably hired by your friend Bruno." He shook his head. "Seems Bruno isn't pleased you slipped away from his guys."

"You mean melty face driver guy." I shivered dramatically and huffed then looked at John. "How do you know about me working for Bruno?" I glanced at Mark, who seemed to have no problem letting me in.

"Paul had us on the phone at that point." Mark gave me a small smile. "It's what we do."

I should have known.

"So, you're up to speed?" I felt tired as my adrenaline fizzled out.

Cole handed me a bottle of water and a chocolate bar. "Somewhat. But I have a few questions if you feel up to talking a bit more."

"Can I freshen up real fast?"

"Sorry," he pointed to my duffle bag in the corner, "but we need to hit the road. Finding the tracker only bought us a little time. You'll have to wait until we find a new place." *When the hell did they go into my room and get my stuff?*

"You're a part of the team now," Keith muttered behind me.

"Lucky me." I grabbed my bag, purse, and dress and followed them out the door.

Exiting the hotel was even scarier than when we arrived. Maybe because I kept thinking I was seeing Mr. Melty Face. I tried to convince myself he might not even be alive.

I don't remember much of the drive, as I was dead tired and wired at the same time. Everything seemed to morph into a blur inside my head. I was in the front per Cole's request, and Paul drove. The rest of the guys were passed out in the back. At one point, I turned to say something to Paul but changed my mind. I was good with people. It was what made me good at my job, but Paul seemed to dislike me being around, and I wasn't sure why.

Bruno popped into my thoughts, and the memories from the first time I met him pricked away at the door I kept under lock and key in my head. I'd been about two years into my job when I had caught his attention, and it was a time I'd like to forget.

I pulled my legs up on the seat of the van and curled into a ball and tried to sleep, but with the sleep came the nightmare. *Stop. Stop. Stop.* My muscles clenched as I instantly came awake, and I pressed my head into my kneecaps in fear I'd yell out. Ben had warned me the nightmares would get worse if I didn't deal with my trauma, but I thought I had them under control, until now.

"Have you ever been to Holbox?" Paul asked just above a whisper, careful not to wake the others.

"No." I tried to use his distraction to bring myself down, but it wasn't easy. "I mostly worked Oaxaca,

Guerrero, and Chiapas. I occasionally jumped the border into El Salvador."

"Never mid- or northern Mexico?"

Again, the memories made their way to the surface and smothered my sanity, testing its limits. "Do you have any family in the States?" I asked him, and he glanced at me. I knew he hadn't missed my change in subject.

His hand flexed on the steering wheel, and I wondered if I'd hit a nerve. "No."

I quickly asked a different question. "What made you want to join Blackstone?"

"To make a difference. Why did you become a war correspondent?"

"To make a difference," I repeated.

His lips finally broke into a smile, and I liked how his face looked when he did. "Fair." He thought for a moment. "Do you have any family back in the States?"

I turned to look out the window and thought about how that question made me feel empty and hollow inside.

"I did," I confessed, "but I don't anymore."

"Sorry," he muttered.

"Sorry would mean someone loved me enough for me to miss them." My mouth moved before my brain could stop it. "I think I'm destined to be alone."

His hand tightened on the wheel again. "Now, that's something I understand."

"At least you have them." I nodded over my

shoulder. "All I have is a plant that might or might not be alive. He's living with my doorman." Tears prickled my eyes, and I realized how much I missed having someone, anyone. "How sad is that?"

"I killed a succulent once," he remarked, and I laughed but quickly covered my mouth so as not to wake anyone. I dropped my feet to the floor and sighed as I dried my cheeks. "What about Ben Bale?"

"Ben? He's a good friend, but we see the world too differently to ever have any kind of relationship, if that's what you mean." I thought about Ben. "He's a great guy and the best at getting pictures that show all the ugly truths, but they only scratch the surface. I want to dig deep and report the stories with all the details."

"You two have worked together for a long time, then?"

"Long enough." I didn't elaborate. I blew out a puff of air as I remembered how he was when I was released from Bruno the first time. He'd been there for me, but he made sure I knew how disappointed he was at the risks I took to get a story. He hated how I had gained the trust of men like Sully Sanchez. Little did he know the real truth…I lived my life on the edge because I had nothing to lose.

"When you work with someone long enough, they become family," he said.

"I have a story that's going to change the way things are here in Mexico. I'm just waiting for the day I can lay out all the facts and take down a tier of my own." I didn't know why I'd just dropped that little bombshell, but he took it in stride.

"Well, we're on a drive. Why don't you tell me about it, and maybe we can help."

I let a smile form on my lips as I sorted through my tangled thoughts. "No, this story is something I have to do on my own." He didn't push, and I liked that about him. Instead, we sat in silence and watched the moon ride along with us.

A while later, Paul pulled up to a set of gates, said something I couldn't hear, and waited for them to open. We drove down a tiny street that was only large enough for one car, and after a few turns, my jaw dropped at the sight. A sign read Aguas Brillantes. Roughly translated, it meant Shining Waters. The ocean looked black against the moonlight that seemed to dance among the waves. They made a peaceful sound as they lapped at the shoreline.

"What is this place? It's so beautiful."

"Mike's wife, Catalina, has an old friend who agreed to let us stay at one of his cabins. At least here we'll have some protection, and we'll be hidden away from the public." He parked and looked around before he opened his door and stepped out. I joined him as the others slowly woke. Paul handed me my bags, and I followed him to the stairs of the cabin. He felt along the gutter until he snagged a key.

The smell of something freshly baked filled my senses when he swung open the door. "Wait here." He pulled his gun, and I stepped out of his way as he cleared the cabin. A moment later, he returned. "All clear." While Paul clicked on some lights, I took in the large windows and French doors that led out to a patio and dock. I set my bags down and opened the doors and stepped outside to let the salty air brush over me.

"Mike, thank the wife," Mark sighed. "Am I delirious, or do I smell cookies?" He put a hand over his heart. "Man, this is way better than a hotel room."

I came back in and leaned my hip on the doorframe as I watched them set up their command station. They made it look as simple as breathing. They worked in unison. Each one knew exactly what they had to do, and I suddenly felt out of place.

"All right, there's seven of us and three bedrooms," Cole announced. "There's two queens in that room." He pointed. "Paul and Mark, you're with me in one room. That one has one king, so Keith, John, and Mike in that room, and there's a king in that one. You take that one, Nicole."

"So, there's a bed for all except one of you?" I didn't like that idea.

"Trust me, we're used to it." Mike smiled.

Though I liked my space, I was supposed to be a part of the team, and if they were all bunking up, so could I. "I can share a bed with someone." They all stopped and looked at me. "Seriously, I've bunked with Ben many times."

"Paul." Cole nodded. He didn't miss a beat, and I liked that, but I saw the smirk on Mark's face when

Paul grabbed his bag from the other room and brought it into mine. I was hoping for anyone else, but I also knew he was the only one who didn't have a wife. The last thing I wanted to do was cause trouble for any of them later.

Paul tossed his bag on the couch, and I stepped into the room, I hoped he wasn't pissed off.

"Sorry if I made things weird."

"You didn't," he mumbled as he rubbed his eyes. He looked tired and stressed.

"Okay." I pulled out my laptop and plugged it into the wall and checked my email. My phone buzzed, and I pulled it out of my purse and stepped outside into the warm breeze.

"Hello?"

"Where are you?" *His* tone had a bite to it, and I took notice of the time, somewhat regretting giving him this new number.

"Holbox."

"Good. You're nice and close. You ready for the party?"

"Yes."

"You know what you need to do?"

"Yes." I hesitated and knew he wasn't going to like me asking questions. "The guest list hasn't changed?" Silence.

"No."

"Good." I felt my shoulders relax.

"Don't get sidetracked. Get in and get out, but not until you have what I need."

I nodded like he could see me. "When have I not?" This time I hung up on him and closed my eyes. He was such a dick.

I turned to go back inside but jumped when I saw Paul leaning against the door, watching me.

"Who was that?"

"Jack," I lied.

"Since when do *Washington Post* employees call this time of night?"

"One step forward and three steps back, huh?" I moved past him, but he grabbed my arm and swung me to look at him. He stared into my eyes as if to read my thoughts. "I see we're right back to where we were before the taco truck." My voice was low and there was a level of hurt to it.

He let me go, and I grabbed my bag and headed for the bathroom.

"Ah!" Mark screamed like a teenage girl as I walked in. He covered his nipples with his hands dramatically, and I rolled my eyes and stepped back. He had pants on; he was just shirtless.

"So, one bathroom and six guys. Aren't I lucky?" I huffed, and Mark popped his head out.

"Like what you saw?"

"Tune him out," Keith muttered beside me. "It's what we all do."

"You know, Keith," Mark came strolling out in his camo pants as he hiked a t-shirt over his head, "I think sharing a room is going to be a good thing for us. We need a little us time." Keith flipped him the finger, and Mark sent me a playful smile. "It's just so much fun." He winked, and I grinned at how light and playful he was with the other guys. "Bathroom's all yours."

The shower felt amazing, as did my clean shorts and tank, but bed was calling my name. I tidied up the bathroom as best I could, then slipped back out to the living room. It was quiet except for Cole and Mark on their phones. The rest of the guys seemed to have gone to bed. They probably worked in shifts in these situations.

Quietly, I opened the bedroom door and found Paul doing shirtless push-ups on the floor. His earbuds showed below his ball hat, and I could hear the beat of his music. I put my bag on a table and sat on the side of the bed and attempted to finger comb my hair. I found myself drawn to him when he was on roughly his sixtieth push-up. My arms would have given out after ten. The moonlight cast shadows in the grooves of his muscular back. He was incredibly fit, and I hated to admit he was incredibly handsome when he wasn't questioning me and my loyalty.

I inched down under the covers, and my head started to swim with all the events that were going on. I closed my eyes and wished I could turn the chatter off.

"Any hot water left?"

My eyes popped open. I looked up and saw him breathing heavily over me. "There is."

He gave a quiet nod. "Cole wants to see you."

"Now?" I knew he was on the phone.

"That's what that statement means."

I rolled my eyes and knew sleep would have to wait. "Sometimes, you can just answer a question without the dickiness." I flipped off the covers and stood but watched as his eyes dragged down my front, and I instantly got hot and flustered.

"Here." He handed me his zipper hoodie, and I looked down and saw my nipples were poking through the fabric.

"Thanks." I tugged it on, grabbed the laptop in case Cole wanted it back, and left the room, undoubtedly scarlet red from embarrassment. A moment later, he walked into the bathroom, and I was thankful when Cole came out of the kitchen and said he wanted to talk.

We sat down, and he slid a phone across the table. "If we're doing this," he swiveled his finger around the room, and I took it to mean as a team, "then we're doing it right. First thing, lose the burner phone and take this one. It's secure, and you won't need to keep buying minutes. That's too risky in our line of work."

"Agreed." I quickly sent off the new number to the people who needed it then removed the battery from the burner phone and left it for him to dispose of.

"All our numbers are programmed in there under the first letter of our name, with the exception of Mark. He's under his last name, Lopez." Made sense, because there was Mike and Mark. "We have yours too. Second, you hold on to that laptop." He indicated the laptop Mark had given me. "Again, its secure, and I don't want you bringing in any other kind of technology that could potentially be bugged or hacked."

"I have my GoPro camera." At his nod, I went on. "Other than that, I understand, and I'm good." I liked Cole. He was kind, but clear. I knew where I stood with him.

"Paul mentioned you want to attend a party to try to make contact with someone who might have info about the child. Explain this to me."

I opened the laptop and turned it around to show him. "Yes, a friend sent me the guest list for Sully Sanchez's party. He wanted me to see this guy's name right here." I pointed to the name Rafael Cruz. "He's a high ranked soldier for the Canos family, so you can see why his name would stand out at a Perez party. He also plays a major role in distributing drugs for the Canos family right through to Texas." I figured it was best to share everything, and they could take or leave what they wanted from it. At least I was forthcoming with the reasons I wanted to go.

"That's intriguing, and I think you're right that it's a red flag. How do you plan on getting in?"

"I've been added to the guest list. Even though I wasn't originally invited by Sully, he loves to flaunt his wealth in front of me, and as a reporter, I can show the world how important he is." I rolled my eyes. "It wouldn't be the first time I've surprised him by showing up somewhere. It's a game I play to keep him close."

"So, he wouldn't question how you got on the guest list?"

"He might wonder, but he knows how resourceful I am."

"Okay. Smart." He scrolled down and saw my name with a plus one next to it.

"What could be the reason for Rafael Cruz being there, in your opinion?"

"There's been a lot of action going on, particularly between those two families, since that baby was discovered. They seem to have everyone on it. It's an all-out blood war with a 'shoot first, give a shit later' mentality like yesterday's shootout in town, for example. It's obvious that no one has a clue where the baby is. Why is that?"

Cole nodded. "What do you think?"

I leaned back and crossed my legs as I thought. "These people have spies everywhere, and endless funds. There has to be someone else calling the shots. Someone outside those families has that baby hidden, and I think Rafael knows who. We know that if you're a Perez or Canos soldier and you cross over into the other's territory, you're dead. So, why is this guy attending a Perez party?"

"My thoughts too." He rubbed a finger along his lip. "A guest list like that would be hard to come by." He studied me like he wanted to know who gave it to me. I didn't offer anything unless he asked me outright, and then I'd have to be honest that I couldn't share. "Do you feel safe going to the party? What if Bruno Perez shows up?"

"His name isn't on the guest list. I've double checked that. As for feeling safe, I'm not even sure I know what safe feels like anymore. But I can assure you that I'd attend the party either way. I don't back down from a story, no matter what the risks. I have nothing to lose, and that makes running into a Cartel party headfirst kind of fun, don't you think?" I tried to make a joke, but it came off as sad instead.

He looked away and nodded as he absorbed what I said. "I respect your dedication to your job, and to be honest, we're at a standstill here. We need to find the child, so this'll be our next play. Paul," he said over my head, "you'll be Nicole's date for the party."

"Copy that," Paul grunted. I hadn't heard him come out of the bathroom and wondered how long he'd been standing there.

"I'll make a call and get some prosthetics here so we can alter your appearance. Sully and Bruno know what you look like, and I'm sure his facial recognition system is up to date, so we'll have to play this one carefully." He looked at me. "You'll wear an earpiece so Paul can hear everything you hear and communicate with you from afar, plus you'll wear a camera for us to watch. We'll need as many eyes and ears as possible on this. The rest of us will be on standby, ready to leave the moment you get something." Paul came around and sat in a chair near me. "This could be just the break we need, Paul, so use it wisely."

"Agreed." Paul nodded at Cole.

"Just a heads-up," I glanced quickly at Paul then back to Cole, "Rafael has a reputation with American women. I want you all to know I can handle myself with him and don't need anyone to intervene."

"I'll be the judge of that," Paul cut in, and Cole nodded like he agreed.

"No," I inched forward on the seat, "Sully and I have an understanding, and if you step in, it might set him off."

"Would Sully know if you're dating anyone?" Cole asked, and I shook my head. "If you act like you and Paul are together, so to speak, then it would be normal for him to step in and protect." I stood. "Nicole," Cole's voice held a warning, "I know you two started off on the wrong foot, but we've agreed to be a team here, so if you need to act like you're in love, you'll do it because that's the assignment."

He's right.

"Okay." I sat back down and nodded as a yawn escaped. "Sorry."

"Don't be. Go get some sleep. I'll catch the other guys up to speed later. We'll run through everything one more time before you leave."

I trudged toward the bedroom but turned around before I opened the door. I needed them to understand. "At some point, I'll need to look available if I'm going to rein in Rafael, and if Bruno shows up…" I couldn't finish the sentence.

"Then I'll make a judgement call when we're in the situation," Paul said over his shoulder. "Remember this is what we do."

"As long as you remember this is what *I* do." I glanced at Cole then headed inside the bedroom, flipped back the covers, and the moment I hit the pillow, I was out cold.

THIRTEEN

The previous night

BRUNO

Mama sat across from me, her fingers silently drumming against the arm of the chair. Her shiny black shoes were crossed at the ankles and were as expensive as her perfectly pressed Italian blouse. My office always felt smaller when she was in it. I tugged at my tie and wondered what brought her by without so much as a call or text.

"Bruno, I'm worried about you." She studied me carefully, and I shifted in my seat.

"Worried about me? Why?"

She nodded at her right-hand man, Rio, and he handed me his phone. I looked at the photo of Nicole and me on the small screen. *How the hell did he get that?*

"You told me she wasn't going to be a problem. You told me you could control her. Rio," she nodded again, and he swiped to the left to reveal another photo. This one was of an angry Nicole as she yelled at me before I sent her away. "That doesn't look like control. That looks like you're thinking with your *verga* again." Her voice held a note of steel, and I had to stop myself from reaching down to pat my crotch.

I pushed Rio's phone away. "Photos can be interpreted a thousand different ways, Mama. What you see there is a woman with a temper. A woman who doesn't like being told what to do, yet she's out there doing it anyway." I shrugged and made sure I seemed unaffected by what they showed me. Inside, though, I seethed with anger. I'd have to watch my men more closely and see who would take photos and send them to Rio.

She leaned forward and stared more intently. A shiver ran up by spine. My mother could always chill me to the bone with one of her looks. She was a woman to be reckoned with, and you didn't want to be on her bad side.

"*Mijo*, you're a smart man, but you should have killed that damn reporter long ago when you had the chance. *No te engañes, mijo.* Your little games don't work—and you sure as hell can't fool her," she lowered her voice to just above a whisper, "but that *puta* will get you killed." She held my gaze a moment longer before she eased herself to her feet.

A sudden movement made us both look toward the door as Armondo whisked into the room. He bent down to whisper in my ear, and my blood boiled as his words sank in.

"Where is he?"

"Campeche." I fought not to curse and instead waved him off to get the jet ready. I rubbed my head then remembered I needed to look calm and in control. Little got past my mother.

"As for the child," Mama went on as if we hadn't been interrupted, "I don't care if he has a few drops of that traitor's blood in his veins. He also needs to go. By whatever means necessary." She kissed the top of my head and swept out of the room.

I tugged at my tie again and angrily waved at the rest of my men, and they scurried out of the room before I could take my anger out on them.

"We're ready." Armondo stood in the doorway.

"Fuck." I flung my crystal glass across the room and enjoyed the sound it made as it shattered on the tiled floor as I hurried off to pack my bag.

I settled into my seat on the jet, and my mind spun as we took off. Maybe Mama was right, and I should have killed Nicole. I wondered if she would really do what I asked. I knew she cared for her cameraman, but it would take more than that for her to bend to my will. I wanted to believe Sully was right and she could be trusted. Still, what if she had Sully wrapped around her finger and was playing with both of us? Mama was smart, and she didn't get to where she was without fear blazing her trail. She and I both knew I had a weakness for that woman.

I got some sleep before we landed, and soon we were waiting for Nando to finally show himself.

"That's twice now you lost her," I said quietly in English as I put a gun to Nando's ugly, mutilated face when he jumped in the back of the car. He was shocked to see me because I was supposed to still be attending that very important meeting with Mama, but instead, I was now in Campeche dealing with his fucking mess. "What the hell happened?"

"I don't know. One second, I had her, and the next, a grenade went off and we were separated. Canos has soldiers everywhere."

I dropped the hand that held the gun and pressed the heels of my palms against my aching eyes. *"Dios mío! Qué desastre!"*

"Sí, it is a disaster." He raised his hands when I glared at him and spoke English. "But I believe she is still looking."

"And how could you know that?" I held up a finger when my phone rang. "What?" I snapped.

"She's on her way to the airport." Gabriel sounded off, and I knew something had happened.

I leaned forward as I tried to calm myself. "Do you have eyes on her?"

"Non, monsieur, she's on a bus that left the hotel. It travels to the airport, but I am following."

It was hard to deal with the level of incompetence I had to put up with. I tapped the gun to my head as I thought.

"Also," he stumbled, "her boyfriend is here."

I sat straight and repeated his words. "Boyfriend?"

"*Oui, monsieur.* I mean—*sí, señor.*" He took a breath and switched to English. "I met him at the hotel when I first made contact."

"You sure it was her boyfriend?"

"*Sí,*" he stopped himself, "yes, he was very protective, and later I watched them go dress shopping and to dinner."

Nicole would never speak about her life back in the States. I wondered what was really going on. Who was this mystery man who would risk his life to be with her while she worked in Mexico? *For me.* I ground my teeth together when I thought of another man touching her. Apparently, the scars I left must have healed. I guessed she'd need another reminder.

"I am at the airport now." Gabriel sounded stressed, and I heard a car door slam shut on his end. "It is very crowded here."

"Find her," I ordered.

"I see the passengers." He sounded out of breath, and I grew more and more impatient. "Sir, I don't see her. Perhaps she is in the bathroom."

"No," I leaned my head back and closed my eyes, "she found the tracker, and you fell for it."

"Sir," Nando held up his phone, "I think I might know where she's going to be."

I snatched his phone from his hand and read the tiny font off the screen. "Go, get her, and if you don't get her, don't come back."

I waved, and my driver, Armondo, got out and opened Nando's door. He yanked him out by the scruff of his shirt and dumped him on the ground.

"Where to now, sir?" Armondo said in English as he got back behind the wheel.

I tapped my chin with my fingers and suddenly got an idea.

FOURTEEN

PAUL

Nicole was fast asleep by the time I crawled into bed. I decided to sleep on top of the covers instead of under because it felt too intimate. I stared at the ceiling for a bit but found myself wondering what she looked like when her guard was down. I carefully turned onto my side and took in how pretty she was in the pale light. Talya's face pushed through my thoughts, and I remembered when I'd lie next to her in the morning and trace the tattoo along her back for hours. It was our alone time when no one would bother us.

The memory faded, and I refocused on Nicole. For someone living out of a knapsack, she definitely took care of herself. I guessed she'd have to consider that she might have to jump on live TV at any time. I followed her hair down to her collarbone and noticed her necklace. The chain disappeared between her breasts, and I wished I could see what the pendant was. I had no idea why I cared so much, but I did.

Her phone made a small ping sound, and her eyes instantly popped open. She stared at me for a moment as she blinked to clear her vision.

"Hey," she whispered, "sorry if my phone woke you."

"It didn't, but it sure woke you in a hurry." I hated that my voice sounded almost like an accusation. She seemed jumpy as she pushed up on her arms and snatched the phone off the night table.

"Can you blame me?" She huffed as she studied the screen. "I work around the Cartel for a living, I play their games, and all the while, I try not to piss anyone off to stay alive." She flipped the covers off. "Shit." She grabbed the hoodie I'd offered her the night before. "Do you mind?"

"Nope." I propped the pillow up and watched her slip outside to the patio. Once the phone was up to her ear, I leaned over and quietly opened the window a little so I could hear. Something deep inside told me she was hiding more than her contacts from us, but it was too early to call her out on it. She was our only hope for a fresh lead on my son, and I wasn't about to jeopardize that.

"Hello, sir." She seemed uneasy as she listened. "What?" Her hand moved to her mouth. "No sir, I haven't been— I mean, I don't think I've been." Her hand slid down to her throat. "Yes, of course, right away." She lowered the phone and looked at it, and I figured the call was over.

I eased down on the bed just as she came inside.

"Everything all right?" I yawned. "You didn't sleep very long."

She slipped my hoodie off and turned the lamp on. She ran her fingers through her hair, then down her neck, down her chest, stomach, hips, legs, and all the while, her breathing picked up.

"Nicole?" I sat up and saw how worried she looked. I swung my legs off the bed and walked over to her. "Hey? What's going on?"

"He fucking got to Ben," she muttered, still in her own thoughts, and I was instantly on high alert. She pulled off her t-shirt and shorts then stood there in front of me in her bra and panties. She slowly turned herself around. Holy shit, she was gorgeous.

"Do you see anything?" She pulled her hair off to the side. "Any cuts or anything?"

I did a quick scan of her body. "No."

"Look again." Her voice shook. "I was alone with him."

"Who?"

"Bruno," she cried. "Please look harder." I humored her, and after I ran my fingers over every inch of her exposed skin, she seemed reassured.

"If I knew what I was looking for, maybe I could be more helpful." I grabbed my hoodie and wrapped her bare shoulders with it.

"That was General Bruce on the phone." She

pulled her jeans on and threaded her arms through the hoodie but didn't zip it. "Bruno planted a tracking device under Ben's skin!"

"What?" My blood pumped ice water.

"The chopper you guys were in took a hard swing to the side or something, and he hit his shoulder. I guess it deactivated the device. He was complaining of shoulder pain."

"I remember that." He had rubbed his shoulder a lot after we brought him out. "We just assumed he'd bruised it."

"Well, it got infected, and now Ben's getting treatment. But shit, they were trying to see where he was."

"No," I ran a hand through my hair, "they were trying to find our safehouse."

"Don't you guys scan for those things?"

I nodded and thought about how horrible things might have gone if they had tracked him to Shadows. "We do whenever we cross the border, and it means their trackers are better than our equipment." I snagged my hat off the chair. "I need to talk to Cole."

She followed me out to the living room where the guys had Frank on speaker phone getting the same story from him.

"It seems it stopped tracking him once his shoulder impacted with the chopper," Frank explained, and by the look on Cole's face, the news had shaken him as much as the rest of us. "We won't know much more until the boys here in Washington work their magic. For now, we just sit tight. Cole, make damn sure Nicole isn't chipped."

"She's not," I replied. "I just checked her out. Not that I can be positive, but I don't see any marks on her."

"Copy that." Frank sighed heavily. "I don't have to tell you boys how serious this is. We need to change the way we handle things from now on, especially after you cross a border. Maybe check Nicole again just to be sure."

"Agreed." Cole cleared his throat. "Thanks, Frank. We'll be in touch."

Keith whistled. "That's way too close for me. I think it's time we beefed up security at the house as well."

"Mike," Cole looked at him, "maybe get Trigger and Grim on the phone, ask them to check for any Cartel trackers on their men as well. They should know about the threat."

"On it." Mike dipped into the next room, and I glanced at Nicole. She looked pale and uncomfortable.

"Nicole, do you mind if I give you a once-over? We need to be sure."

"Of course, Cole. I'm not shy, and I sure as hell don't like the idea of being chipped like a damn dog." They went into the bedroom, and John followed out of respect for Savannah and Nicole.

"You should get some sleep. We've got a big night tonight," I said once they were done.

She rubbed her head and nodded then disappeared into the bedroom again. I was wired, so I stayed up with Mark and John, who were on shift. I leaned back in the chair and rested my tired head. All I could think about was where my son was and if he was all right.

"How is she?" John broke my thoughts.

"Jumpy but focused. I think."

"You think she'll be able to handle the party?"

"I do. She's used to working solo, minus her cameraman and protective team, but I think they follow her lead to a point, so this will be an adjustment for her." I looked at the ground and thought about her other phone calls.

"What?" John read my mind.

"I'm not sure yet. Something's bothering me about her. She's had a few private phone calls, and they're never more than a minute long."

Mark rubbed his hands together. "Well, she's got one of our phones, so we can track the number if you feel it's needed."

I didn't like the idea of spying on her, but if it came down to it, I would. "Not yet, but the thought's crossed my mind."

"All right, guys." Cole sat down and rubbed his face. "Paul, when you guys are at the party, we'll take a sweep of Selena's house. See what we can discover. It's not far from where you will be, so if any trouble or any leads come in, we'll meet up."

"Sounds good." I let that sink in.

We all went silent after that, and not long afterward, I passed out.

———

I stood in front of the mirror, and if I didn't know it was me, I'd never have recognized myself. The bright blue contacts concealed my dark green eyes, and the tribal tattoo that showed below my t-shirt made me laugh. I knew I could never pull off a neck tattoo; that one, I was happy to leave to Grim Gates. My cheeks were puffy, and my hair went from short to shaggy with a slight gray to it. I still looked my age, but I no longer screamed *intense army,* as Savannah so lovingly described me.

"Not bad, John," I turned and held out my arms to show him how impressed I was, "not bad at all. There's not a chance they'd recognize me."

"Well," he whispered, "Eric's supposed to be dead, so we have to make sure I did a good enough job." He nodded toward the bedroom where Nicole was getting ready. "Activate your vocal box and see if she recognizes you." I pressed the tiny button under the prosthetic and tested out my voice. It was low and raspy. "You made me a stage four smoker?" I glared.

"I had to get creative."

"Right." I gave myself one last once-over in the mirror and brushed my hands down the fine material of the tux. I crossed the room and knocked on the door.

"Come in."

My stomach clenched as I took in how stunning she looked in that black halter dress. The damn thing hugged her body in all the right places, and I blinked hard when she turned, and I saw once again how low the rectangular cutout sat on her pelvis. Her hair was up in a low French twist, and a few pieces fell out to soften the look. Her sparkly heels peeked out from below, and a glimmering see-through skirt showed a chain wrapped around her upper thigh. I'd never seen anything so sexy in my life. The memory of how she felt under my fingers as I checked her for the tracker made my head swim.

"Can I help you?" She pushed a long, sparkly earring through her tiny lobe as she glanced up at me in the mirror.

"Sorry." I cleared my throat and was glad the prosthetics hid my embarrassment as I gawked. "I'm Dan. I'm stepping in for Paul tonight." It felt good when her face fell. "I'm a friend of the team's and your escort tonight."

"When was this decided?" Her hand moved to her stomach like she was uneasy.

"About an hour ago."

"I see." She picked up her lipstick then dropped it, giving away her nerves. "Um, excuse me." She brushed by, and I grinned, pleased it worked.

"Nicole," I called to tell her it was me, but she marched up to Cole who had a hard time keeping a straight face.

"Something tells me Blackstone keeps their team in the know, so why am I minutes away from walking into that den of vipers with Dan here?" She pointed at me, and Cole rolled his eyes. "Where's Paul? Why isn't he taking me?"

"Nicole," Cole's smile appeared, which only seemed to piss her off more, "you're missing—"

"Do you know how hard this job is for me?" she blurted. "I try to act like I'm not terrified, but I am. When I found out what happened to my last team, and Ben was taken, I couldn't sleep for days. Those men are ruthless heathens who will stop at nothing to get what they want, believe me!" Bruno's face flashed before me; whatever he did to her sure left a mark. "I'm putting my life in danger here, for good reason, but that doesn't mean you can pivot the plan at the last second."

"I didn't," Cole said calmly, "and Dan isn't taking you."

She looked at me in confusion. "But he said—"

I pressed the button on my vocal box so she could hear my real voice. "It's me, Paul. We had to know that I didn't look or sound like me."

"Seems to me someone could use a Marcus Martini." Mark beamed and handed Nicole a drink. She took a deep swallow.

"Sorry for upsetting you." I felt bad when I saw her finish the entire martini.

She handed Mark the glass. "How very *Day of the Jackal* of you." She screwed up her face then ran her finger along her bottom lip. "We should get going."

Cole brought the computer over to show me the map of where Talya's oldest friend lived. "I know you know the plan, but I want to run through it one more time. You and Nicole work the party, and the rest of us will check out the friend's house. Keith has altered his look a bit and will act as your driver and will be your eyes outside. If any of us gets anything, we share it real time."

"Got it. What are the odds her friend will be there?" Nicole crossed her arms. "The Cartel will be turning over every rock in this country, especially the Canos and Perez families. God only knows who else is after that child."

"It's a start." I knew I sounded snarky, but my lack of patience with all this was eating me up inside.

"Are you two able to act like you don't want to kill one another?" John piped in with a smirk, and she shot me a nasty look.

"We're professionals. We got this." I handed Nicole her purse. "Okay, let's go."

Cole stood and opened a box. "Earpiece," he handed it to her, "and a tiny pin camera that will look like it's part of your dress." He watched as she pinned it through the fabric. "Just push the front and back of it to activate, but they'll do a sweep of you when you first arrive, so only turn it on once you're in."

"Copy that." She tested out the earpiece. "Can you hear me?"

"Loud and clear," I confirmed.

"One last thing, if you ever need Paul to intervene, you need a safe word."

"I'll order a dirty martini, because Sully normally has champagne circling at these parties."

Cole nodded at me. "Dirty martini is her safe word."

"Copy that." I took her arm and headed for the door. A limo was parked and waiting. If we were going to this thing, we were going to look like we belonged.

"Nicole," Cole addressed her one more time, "if you get any tip at all on where the child might be, repeat it when you're alone. We'll be listening. We just need one lead, so let's make it count."

I opened the door to the limo, and she slipped inside. I signaled to Cole that I was good and joined her.

"You know where," I called to Keith, who was dressed as our driver. He would stay outside in case we needed him.

Nicole kept her eyes on the window while I began to channel my head into my new character. I was Dan from LA and worked in international trading. I figured it was something that would catch their attention. I knew enough to carry on a decent conversation from when I was Eric, so I shouldn't get tripped up with any of their questions.

When we arrived, we were stopped at the gate, and once Nicole showed her invitation, we were let through to drive down a very long driveway. The house reeked of drug lord. Their homes were always big, grand, totally over the top.

"Very John Gotti," I whispered. "Have you been here before?"

She opened her purse and pulled out a small mirror. "Just once a long time ago." She snapped her mirror closed and kept her gaze out the window. "Let's just say I'm breaking a promise to myself by returning." I wondered if that was the place she first met Bruno.

We pulled up, and I acknowledged Keith's glance in the mirror before he stepped out and opened our door.

"Ready?" I asked her.

"Yeah." She waited for me to step out and offer her a hand. She had slipped into character instantly. She was good. Her smile was wide, and she looked pleased to be there. I slid my hand down her back and rested it above her tailbone to show ownership, as one would with such a beautiful woman on their arm. The second we stepped out of the limo, I knew they'd be watching us. Nicole might be welcome here, as she was with the American press, but I was an unknown American, and there'd be plenty of questions and speculation. These were dangerous people, and they wouldn't hesitate to kill. We had to tread very carefully.

We showed our invitation again as we stepped through the security. The moment I spotted the champagne flutes I grabbed two and snagged a napkin off the tray. I handed her one and pretended it dripped on her dress.

"Shoot, sorry." I used the napkin to shield my hand as I slid it into the side of her dress to activate the camera. Her smooth skin and the curve of her breast caught me off guard, and I paused for a moment at the sudden warmth that went through me.

"Thanks." She smiled up at me as I removed my hand and took a small sip of the drink.

I did a sweep of the guests and was shocked to see I knew some of them. Well, Eric did.

She raised her glass to her mouth as she spoke. "Sully is coming up behind you. He'll be a hard sell."

"Copy that." I loved a good challenge.

"Well, if it isn't our latest escape artist." Sully lifted a brow at Nicole. "May I say, you look lovely."

Nicole leaned in for an air kiss, and as she stepped back, I wrapped an arm around her waist and pulled her to me. She played along well and ran her hand over mine.

"Sully, this is Dan Brandel from LA and my date for this evening." Her eyes sparkled as she looked up at me. Her hand ran down my chest as she leaned in.

"Nice to meet you, Sully. You have quite the house." I shook his hand as he studied me.

"Thank you. It's nice to meet you too." He tilted his head back a little as if to raise his nose. "What is it that you do?"

"Let's just say I have a knack for moving people around." I hoped that comment might intrigue him.

"Is that so?" He smiled like he was impressed. "Perhaps we should talk more later." *Perfect.*

"I'd like that."

He looked at Nicole, and she jumped right back in.

"I wasn't running, Sully, but I wasn't about to be babysat by one of Bruno's greasers who thinks he can hit me whenever he feels like it."

"Are we talking about Nando or Bruno?" He made a poor attempt at a joke, but she handled it like a pro.

"Both." She chuckled darkly. "How is our mutual *friend* doing?" She made a face. "You do know the man is completely unhinged."

"I will not comment on Bruno's mental state, Nicole. He is very upset that the child hasn't been located yet." I knew Nicole felt my flinch at his words, but I kept my face unfazed as Sully watched me closely. "You have disappointed him with your lack of information. I'd be careful if I were you. You of all people should know he's out for blood."

"He just hates to lose." Nicole waved a hand as if to brush off Sully's remarks. I wished I knew more about their past. I could sense there was a lot being left unsaid.

"That, he does." Sully sighed dramatically. "Well, I'd say there is more at play here than just the whereabouts of the child."

"Meaning?" She nonchalantly brushed an invisible speck from her dress.

"Oh, you know, this and that." He waved her off, but I felt her hand flex on my back as if she understood what he might mean.

"Come, Dan." Sully motioned at me. "I have some people you should meet."

This could be interesting. I pressed my lips to her cheek then smiled lovingly. "I'll be back."

PRESS

FIFTEEN

As much as it was a mind trip to be with Paul while he was so well disguised as a completely different person, I was glad for the opportunity to do what I did best. Dig.

I spotted someone I needed to see, so he was first up. I made my way over to the bar and ordered a glass of white wine. Then I slipped onto a free stool as close as I could. I sipped my drink and pretended to search through my purse, while I tapped record on my phone, but without warning, they decided to take their conversation elsewhere. *Damn!* I twisted on my chair and looked around the room. That was okay; I'd find him later.

I watched Paul for a moment as he worked the crowd like a champ. He smiled, shook hands, laughed, everything he needed to do to fit in with these people. The Cartel were rich and their friends even richer. They'd lost their moral compass soon after they slid out of their mothers' wombs. They had zero respect for anyone or anything except the almighty dollar.

"Spill the tea, Nicole." Sully accepted a drink from a waiter as he approached me. "Why did you bring a date to my party?"

"You mean a party I wasn't invited to?" I raised a brow. "We had a deal."

"I felt you were needed elsewhere. I assured our mutual friend that you were to be trusted. He gave you a job to do. You'll have to forgive me for not extending an invitation, but—" He raised his glass to his lips.

I instantly felt nervous. "I understand he isn't coming?"

"He's not," he twisted the glass between his fingers, "but Rafael Cruz is. I also have a job to do. Again, I'm going to ask, who is your date?"

"You mean my shiny new penny?" I wiggled my brows as I roped him in. "He's actually a *regalito*."

"I do enjoy *regalito*." He stepped closer.

"As he mentioned, Dan is from LA and works at importing-exporting things such as artwork, artifacts," I slid my gaze over to him, "humans who just so happen to carry high amounts of *cocaína*."

"Really?"

"I figured he should come here and meet you. Dip his feet in your world so that should you decide to ask him for help with your little California problem, he might be more open to it."

He studied my face the way he did when he was happy about something, but didn't want to seem too eager. "You two seem very close."

"It's all part of the game, Sully." I winked as I took a sip of my drink.

"All right, well, I appreciate the offering. I'll be sure to speak with him again tonight and see if we can't find something that would benefit us both."

"Do that, and you're welcome." I hoped he'd pull his men off Paul so he could do what he needed to do. I steered the conversation back to the situation at hand. "Now tell me, Sully, why you and I are both doing the job of one." He hesitated, and my temper got the best of me, or at least I made it look that way.

"I don't understand." He lifted his hands.

"That child. I don't like being blackmailed into doing someone's dirty work. I couldn't give two fucks about the child. He's not the story I'm interested in telling," I lied with ease. "So, I'm supposed to be off looking for some child and you're hosting a party here, I suspect for the same reason." I waved my arm around. "Add to that a high-powered Canos soldier is in attendance. Doesn't that tell you something? Sounds to me like we're being played against each other. Tell me I'm wrong, Sully." He scrunched up his nose and glanced around. I knew he must have had the same thoughts himself. I might hate Sully, but he wasn't stupid.

"Nicole, Bruno has made it clear what he'll do if you don't do as he asked. You need to find that child—"

"I'm done playing Bruno's games," I glared at him, "and I know that son of a bitch doesn't have my cameraman. Ben called me yesterday and confirmed he's okay." I hopped off the stool and sent him a look to show him I was done with it all. "So, let me clarify." I placed a hand on the bar. "I have proven to you time and again you can trust me. I even brought Dan to your party because I know he can be of help to you, yet you still sit here and let Bruno call the shots when it comes to our friendship? Do me a favor and don't call on me again."

"Wait, wait, wait." He pointed with his head to sit back down, and I knew something was up. Careful not to seem too intrigued, I hesitated and pretended to think for a moment before I did as he asked. "I can't get close to him."

"Him. Who? Rafael?"

"Yes," he hissed, clearly unhappy. "We don't have the best relationship. Bruno seems to think we do, but he won't give me the time of day, as you Americans say..." He took a sip of his drink.

This was an interesting development. I had to play my cards right. "So, get someone else to speak to him."

"It's not that simple." He actually looked worried. "I could use your help with this."

I laughed and shook my head. "No."

"Nicole, seriously, I need you to find out what his next move is with the child."

"So, you're saying he has information on the child's whereabouts?" His expression showed he didn't want to answer. "Sully, fill me in with what you know, or I walk."

"Yes," he reluctantly answered and lowered his voice. "The original story was the kid was to be given to the first one who came for him."

"Where? Do you know where they have him?"

"No. And now there are new players," he nodded toward Rafael, "and they have changed the game. Like everything in this country, it has become about money. The child has shown its value, and now there is a bidding war. Not so unusual these days, *comprende*?"

I nodded. "I understand all too well the way things work here."

"So, now the child will stay hidden until that man gets what he wants."

"All right, so he's calling the shots," I repeated to make sure the others heard, and Sully nodded. "So how am I supposed to play into this?"

"Get his attention, use those." He looked down at my breasts. "He'll tell you anything if he thinks he might have a chance with you." He simply shrugged at my disgusted look. "This is also how the world works, Nicole, and we want the same thing. No?"

"No, we don't, but I want a story, and I want a

good one. I told you I'm not interested in some kid, and you can tell Bruno that."

"Please, I just want you to let him talk then tell me what he said."

"Why should I?" I turned and watched Rafael as he spoke to some men who looked to be in their late eighties.

"I know things," his expression was unreadable, "things that involve you and Bruno."

I gave him an annoyed look. "There's nothing between that fuck weasel and me." I was tired of this.

"Not like that." He cleared his throat. "I mean what Bruno really has planned for you."

I huffed. "And what would that be?"

He licked his lips and ran a shaky hand through his hair. Why was he nervous? "I'm assuming that if you spoke to Ben, he told you he was chipped." I didn't say anything, and he went on. "Bruno was furious because it didn't work. Something happened, and it has only fueled Bruno's revenge."

"Revenge?"

"Yes. You remember his uncle, Martin Castillo?" At my nod, he went on. "You know his empire was reduced to rubble by those *Americanos*?" I nodded. "Now there will be," he struggled to find the word in English, "*repercusiones*."

"Repercussions."

"Yes, repercussions to that downfall."

I scratched my face. "What's that got to do with me or with Ben being chipped?"

"There's much more to tell you about this. I think you need to know—" He stopped talking when one of his men whispered something in his ear. His face showed he wasn't happy at whatever was said, and he nodded once, finished his drink, then stood.

"What?"

"You should meet with Rafael now."

"No, you should finish your story now."

He rubbed his mouth nervously. "Please forget what I said."

"Not possible."

"I'll give you something else for your news. Something very interesting about Bruno's mother and what she has been up to. I'm sure your American viewers will be very interested in what she has planned for the border. This will be an international story, Nicole. You will want this."

I wanted to know more about what he'd referred to with Bruno's uncle and Ben's chip, but something told me now wasn't the time to push. My brain spun with all the possibilities. I tapped my finger on the bar and took a moment to let him sweat it out.

"You better not screw me on this, or I'm out, Sully. I'll be gone tomorrow, and I'll take Dan with me." I knew I had to threaten, or he'd never believe me. "Gather up the shit on his mother, and so help me God, if it's not juicy, I'll write a story you'll both regret."

He swallowed back his pride and looked me straight in the eye. "Understood."

"And whatever it was you started to tell me about, I want that story too. This isn't a one-sided business relationship."

"I understand that too."

I rolled my eyes and turned away. Then I spotted Rafael Cruz at a table with another man I didn't know. *Time to play.*

I tugged my dress back so my bare thigh showed through. It was at his eye level and could hardly be missed. I carefully tilted my wine glass and let a little drip onto the front of my breasts.

"Oh, my goodness," I said out loud and acted as if the cold liquid was a shock. "May I have one of those?" I pointed to his napkin as I leaned over to give him a better view, and he didn't disappoint.

"Allow me." He got quickly to his feet, took the napkin from me, and boldly dabbed my chest. Yup, he definitely lived up to his reputation. I'd done my research, and it had just been confirmed by Sully.

"Such a gentleman." I internally rolled my eyes. "Thank you." I smiled and made sure my eyes sparkled with interest while my stomach rolled a little in disgust. I should get an Oscar for that performance.

"Tell me your name." He stood above me, and it took everything for me not to step back. "Someone as sexy as you must have an equally sexy name."

"Nicole Winter." I made sure the name came out in a slow crisp tone. "I'm an American press correspondent." His jaw locked in place, so I hurried to smooth things out. "I've been working in Mexico for the past decade and have found I enjoy many," I paused dramatically, "opportunities on this side of the border. It's how I became good friends with our host. Sully and I often share the same view on things. It has proven to be mutually beneficial, if you understand my meaning."

"You work with Sully?"

"You could say that, off the record, of course." I grinned playfully, and it seemed to catch his attention.

"Maybe you and I could work on something together."

"Oh. Did you have something specific in mind?" I felt my heart race as I stood in front of a man who was a high-ranking soldier for the Canos family, yet he was here in the middle of his supposed enemy's party still with a heartbeat. The fact he hadn't been slaughtered for entertainment the moment he walked in confirmed he held all the power.

"I'm sure someone as powerful as you," I ran a finger along the buttons of his dress shirt, "knows everything that happens in Mexico."

"You are correct." The corners of his mouth drew up like a sleazy alley cat about to pounce. "I know everything. I'm a very big deal here, and not to be underestimated. Soon everyone will see that." The tip of his finger toyed with my sparkly earring.

"Well, you have my undivided attention."

The band started to play, so he had to lean in and

whisper the details. A cold feeling crept over me as he spoke, and I wondered how much the guys could hear.

"What do you think?" He leaned back and gave me a cocky look.

"I do love a little danger," I purred. "But I have to ask, what if no one bites?"

"Then the prize becomes fish food, but I will have my cash in hand either way."

It all felt very mafia to me, but I wasn't about to point that out. The Cartel and the mafia did things very differently, and I found over the years the Cartel don't like to be compared to anyone but themselves. So, I decided to play Rafael's game and see what I could find out.

"That's very impressive," I drawled and nodded at him.

"Yes?" He ran a finger along the collar of my dress, and his eyes danced with excitement. "Maybe we should go somewhere and discuss this further."

"There you are." Paul slid his warm hands along my hips then leaned down and tilted my chin to look up at him. I was barely able to contain my shock as he pressed his lips to mine for an intimate kiss. He pulled away with a hungry look then turned to look Rafael square in the eye.

"You found me." My voice hitched a little as I struggled not to betray what he'd just done to my insides. And it apparently kick-started my libido as well. "Hun," I tried out the nickname and wasn't sure how it sounded, "this is Rafael Cruz."

"Nice to meet you." Paul pulled me in front of him and dropped a kiss on the bare part of my shoulder. "I see you've met *my* Nicole."

"I have," Rafael said, his annoyance clear. He was used to having the upper hand when it came to women, and I knew he wouldn't appreciate Paul's interference. I was worried it would ruin the offer Rafael had made. We needed this.

"Go away!" I hissed in Paul's ear.

"Judgement call," he hissed back, and I couldn't believe he'd chosen that moment to intervene.

"Mr. Cruz," I drew his attention from Paul back to me, "I will pass along the information as you requested and will let you know how it's received." I reached forward and offered my hand. He brought it to his mouth and kissed the back of it, and as he did, he shot a glare at Paul.

"I can't wait until we get to speak more about it, *alone*."

"I agree." I smiled warmly at him and gently squeezed his hand, feeling his response. I waited for him to let go, then he excused himself and walked away. Once he was out of earshot, I turned to Paul. "Are you crazy?"

"A little." He scanned the room over my head. "Did you get anything?"

"I did and was about to get more when you came in and ruined my chance."

Paul suddenly seemed to lock in on someone who made his jaw clench. "Just give me a moment. I see someone I need to speak with."

"No, seriously, Paul, we need to talk."

"I really want to hear what you know but, damn, it'll have to wait a minute. The team's listening. Tell them," he ordered. "Sorry, but I need to deal with this."

"Deal with what?" I grabbed his arm, but he shrugged me off. "Who do you know here?" I called after him, and he turned and smiled then raced off. I wondered who I missed on the guest list.

"Hey, guys?" I whispered. Then Sully caught my eye as he approached. His face was rigid, and I wondered what was up.

"We're here, go ahead," Cole answered, and I wanted to fill them in on everything, but I couldn't because Sully was now in earshot.

"Stand by." I walked toward Sully. "Sully."

"Nicole," he shot back in a cold voice. *What's happening?*

"You need to finish what you told me. You can't start a story and—"

"I can't, Nicole."

"Why?"

"Because we have company." He nodded over my shoulder, and I turned, expecting Paul was back, but instead I locked eyes with a pissed off Bruno.

"Sully," my fear got the best of me, "order me a dirty martini, please."

SIXTEEN

PAUL

The radio in my ear suddenly crackled loudly, and I fought not to react to it as I made my way across the room. That was strange. I picked up a plate and added a few pieces of fruit to it and carried it with me. I hated to leave Nicole so quickly, but I spotted a guy I'd once been close with when I was Eric. I lipread him say my friend Chili's name in conversation with another man. I had to get close to them in a hurry. They seemed intense, and my Spidey sense tingled. When I heard them mention Chili again, my hackles went up and I got closer. I fished around the serving sets on a side table to find a fork as I tuned them in.

"Something is not right." The man I knew was definitely on edge. "Chili has never worked this far south before." He spoke English, as most of the guests were speaking Spanish, but they kept their voices low.

"Maybe he's moving his operation down here?"

"No way," he shook his head, "not since Noah died and he took over the tunnel. He wouldn't risk losing that territory. Besides, Bruno would kill him."

"Then what do you think he's doing here?"

I kept my back to my old friend but was able to see his face through the top of the shiny serving tray cover. "I'm not sure, but he's poking around in places he shouldn't. The fact that he's been seen has kicked up dust, and there is now a target on his back. The Canoses have put someone to watch his next run. If there is something going on they don't like, they'll take him."

"That's smart."

Fuck, I needed to warn him.

I glanced around and couldn't spot Nicole or Sully. Time was ticking, and I had to reach Chili before he was caught. I told him what was going on and had sent him to check out a few places my son might be. I spotted a lady's purse hanging on the back of a chair, the top open. Her phone was visible, so I put my plate on a table and walked toward her table and bumped it with my hip.

"Oh!" The lady jumped, and I dropped to my knee, snatched her phone, and tucked it up my sleeve.

"My apologies. Are you all right? Did I hurt you?" I asked in Spanish while I held her hand.

Her face immediately warmed, and she smiled and patted my shoulder.

"Good." I didn't wait for a response. I headed for the stairs and slipped out of view. I checked a few doors until I found one that wasn't locked and carefully let myself in. It was some sort of guest room, and once I cleared it, I locked the door behind me. I went to the window and peeped out through the curtains then held up the phone and prayed the reception would be good. I couldn't hear any crackling. I breathed a sigh of relief as I silenced the ringer.

It had been a while since I texted Chili in code, but it came to me easily.

Unknown Number: 5579

A moment later, the phone buzzed and once it connected, I spoke.

"Your order has been cancelled."

Silence. "Understood."

I took a deep breath as I crushed the phone against the sill then tossed the remains into a planter.

"I said enough!"

The voice was familiar, and I peeked through the curtains again to try to spot her. I couldn't see anything.

"Let go," I heard her snap.

I wasted no time and eased the double patio doors open and crossed the balcony. I saw Nicole struggling with a man, and I made a beeline to where they were.

"Bruno, please, I told you everything. You're hurting me." I heard fear in her voice.

"Don't make me repeat myself." He lifted his hand as if to hit her, but I grabbed it and twisted it backward. Nicole's eyes widened and she immediately backed away.

Bruno yelped and swung around to face me. If he only knew who it was who stared right back at him.

"You touch my girlfriend again and you'll deal with me," I threatened then ducked when I saw his fist coming. I shoved him back, and he flew into the same pillar he had just pushed Nicole into. He whirled around and touched his lip then casually wiped the drop of blood from his finger with a tissue. He removed his jacket, laid it over a chair, and put his hands up to fight. I would have loved to indulge myself, but I didn't have time for it, so when he lunged at me, I wrapped my arm around his neck and pressed into his kidney, slowly putting him to sleep. I lowered him to the ground, waited for a beat, and looked up at Nicole.

"You okay?"

"Your judgement calls are way out of whack." She rubbed her arm where he'd held her. "You took your sweet time," she spat. "What the hell happened? Where did you go?"

"Not now." I stood and shook my head then took her hand and whisked her down the stairs. "Where are you?" I asked Keith through my radio.

"East gate."

"Copy that." I changed direction, and we circled the property using the shadow of the fence as cover. I pushed her ahead of me and helped her slip through the tiny garden gate. Once outside, I cautioned her to keep low, and we made it to the road where Keith waited with the car.

"You good?" he asked as we crawled inside.

"Define good." Nicole snickered, but I signaled we were, and Keith took off. I tossed my head back and took a deep breath.

"So?" she asked.

"So?" I pulled out my phone.

"What the hell happened back there?"

"I had to follow up on something."

"Which was?" She wasn't letting it go.

I pinched the bridge of my nose. I wasn't used to explaining myself. "I heard something, and I needed to deal with it." At her expression, I continued. "It was someone's name I knew from a long time ago. I had to know if they were connected to this shitstorm."

"Were they?"

"No." I glanced at her and saw she was seriously angry with me. "What are you really upset about, Nicole? That I left you alone for a few minutes? You said you could handle yourself, remember. Or are you still mad that I interrupted Rafael while he gawked at you?"

She looked ready to punch me. "What I'm upset about, Paul, is that you guys assured me that you'd watch my back. You told me to use a safe word if I was in trouble, I said that safe word, and you didn't show up for another ten minutes."

"What?" I hadn't heard her use the safe word.

"We were all unreachable for eleven minutes," Keith said, and I glanced at his face in the mirror. "Seems pretty convenient that Bruno showed up right when our coms went offline."

"He must have had a scrambler." That was why my comms had crackled in my ear. I should've caught it. My mind was a mess, and I realized my skills were less than they should have been. I pushed the fog away and changed the subject. "What did Rafael say?"

"We have company," Keith cut in before she could answer. He quickly pulled his wig back on and grabbed his pair of thick glasses. It was doubly difficult to do our job since most of the Blackstone team's faces had been leaked to the Cartel families.

My hand fell heavily on Nicole's bare thigh to catch her attention. "Keith is going to speed up, and when he turns the next corner, he'll slow as much as he can, then we're going to jump out." At her shocked expression, I raised my brow and shrugged. "Then we're going to walk along the water back to the cottage." She didn't answer, but she didn't protest either.

"Ready?" Keith called. "One, two," I waited for Keith to swing around the corner and slow, "three, go!" I swung her over my lap, kicked the door open, and we rolled out together. I held her tightly to me until we stopped then hauled her up until we had our backs flush to a concrete wall. "Just wait," I warned as tires squealed and a black car zoomed past where we huddled in the shadows. They had followed the bait. "Come on."

I helped her over the low wall and down the bank to the sand where she took off her heels and hiked up her dress. I held a finger to my lips and motioned her to follow. We waded waist deep into the water so our footprints couldn't be tracked. She didn't speak as we made our way along the rocky sea floor. She fell behind a few times, and I waited for her to catch up. It was a long, exhausting walk, as we were both fully dressed, but we didn't dare shed an article of clothing that could give away our location.

I put my hand in the air when I heard a boat engine. She had already stopped dead in her tracks.

"Do you hear that?" Her whisper was shaky, a dead giveaway that she was cold and scared.

"Get down." I dropped until my chin hit the water, and she did the same.

"Do you think they're Bruno's men?" she whispered as the boat slowed and they started to use a big spotlight to scan the water's edge.

"Can you hold your breath?"

"Yes."

"Good. When I say, go below the water, and I'll tap you when you can come back up." I hoped she could do this. I waited for the light to get closer, and when it was a few feet away, we both took a deep breath and submerged.

The moonlight was filtered from the salty sea, so everything was black. I felt Nicole touch my hand, and I threaded my fingers through hers. I needed her to stay calm. Their strong light slowly moved over us, and for a moment I thought we would be seen. Perhaps they saw the ripples and wondered what had caused them.

She squeezed my hand, and I saw she had to go back up. We resurfaced, only to come face to face with the side of the boat. She dove back down, and I did the same, but I lost track of where she went. The ocean floor dipped, and I dropped lower as the boat engine roared to life again, and I could barely make out anything in the foam it created as it moved away. I kicked hard and shot up to take in a deep gulp of air as I spun in search of Nicole.

"Nicole," I called quietly, but I couldn't spot her. "Nicole!" I said a little louder as dread started to come over me. "Nicole?" I studied the top of the water for any signs that she could be submerged. I found myself getting upset, and that was very unlike me. I was good at not getting attached or letting my emotions get the best of me.

Suddenly, she popped up, coughing and sputtering. I swam toward her, grabbed her by the waist, and swam her back toward shore until I could stand.

"Hey," I tried to soothe her, "you're okay. Take a deep breath." She coughed some more then rolled to face me with a terrified expression. Her chin quivered so hard I could hear her teeth rattle. My heart squeezed to the point of pain. "I got you." I pushed her hair back and studied her face to make sure she was really all right.

"That was way too close." I wasn't sure if she meant the men or too close to death. Tears mixed with the beads of water on her face, and I wasn't sure what to do to help her, so I went with what my body said to do. I moved my hand to her head and slowly lowered my face to hers. I stopped inches from her lips and waited for her to tell me it was what she wanted, too. Her eyes moved to mine then to my lips, and that was enough for me. I pulled her to me, our lips connected, and we both threw our terror of almost dying into the kiss. Her legs wrapped around my waist, and I pulled her closer to me. My body came alive, and for a brief moment, I felt a rush I hadn't felt in years.

She moaned when I shifted her on my waist and she felt how turned on I had become. It was the worst timing, and the worst place to let my guard down, but we were caught up in the heat of the moment.

Only the sound of the boat engine returning made me tear away from her.

"Paul," she cried against my lips.

"It's coming back. We need to go." I helped her stand, took her hand, and we dashed up the sand and hid until the boat was gone. Then we trudged the last fifteen minutes to the cottage.

"What the hell happened to you two?" Mark looked at us, covered in sand and dripping wet.

"Any word on the child?" I ignored his question.

"No, but we'll fill you in asap."

"Where's Keith?" I needed to know he was okay.

"Here," he answered, coming in behind us. "I lost them. They think we're in town."

"They're smart." I removed my heavy jacket and pulled off my sagging prosthetics and tossed the nasty fake skin into the trash. "A group of them searched the shoreline, too." Nicole headed for the bathroom, and I hoped what happened hadn't rocked her too badly. I knew that in her job she'd have been through some nasty stuff, but after that party, it had gone from bad to worse in a hurry. "We had a few close calls." I nodded toward the bathroom.

John handed me a towel. "Is she okay?"

I dried my hair then toed off my wet shoes. "Yeah." I looked around the cabin. "So, how'd tonight go? What happened?"

"Get cleaned up." Cole tossed his burger wrapper on the table. "We'll fill you in then."

I bit my lower lip in frustration and pulled from my training. "Copy that."

I headed for the bedroom to get cleaned up. I stripped, wrapped a towel around me, grabbed some soap from my bag, and went outside to use the pool shower since Nicole was in the bathroom.

The shower felt great, but I kept it short and

hurried back inside to get into some dry clothes. Just as I pulled up my camo pants, the door opened.

"Sorry." She turned away, holding the towel tightly around her.

"It's fine." I pulled on my ball hat then snagged my t-shirt off the bed as I moved toward her. "How are you doing?"

"Fine," she answered too quickly, "just tired." She lowered herself onto the mattress.

"Do you want to come hear how things went at Selena's?"

She looked away, and I could see she needed a moment to gather herself. "Since there's no child out there, I'll assume they had no luck. I think I'll skip this one. You can fill me in later."

"Fair enough." I understood that. "Hungry?" When she didn't answer, I tugged on my shirt. "Come out as soon as you feel like it, then. Just remember the team needs to know what you do so we can plan our next move." She slowly nodded, so I let her be.

"Heads up." Mike tossed me a wrapped burger, and I caught it as I sat down next to Cole. "It's old, but it's food."

I was so hungry I didn't care what I was putting in my body tonight. I had that thing gone in three bites. Mike slid another over, and I inhaled that one too. "Nicole hungry?"

"I'll take one to her later. She needs a second." I nodded for Cole to start. I was anxious to know what they found, if anything.

"Before I start this," Cole brought up the body camera footage from their evening, "you need to know that the boy," he lowered his voice, "wasn't there." I knew by his look I was in for some blood. He hit play, and I watched as they approached the house and entered through the side door. I could see three bodies that looked like they'd been flung around the place at random, and another was tied to a chair. It was obvious he'd been tortured.

"We immediately checked for the child. There was no sign of him anywhere and no sign of the friend. We tracked down the landlady. She said Talya and the baby moved in with Selena about a year or so ago. She told us she often heard Selena arguing with her boyfriend after that about wanting time alone but how she couldn't get it.

"It was obvious that the landlady didn't like Selena's boyfriend and was sympathetic to Talya and the baby. She said Selena was two-faced. She seemed really great when Talya was there but turned nasty about her when the boyfriend came around. I guess after Talya died," he cleared his throat, and I knew he was trying to be sensitive, "the friend struggled with the baby. I guess he cried a lot. Then once the boyfriend moved in, she said things got really strained."

"Jesus, the poor kid lost his mother. What'd they expect?" My stomach was in turmoil over what my poor son must have gone through. "What else did she say?"

"Not much. She said she had a strange feeling that things weren't good and was worried about the baby. Then a few weeks ago she came by to collect the rent, and the place had been abandoned. She said they left in a hurry, since there were still dirty dishes in the sink, laundry in the washer, things like that. Tonight, about three hours before we got there, she got word from a neighbor that they heard gun shots. She arrived and found this." He pointed to the video. "They're Canos' people." Cole showed me a photo of the inside of a man's wrist. It had been inked with a Canos honor tattoo. "From what the neighbors saw, sounds like Perez's guys showed up and killed them."

"Doesn't seem like they wrecked the place." I watched the screen replay the video.

"No, lucky for the landlady." Mark handed me a bottle of water. "They were on a mission to find the kid. They found Canos' guys instead." He chuckled. "Sorry." He looked at me.

"We're getting closer. That's what matters," I said more for myself than for him.

"I heard your night ended in the water." Mark leaned his arms on his thighs. "Did you get anything from the party?"

"I think Nicole did, but we haven't had a chance to talk. I lucked out and recognized a guy I knew from before. I lipread him saying Chili's name and had to get close to find out what they were saying. The gist is I guess he was kicking up too much dust and they were on to him. I managed to let him know he needed to abort and get out."

"Shit," Cole huffed.

"Yeah," I rubbed my tired face, "then Bruno showed up, and he had a scrambler on him. I didn't hear her say her code word, and he got his hands on Nicole. It was just one mess after another. But she knows something, and once she gets her head back on straight, she'll be out to share it."

Nicole appeared a few minutes later, freshly changed with towel-dried hair. I closed the laptop and reached for the bag of food. "I thought you might want a cold, nine-hour-old burger." I handed it to her with a shrug. "Sorry, but it's the best we could do."

"How'd you know?" She tried to banter back, but I could tell something was really bothering her. "Thanks."

"So, how was the party?" Mark asked as he kicked up his feet at an attempt to relax the room.

She tugged at her sleeve, and it was hard to miss the raw marks on her wrist. My guess, it was Bruno. "Eventful." She tore at the wrapper and started in on the burger. She swallowed and wiped her mouth. "I better share this now, so I don't forget anything." She put the burger down on the table.

"All right." Cole nodded, and all attention was on her.

"Turns out Bruno has Sully and me both looking for the child. He's playing us but doesn't realize that Sully and I go way back, and we talk. I have no loyalty to any Cartel members, of course, but if I did, it would be with Sully. He held that party to attract the attention of Rafael, but he couldn't get close enough to him to do what Bruno ordered.

"As I've mentioned before, Rafael has a type, and it's not men. So, I worked him, and he let me in a little, baited me with some possible new stories." Her face dipped, and I wondered what kind of stories he offered. "I got his attention and pulled him away from his friends then did my thing. I told him how I had the media basically in the palm of my hand and how useful that could be to him. He got cocky and started to brag about this new business deal he had going on."

"Do you think he thought you already knew about the child?" John asked.

"Not positive, but I think so because I made sure he knew Sully and I worked together from time to time. The fact that I'd been invited to the party may have helped. I played it cool. I made sure to act more interested in him than what he was sharing."

"Smart," I chimed in.

"Thanks." She gave me a quick glance. "He told me that his girlfriend got her hands on something that would be worth a lot of money to some people. He wanted me to help spread the word that this *something* is up for sale, and the highest bidder wins. The auction, for want of a better word, closes in two days."

"Anything else?" Cole probed. "Did he give you

any idea of where this item, obviously the child, is being held?"

"No, but he did make an off-the-wall comment about how the prize would become fish food if he didn't get what he wanted. He laughed and said he'd get his cash either way." She looked over when we all went silent. I knew she caught the sympathetic looks John and Keith threw my way. "I know. It's terrible, isn't it? He has no regard at all for human life."

"He's an animal," John agreed, "but the fact there's a deadline means we need to work fast."

"Nicole," Cole leaned forward from where he sat on the couch, "can you tell us what Bruno was doing at the party? I thought Sully told you he wasn't going to be there."

She had just picked the burger back up, but at Cole's words, she dropped it on the table, unfinished. "Sully had no idea, and I could tell he was just as blindsided as I was that he showed." She seemed about to say something, then paused as if she didn't want to share the rest.

"And?" I encouraged her.

"And he reminded me that I worked for him, which is a joke. I've never worked for Bruno. He's delusional." She rubbed her face. "Though you're definitely on his radar now." She looked at me. "Be careful, Paul. There's something bigger going on here. I can feel it."

I glanced at John then back to her. "Meaning?"

"Bruno's got bigger plans for me. Sully hinted at

it. I have no idea what because he got pulled away before I could press him on it. I've been thinking about it." She bit her lip. "Sully knew about Ben being chipped and how furious Bruno was about the tracker not working. He's up to something, and Sully thinks it's to do with getting revenge for his uncle's death."

John looked at Cole. "We need to find out what Sully knows about Bruno."

Nicole's face fell, and I wondered what she hadn't said. She rubbed her neck and looked tired, and I decided not to push.

"We leave before sunup to sweep Selena's place." Nicole looked at me. "I need to see it for myself. We may find something they missed," I explained. "For now, why don't you get some sleep?"

"Yeah," she stood in a zombie-like state, "I think I need to."

SEVENTEEN

BRUNO

I watched the party from the back of the room. Some of the guests began to retire for the evening. It wasn't lost on me that Sully had avoided me the whole evening. When I saw Nicole would be there, I knew I had to leave my meeting with Mama early to drive down and deal with the situation myself.

My phone buzzed, and I read the screen.

> J: There's been some chatter. Call when you can.

> Bruno: Tomorrow.

I tucked it away with a smile. *Excellent.*

The moment I walked in, I could see by Sully's face that he hadn't been able to get the information I asked for and hadn't thought I'd show up. Then when I saw Nicole with an American on her arm, it sent my blood pressure to new heights. I had sent her to find out where the child was, not to enjoy herself at a party with some American. Sully made some excuse that she was working the party to get close to Rafael, but she wasn't originally invited, so how did she even know he'd be there? It was becoming evident that I needed to keep a closer eye on what was happening here.

I called my driver over. "Armondo, I want you to investigate that American Nicole is with. I want to know who this Dan is." Armando left with his phone to his ear.

The man who had been hovering around Rafael finally left him alone, so I crossed the room to intercept. Rafael held all the power in this situation, and he was enjoying his moment. He was puffed up like a peacock as he sipped his drink, but he was a soldier for the Canos family, and the moment he made one misstep, I'd be there to help him into an early grave. For now, I'd play the game, because I would win. I always won.

I grabbed a drink off the waiter's tray and stepped in front of Rafael.

"Well, if it isn't Bruno Perez." He gave me a sly grin like we were old friends. "I was hoping I'd run into you." I noticed he spoke in English, which I preferred. It helped to eliminate some of the eavesdroppers.

"Rafael." I didn't offer my hand or use his last name. "I understand you have a little project that brings you to our side of the street."

He held up the crystal glass of some of our finest brandy. "Yes, I recently came into possession of a bargaining chip that should interest several parties. I was invited to come tonight to see how interested they are." He raised his brow, but I refused to bite.

"Come, now, Bruno. Surely, you've heard that the Canos family has a secret son in the wind?"

"I did, actually." I casually glanced around the room. I wasn't going to show him how much power he had. "I wasn't aware you had anything to do with that."

One thing about Rafael was that he loved to brag. "Oh, I have everything to do with it. I was the one who found the kid and put this whole game in motion." He positively radiated with glee. "My buddy's girlfriend and the boy's mother were living together when the mother was killed. The girl wanted nothing to do with *el mocoso* after that. I was smart and saw the opportunity and took it."

"You're playing the families off each other." I nodded and gave him an admiring glance. I wanted him to know I was impressed by his intelligence. "I would have done the same."

"Of course you would have. It's a great plan, and now look." He waved a hand. "I'm at a Perez party, sipping your *tragos,* while you all consider the wonderful *oportunidad* I have provided you. Think of how valuable this child would be. What a bargaining chip to hold over the Canos family, eh?"

I fought not to drive a bullet through his smug mouth. "Well, it sounds like you have set yourself up well. Good luck with that." I turned to leave, but he cleared his throat.

He tilted his head and lowered his voice. "If you like, we could talk numbers."

"I'm listening."

"Ten million US dollars."

I laughed. I refused to insult myself by accepting such a price. "Six and we have a deal," I countered.

"Eight and throw in that woman you were manhandling outside." I hadn't realized he had seen that. "Nicole, that reporter."

"She's spoken for," I growled. I should rip this idiot's windpipe out and hand him over to my men.

"I'm joking, my friend." He laughed heartily. "I can see you like her body." He made curvy lines with his hands. I ran my tongue along the inside of my mouth as I remembered how he'd gotten between us outside before Nicole's date played hero. The only reason I didn't kill him then was because he held all the cards when it came to where the damn child was. "But the girl will be mine in time." His face hardened and he elbowed me. I bit back my temper.

"Seven and we have a deal." I sipped my drink. I needed something to do with my hands other than to put them on his neck.

"Seven and the girl."

"You're playing a dangerous game here, Rafael," I warned. I was moments from losing everything I'd worked so hard to control.

"*Si*, I am, but I intend to secure enough money for my safety."

I stared into my glass and counted to ten before I looked at him square in the eye and lied. "I admire your drive, and because of that, I will give you seven million US, and as for the girl, if you can handle her, she's all yours." I shrugged, and he held out his hand.

"Deal." I shook his hand and led him to a room to swap bank information.

"Once the money clears, I will send you the address." I opened my mouth to protest, but he handed me a card. "For good faith on my part, here is the city they're in. Pleasure doing business with you, Mr. Perez." He smiled and walked from the room. I opened the paper. *Cozumel.*

Excelente. I'd have easily paid twice his original amount.

"*Jefe*," Armondo leaned in close, "it would seem Nicole's boyfriend has information that goes back only ten years. Then *nada*." He raised a brow, and my blood boiled.

What game was Nicole playing?

"Get the car. We leave tonight."

EIGHTEEN

PAUL

I smeared the last of the camouflage paint on my face, and the rest of the guys did the same. Concealing our identities had become a necessary part of every mission. It made everything more difficult, but gone were the good old days when the internet was dial-up and social media hadn't been thought of.

Nicole strapped her GoPro to her chest and inched toward the door of the SUV we had borrowed. We couldn't risk being followed again.

"You're documenting this?" I checked the clip of my gun.

"Of course. Do you know how much is missed by the human eye? Besides, if something big happens, I have my next story." She hopped out. I wasn't sure how I felt about that.

"Hey," I stepped closer and folded my arms across my bulletproof vest, "stay behind me, keep your head on a swivel, and if I tell you stay back, stay back."

"I know." She rolled her eyes as she pushed in the earpiece we gave her. "I told you before, this isn't my first rodeo." At my warning look, she made a face. "Paul, I've worked with soldiers before."

"Maybe, but you haven't worked with Blackstone."

"Hate to break it to ya, Ace, but I've worked with some pretty elite teams. I promise I got this." She smiled at me then raised her fingers and ran them down my painted neck then stroked them across the tops of her cheeks, smearing the paint across her own face. "Hooah!"

"Hooah," I muttered as she left to join Mark.

Cole came up next to me. "No one would fault you if you wanted to hang back." I shot him a crazed look. He chuckled lightly. "I figured. Remember, comb through everything—"

"Because somewhere there's something to point you in a direction." I slapped his shoulder. "I got this, brother, I promise."

"I know you do." He walked with me over to the others. "All right, boys," Nicole cleared her throat, "and girls," he acknowledged her. "We all know what our jobs are. Let's get in and out in under ten minutes. The moment we enter the property, start your watches. If anything goes wrong and we get separated, we know where to meet up. Copy?"

"Copy," we all said in unison.

He signaled for us to approach the place, and we spread out with our rifles raised and eyes constantly scanning the area.

John and I took the side entrance while Mark and Cole took the driveway, and Keith and Mike took the back yard. Nicole was behind John, and I gave him a nod that we were clear to enter. She tapped his arm to signal she was ready. I bent low and moved across the straw-like grass then pressed my back flush to the house. The others followed, and once they were with me, I tried the handle and felt it was locked. I used my shoulder and carefully broke the lock from the wall.

We moved inside, and after a quick glance around the house, I felt as though I'd stepped back in time. Talya's face was in several of the photos that lined the wall. It was like a kick to the heart. I hadn't had time to process her death, and I knew that would have to be dealt with at some point. I stopped short, and John ran into me. Out of the corner of my eye, I saw him follow my line of sight to the baby photo of my son. It suddenly dawned on me how much I'd missed. If only the circumstances had been different. It was hard to drag my eyes away.

"What a cutie," Nicole whispered behind us. I snapped out of it and shoved my sorrow down as I moved deeper into the house. It appeared they'd left in a hurry. There was a half glass of juice on the counter, along with a baby bowl and spoon in the sink. Diapers were scattered by the back door, and a tiny sock lay on the floor in the corner. That tiny sock got under my skin like a punch to the gut.

Then I smelled her, and my body locked in place as I searched for the source. A familiar sweater hung on a peg next to me. I picked it up and held it close to my face so I could drink in her scent. I closed my eyes and fought all the memories it unlocked inside my head. When I opened them again, I saw Nicole watching me, and I quickly tossed it aside and moved on.

"All clear in the bedrooms," Cole said softly through the radio. "Moving toward you guys."

As I turned to exit the kitchen, I caught sight of a photo propped against the windowsill above the sink. I picked it up and studied it carefully. It was of Talya, and she held my son. Her face looked a little fuller, and there was a small, raised scar along her jawline that hadn't been there when I knew her. She had tiny lines at the corners of her beautiful brown eyes. I moved my attention to my son, and a lump built in my throat.

Nicole was suddenly by my side. "That had to be taken this month. Look at the newspaper." She pointed to the background. "That story was printed only a few weeks ago."

Well, shit, she was right.

The photo had been taken in the room where we stood, so I turned and looked to see where she'd been standing. I stood in front of the wall by the back door and held the photo up as if I were taking it myself. Then I lowered it, moved it up again, then lowered it again.

Nicole's voice came from behind me. "What do you see?"

"It's what I don't see that interests me." *The prize becomes fish food* circled back in my mind from when Nicole shared what Rafael had said. Cole and Mike joined us. "I think I might know where they went." I pointed to the yellow foam keychain in the photo then moved the photo and showed them it was now gone from the hook. "*Rayo de Sol II*," I read from the tag.

"Any idea where the closest marina is?" Mark asked, and John held up his phone and nodded like he found it.

"Let's move," Cole ordered and headed back to the SUV. I pocketed the photo as I ran from the house.

The marina was twenty minutes away, and it gave me time to recheck myself as I sat in the back. I needed my head on straight. I pretended I didn't notice Nicole as she checked her phone every few minutes.

Stress ate away at me, and I closed my eyes and leaned my head on my propped-up arm. I never imagined myself ready to be a father, but that meant nothing now. I knew I'd have endless support and love from everyone at Shadows. Still, it was a lot to process. I wanted to pull out the photo and study every line and curve of their faces but couldn't risk Nicole seeing. She was anything if not observant.

Of course, the most important questions were who killed Talya and where my son was. I was ready to kill. A bullet wouldn't be enough for whoever took the mother of my child from me—from us. I gave in and remembered how she felt under my touch and how much I craved her body on mine. Years ago, I'd come to know that there could be no future for her and me. Her being from a prominent Cartel family and me with my job. Her face came to me, then suddenly it wasn't Talya anymore. It was Nicole looking up at me from under the sheets.

My eyes popped open, and I blinked a few times, then squeezed them tightly shut again as my head was a jumbled mess of confusion.

"Hey," a hand slid over my arm and squeezed it, "we're here," Nicole said softly.

I looked at her and forced away the memory that still clung to my subconscious.

"We're here," she repeated. Her phone vibrated at that moment, and she looked down at it and her mouth gaped. "I need to take this." She rushed out of the SUV and moved a good fifteen feet from the rest of the guys. What I found more interesting was she made sure she kept her back to us. I jumped out, and John handed me a ball hat.

"You good, buddy?"

"Yeah." I started to check my gear. We wouldn't be carrying our rifles into the marina, just our handguns. I snagged my bag from the SUV then Nicole turned around and I read her lips.

"—no right to speak to me that way. I'm doing everything you asked and—" She moved her hand to cover her mouth, and I missed the rest of what she said. John came and stood next to me. His expression told me he was worried about how I was handling everything.

"Who's Nicole speaking to?"

John shrugged. "Probably a friend. You sure you're good?" he asked as I closed the car door rather hard.

"Yeah, all good." I wondered who Nicole really had been talking to, I didn't think it was a friend.

"All right," Cole jogged over, and we gathered around him, "entrance is here, and the boat slip for *Rayo de Sol II* is number twenty-six. Same groups as before. Paul, you guys head right to the slip and see if the boat's there, Mark and I will gather info from the staff, while Mike and Keith, you guys go talk to the locals. Let's go. Nobody does anything until we know what we're up against."

Nicole hurried over and fell into step with John and me. "Good call?" I couldn't help but ask.

"Yeah." She seemed off, and John glanced at me, but let it go. One thing at a time.

The marina was a bit rundown in spots, but the dock itself was high tech and up to date.

I spotted a young kid, maybe sixteen or seventeen, spraying off an expensive looking catamaran. The moment he saw us, he went for his radio.

"Please," I held up a hand and spoke Spanish, "we're looking for someone, and I promise it isn't you."

"Until it is," he huffed and turned off the hose. He tossed it down at his feet. "Americans, yeah?" I nodded. "Let me guess. You're looking for slip twenty-six?"

His words made my chest squeeze to the point of pain. "We are."

"Well, like I said to the other guys, I don't—"

I shifted my weight on my heels. "Other guys?"

"Some Ruiz soldiers showed up here tossing their weight around." Nicole placed a hand on my back as she stepped around me, and the kid's mouth dropped open. I knew she'd probably dealt with the Ruiz family since she mostly worked the southern part of Mexico.

"You're Nicole Winter from the *Washington Post*?" His mouth was open.

She plastered on a smile and shook his hand as he fangirled over her. "Nice to meet you."

He got all excited. "Adan, I'm Adan. My dad has the biggest crush on you." He laughed while I fought not to roll my eyes. "What are you doing here?"

"Adan," she got closer and placed her hand on his arm, and he nearly gushed right out of his skin, "can you tell me what they wanted?"

"They wanted to know about when the boat left the marina and if I knew who was on it."

"Did you tell them anything?"

"No." He rubbed his arm where she'd touched him. "We might live in their territory, but they're terrible men who do nothing for our town. They care nothing for the people here. So, I lied and said I only noticed the boat was gone last week."

"When it was really…" She tried to coach him along, but he looked over at John and me, and I could see him starting to close up. "Hey, Adan," Nicole pulled his focus back to her, "you know me from TV. You know what I'm trying to do here in your country. I always support your people and tell the truth about what is happening in Mexico." He nodded. "Well, something bad has happened, Adan, and if we don't get to that boat first, whoever is on it will be killed."

"The baby, too?" I tried not to react, but that was just the confirmation we needed. My son was still alive and last seen on the boat.

"Everyone, Adan. Everyone will be killed. So, can you help us and tell us when they really left and who was on the boat?" He glanced at me, and I saw his wheels turning. "Don't be fooled by their getup," Nicole said. "They are good people who are trying to do the right thing. Be a part of this story with me, help me tell it." That seemed to get his attention.

"Can I get a picture with you?"

"Picture, video, signature, you name it, and I'll do it. But first, please, the information."

He got excited all over again. "Come with me." He waved us to follow him to a houseboat at the end of the slip. He stepped on board and headed into the cabin. I got on first and did a quick scan then offered Nicole a hand to step down. John stayed on the dock to keep watch.

I leaned in and spoke quietly into her ear. "Get anything you can."

"Copy that."

The kid opened a laptop and started to type in what looked like a boat ID number, and a few moments later a map popped up. "Last year, Selena's boyfriend asked me to install this fancy new GPS on their boat." He kept typing and started to eliminate some tracked boats from the screen. "He's an asshole, as you would say." He kept his eyes on the screen. "Anyway, he asked me to make some adjustments in the program after I did it for him. He gave me a paper with some instructions on it. I did as he asked then told him he was good to go, but I saw what he was doing, and it was kinda strange. Then he only paid me half of what he promised," he complained.

"He really is an asshole." Nicole grinned and leaned closer. "I work with a few of them, too." I wondered if she referred to us.

"You smell nice." His cheeks flamed.

"Thanks." She bumped his shoulder playfully so he'd keep talking. "What's strange?"

"This." He pointed to the screen. "You didn't get this from me, yeah?"

"From who?" Nicole grinned at him again, and he laughed.

"He wants you to think he's here out in open water, but really, he's all the way over here off the southern tip of Cozumel. And to be more specific, they are currently in Isla Paraíso."

I clicked my radio that we had something. Then I said, "And if you were going to that island, what's the best way in without getting seen?"

He thought for a moment. "Honestly, I'd just blend in on a tourist boat but then have another boat for when you want to leave. The tourist boats only run once at night and once in the morning."

I leaned over Nicole's shoulder to study the map. "Is there anyone you trust that we could rent a boat from?"

"Someone who won't sell you out you mean?" He snorted. "Yes, my brother." He pulled out his phone and sent off a quick text, and a second later he got a response. "He'll lend you one, no fee, as long as she's there." He pointed at Nicole.

"That, we can do," she answered before I did. "Thank you, Adan. Now, what can I do for you?"

"Video, please." He turned his phone around, so it faced the two of them. "Guys," he said to the camera, "look who I met today. It's Nicole Winter from the *Washington Post*!" He moved it over, and Nicole smiled warmly and gave a friendly wave.

"Hello everyone. I highly recommend Adan here for all your nautical needs. Look how handsome that face is." She winked at him and put her arm around his shoulder. I thought the boy's heart would burst out of his chest, he was so excited.

"Nic," I used a nickname so she'd look right at me, "can you let Cole know?"

She got the drift that I wanted to speak to Adan alone. "Of course. It was lovely meeting you, Adan."

"You too!" He watched her leave and gave a whistle. "You're so lucky." He looked at me. "I knew she was beautiful, but meeting her in person, wow, she's a real hottie." I had to laugh at the teenage reference. "My dad will be so jealous. I bet you have to fight all the men to keep her."

"She's popular, for sure." I couldn't help but think about all the men we'd met and how many of them fell all over themselves when she was near.

"So, you guys are dating? Because I see the way you look at one another."

I looked back at John, who clearly heard that last comment, because he was trying hard to hide his amusement. I sidestepped the question.

"I appreciate your help, Adan. I know the risk you took to share it. You have our word that no one will know what you told us."

"Thanks." He suddenly looked nervous. I stepped closer and pulled out some money and held it up when he went to take it I moved it higher. "Can I ask that you do the same and hold that video you took of Nicole for a while, maybe at least a week? If people see you with her in that video they'll connect the dots. Understand? Will you help to keep her safe?"

"*Sí, señor.*"

"Good." I gently slapped his shoulder. "Now, let's set up that boat with your brother." I handed him the money once we were done then ducked out of the cabin and hopped over to the dock with John. "Not one word," I grunted as he fell into step behind me, but I heard him chuckle.

"Wouldn't dream of it."

We found the others waiting next to the SUV. Once Cole was up to speed, he thanked Nicole for her efforts and nodded toward the vehicle. "I'll drive." He tossed his bag in the trunk as the rest of us quickly scrubbed our faces clean of the paint. "The rest of you, get some shuteye. We'll talk again once we get there."

Nicole was the first in, and she took the very back seat again. I joined her while the rest rushed to get in, and we hit the road.

A short way into the drive, Nicole shifted to pull her phone from her pocket.

"Wait, what?" She studied the screen with a puzzled look. "Ah, Cole?" she said.

"Yeah?" He looked at her in the rearview mirror.

"Rafael just texted me and said that no bid has been accepted, and that if I hear otherwise, it's not true. I'm not sure what that's all about."

I took the phone from her hand and re-read the message.

"He texted you on the phone I gave you?"

"Yes."

Cole waited for the light to turn red and swiveled in his seat to look at us. "You gave him your number?"

She instantly looked concerned. "Yes. Wait, was that wrong?"

"No," he grinned, "I'm just impressed you did that. You must have left quite the impression for him to keep you in the loop."

"It's because I told him I'd get the info out to all the Cartel families using my resources."

"And did you?" I had to know.

"Yeah," she shrugged like it wasn't a major deal, "but maybe I spread a little misinformation along the way." She grinned. "Like all bidders should meet in Rosarito three days from now and to stay tuned for more details. That should buy us enough time here. They head north, and we head south."

"I'm impressed, Nicole. You'd make one hell of an asset for Shadows if you ever decide to give up the reporter game." He hit the wheel with a laugh, and I looked out the window as I nodded in agreement. She was certainly proving to be an asset on this mission, but something gnawed at my subconscious. I knew she hadn't shared all she knew, and it bothered me that she wouldn't answer her phone. If it was her work, why not answer?

When darkness replaced the warm sun, we were still a few hours away from where we needed to be. There had been multiple roadblocks, and they ate up time we needed. It drove me to the point of almost losing my shit as every second that went by was another second someone could get their hands on my son or worse…

Nicole sank lower in her seat and silenced another call. Instantly, it rang again, and she tossed the phone in her bag. That was the stuff that was bothering me. Who was that? I didn't believe it was her work.

"Your ex?" I dug, since everyone was asleep and Cole had earphones in. He was filling his father in on what was happening.

She ran a hand through her hair, and her forehead creased as she thought about what I asked. "No, not my ex, just someone who wants an answer I don't have."

"That's vague."

"I know." She sighed but didn't offer anything else. She ran a hand over her wrist. I could still see the bruises, and it made me think of Bruno.

"Ben mentioned that you had some history with Bruno back at the start of your career. Do you mind if I asked what happened?"

She stiffened, and every stress line on her face showed through. "You know when people ask you how many people you've killed and how that feeling burns from the inside and makes you want to throw up and run away all at the same time?" I couldn't have described it better myself, so I gave a small nod of appreciation. "That's how it feels when people bring up my past with Bruno."

"I respect that." And I did, but I still wanted to know. "What was he doing at Sully's party?"

She pulled out her necklace and rubbed her pendant as if it comforted her. "He was there for me. He wants to control me." She looked out the window. "He couldn't before, but now he's figured out a way."

"Which is…?"

"You ask a lot of questions."

"I ask a lot of questions when I feel like someone's not being totally straight with me."

Her mouth morphed into a straight line when she looked at me. "Not being straight with you? What do you mean?"

"I don't know. You tell me."

She looked hurt. "I'm a good person, Paul. I've chosen to spend most of my life helping others. I put myself in danger doing it. You Blackstone guys are like family to each other. It's obvious to me that you all care. I wasn't gifted anything like that in my life. I've done nothing but help you since we've met. Just because I keep some things to myself doesn't mean I'm doing anything wrong or I'm not trustworthy." She swiped a tear away in frustration. "I'm beginning to get the feeling that maybe you just don't want to see the good in me."

"Whoa, maybe I went about this in the wrong way." I felt badly she felt that way, but I wasn't used to people not telling me the entire truth. "Why don't you tell me about your family?"

Her gaze moved to the window again, and when a car went by, I saw her jaw was clenched.

"You want to try to understand where I come from to better understand me?" She gave a dark laugh, and I realized I hit another nerve. "Well, let's see if I can sum things up for you. I was dropped off on the steps of an orphanage by my mother in the middle of a snowstorm when I was only a few hours old. Later, I would learn that my father skipped town the moment he found out she was pregnant. The sisters took me in." She rubbed her pendant again.

"When I was eight, my mother came back and said she wanted me. That lasted all of two days before she told me to wait for her on the steps of the orphanage while she went to get me an ice cream. She never returned. She pulled the same shit again when I was fifteen. Fast forward to sixteen when I had to leave the sisters because I was too old and apparently there was never anyone who wanted to adopt me. That felt great." She gave me a glare. "I ended up living on the streets of Billings."

"I forgot you're from Montana." I didn't know what else to say. I felt like a jerk, but I had nothing.

"When I was twenty," she decided to continue, "I was playing around on social media and found my mother had an Instagram page and went through her family contacts. There was a girl with my mom who looked a lot like her, and a man that looked to be her father, and she was showing off an engagement ring. I looked up the girl and saw she worked at a flower shop and decided to go meet her. I mean, she's my half-sister, after all. Let's just say that it didn't go down well.

"I'd barely gotten my reason for being there out when she had my mother on the phone. She flipped out, understandably, so I left, not wanting to make a scene. I went back a week later against my better judgement and tried again, but she flew off the handle and said she wanted nothing to do with me. That I reminded her that her mom was a cheater. I didn't realize our mother was in the back, and she stepped out and nailed the last peg in the coffin. She said I was a mistake and there was a reason she never kept me. She demanded I leave and never return. So, I didn't."

Tears fell, and she didn't bother to hide them. "The sisters at the orphanage gave me this." She showed me the pendant that hung around her neck. "It's the Patron Saint of Orphans. They said he would always be there for me, watching over me."

"I'm sorry, Nicole. I shouldn't have pried."

"Well, you did, so..." Again, I sat there. What was there to say? "I wasn't always alone, though." She looked out the window as if picturing a memory. "There was a field with a stable on the other side of the property. Their horses roamed free in the field. They looked so pretty. I'd watch from the fence, and sometimes they'd get really close. There was a brown one with white; he was my favorite. His markings looked like a map of the world. I used to trace my finger along the edges of the white spots and imagine all the places I wanted to visit. He'd let me touch his nose sometimes, and I'd stay really still and talk to him. He'd just be with me, almost like he knew I needed a friend." She tilted her head and peeked up at my face as I let all that she said wash over me. I wanted her to transfer her pain to me.

She changed the subject. "I might add that it was the pendant that gave me the in with the sisters. And it's why they gave me the baby's birth certificate."

Of course, that would have been a connection for them and opened a door for her. I nodded.

"To finish my life history so I hold nothing back…" She raised a brow at me. "I worked hard to become what I am today. I met Jack, my contact at the *Washington Post* and he saw my potential. Eventually, I gained a reputation for being difficult to work with, but that's only because I let nothing stop me from getting the story I want. Then I met Ben, my cameraman, and we're the best team at the Post." She waited for me to comment, but I just studied her. "You know the best war correspondents are the ones who have no family to use against them, right?" She stuck out her chin. "Shit, I can't even keep a boyfriend. Well, at least one who can keep it in his pants." I saw the pain her ex must have caused her. "So, feel better now?" She dripped with sarcasm and blew out a big huff.

"I like that I know something about you," I shot back. Then I remembered she'd been open with me, and that was what I'd asked for. "You certainly didn't get a fair shake in life. I can't imagine how hard it must have been for you. I'm sorry for that."

She acknowledged my comment with a nod. "And what about you? What's your story?"

Ugh. I figured that question would come, and it was only fair I answered, even if some of it had to be redacted. I took a moment to let my mind wander back to when I was a kid and figured I should share my not so happy childhood with her as well. Maybe she'd see we were a bit alike.

"My parents bounced when I was young. My dad was a piece of shit. My aunt stepped in to raise me, but she had a boyfriend and did the bare minimum. I don't blame her for it. She's still around but has her own family and loves her grandkids. I joined the Army the moment I could. Oh, and I have a sister who's a lot older than me."

"Do you talk to your sister?"

"No, I'm not close with her, and I've no desire to be. She did let me know our father died a year after I joined the service. John and I became close when we met years ago, and then we were both recruited to join Blackstone. I've never looked back."

"What was your mom like? Do you remember her?"

"Not really." I shrugged. "Maybe I've blocked any memories I had. My grandmother, who has now passed, used to tell me a few things about her, but she didn't seem to care much for her either. She probably wasn't impressed that she ran off on us. I guess she was kind but quiet. I had a few photos but nothing I cared to keep. I wished I'd had a chance to get to know her. My father was such a deadbeat, I had no time for him."

"I'm sorry your mom left," she whispered. "I promised myself that whenever I have kids, if I ever get to, I'd do everything I could to let them know they were wanted and loved." She patted my knee with her warm hand, and a calmness washed over me. "There's this—" She started to say something but stopped herself. I covered her small hand with mine and gave it a squeeze to urge her to say it. "Well, there's always this one breath I take at the end of the day that reminds me of how alone I am. It scares the hell outta me."

I let out a long breath. "I understand."

She leaned her head to the side and closed her eyes. "I'm so tired." I flexed my hand over hers where it still lay on my lap and studied how pretty her slim fingers were. Her breathing evened out, and her hand started to slip away as she relaxed. I caught it as it fell away and inched my fingers through hers. I liked it.

"I should mention," she murmured, half asleep, "I don't date soldiers."

PRESS

NINETEEN

NICOLE

"*Look what you made me do, Nicole.*" *Bruno's nasty smile broke out as he proceeded to punish me for not doing what he wanted. "All this pain was your fault.*"

My eyes popped open, and my stomach took a violent roll as the memory faded. I tuned in to the spicy smell of his aftershave. Then everything clicked back into place when I felt movement.

"Oh." I sat up and threw an embarrassed look at the wet spot on Paul's shoulder where I had apparently fallen asleep. "I'm so sorry."

"Don't be." He grabbed his bag from between his legs. "We knew you'd need the sleep, but we're here now."

"Did you sleep?"

"No. I don't need much sleep."

"Oh, well, thanks." I quickly gathered my things. I was embarrassed that he'd probably sat there not moving while I slept on his shoulder, and now I was probably holding them up.

"Must have been some nightmare," he grunted as he slid over and opened the door. I ignored his comment and finger-brushed my hair before I got out to join the others.

"Morning, Sunshine." Mark beamed at me. "Fuel up. We need to be sharp." He tossed me a protein bar.

"Thanks." I wasted no time and swallowed it down. The calories and the little burst of sugar would perk me up in no time.

Cole went over the plan and where we were to meet Adan's brother, and one more location if we were to get separated. It was rather interesting to work with Blackstone. I thought the other teams I'd worked with were great, but none of them even came close to being as thorough as these guys were. The way they knew each other's movements was almost eerie, they always knew exactly where the other guy was. They really were one big working wheel. I was teamed up with Paul and John again, which I liked. John and Paul had a special connection, and I noticed John often watched out for Paul. I tucked that interesting fact away, as I'd noticed a higher degree of stress in Paul compared to the others.

"You see anything, radio it in." Cole looked around. "Let's move."

I noticed Paul slipped on aviator sunglasses and a

dark ball hat. He had a bit of a five o'clock shadow, just enough to darken the skin around his mouth. He could have walked right by me, and I don't know if I would recognize him. Not that I wouldn't have looked anyway because the man was attractive as sin and carried a level of confidence most didn't. That must be a requirement to work on Blackstone. I huffed a silent laugh. I needed to pay attention to where we were going as we threaded through the tourists.

"Here," Paul pulled a dress off a stand and handed the shop owner some cash, "put this on."

I took the white sundress from him and thought how pretty it was. "Why?"

"We need to blend, and you've worn that shirt in too many pictures online. We're one Google search away from your fan club recognizing you."

"You lookin' me up?" I teased, but the way he stared at me from behind his shades made my skin heat. "Give me a second." I asked the store owner if I could change, and he pointed to a small private area. The sleeveless cotton dress fit like a glove. It had buttons down the front and looked clean and crisp. The bottom of the dress hit mid-thigh, so I snagged a pair of flats from a mannequin. I wished they were heels, but if I needed to run, I wanted to have a fighting chance. As I stepped out, I pushed my hair back into a small ponytail and felt like I could play the cruise ship tourist well. "Will this do?"

John slapped Paul's shoulder with a grin. "Yes."

That was all Paul offered me. I shoved my clothes in my bag. We kept moving through the sea of people who waited for the ferry to get over to the island.

"I'm going to check something out." John shot off in a different direction, and Paul never broke stride. I wouldn't ever admit it to Paul, but it was hard to keep up. He had long legs and the endurance of a bull.

Suddenly, someone grabbed my arm and swung me around. "Nicole?" Agustin Ruiz, one of the cousins in the Ruiz family, stared down at me.

I turned to look for Paul, but he'd disappeared, and I was scared he might not have noticed I had stopped. "Agustin." I tried not to show how nervous I was to see him again. He had a reputation, as did a lot of the Cartel, but Agustin had caused a lot of problems between Bruno and me. "Hi, how are you?" My voice shook, and I was sure he could spot my fear.

"Why are you here?" *Shit.* I weighed my options if I should lie or tell the truth. "Where's Bruno?"

"Dead in a ditch somewhere," I joked. "One can dream."

"Yes, one can." His normal smile broke through at the mention of any of the Perez family being killed. "You look fantastic." He moved closer, and I fought not to step back. "Last I heard, you were in Mexico City."

"I was." I tucked a piece of hair back in place, needing something to do. "You know me, I don't spend a lot of time in one place. That's not how you chase stories." Where the hell were the others?

"I have my boat here, so I can give you a lift."

"No, I'm good. I'm here with some people." I kicked myself for speaking without thinking and saw his face harden. I forgot who I was dealing with. These men and their egos, they hated the word *no*.

"It wasn't a question." He reached up and ran his fingers down my cheek, and I looked away and forced myself not to brush off his touch. Something firm and warm touched my back, then a hand settled on my hip. *Finally.*

"Step back," Paul ordered over my head, "and carry on with your day."

Agustin's face scrunched, and I felt my stomach bottom out. "Who the hell are you?"

Paul's chest vibrated against my back as he grunted. "I won't repeat myself."

"She's with me." Agustin wasn't about to back down; our shared history with Bruno had proven that. "Let her go." I kept my mouth pressed in a firm line so I wouldn't say anything. "There's plenty of bitches you can have, but this one is mine."

"What did you call me?" I snapped and tried to jump forward, but Paul's hand kept me firmly against him.

Agustin reached for me, but Paul quickly and smoothly grabbed his hand and snapped it backward. He dropped to his knees with a yelp, then Paul kicked his leg, and he jerked in pain.

Paul took my hand, and I had to run to keep up with him.

"You just have friends everywhere." He snickered over his shoulder.

"Not by choice," I shot back as we raced to distance ourselves from Agustin and whoever he might have with him.

John came into view. He held his phone to his ear as we fell into step. John picked up the pace, and I was soon winded. These guys were crazy fit. We finally slowed as we approached the meeting point. I saw a speedboat and watched Cole shake hands with who I assumed was Adan's brother. We all began to hurry on board. Paul jumped in first then swung around and lifted me off the dock and onto the boat before I could react. The engine roared to life, and I grabbed his shoulders to stabilize myself. I silently moaned when I remembered the last time I was in this position. This time we weren't *in* the water, and his hands on me seared hot. He felt it, too, because when he lowered me, he dragged me down the full length of his front.

"Sit." He pointed, and I rolled my eyes at how quickly he changed moods. I sat, and as the boat swung away from the dock, he plunked down next to me.

"The Ruiz family's here," Paul told the others.

"Damage?" Cole asked.

"Just one of 'em. Hand and knee."

"Copy that."

The speedboat didn't offer much protection from the chilly sea spray. It was a warm day, but out in the open water, the temperature dropped. The engines screamed as they beat through the choppy water, and I did whatever I could to hang on. Mark grinned at me, totally at ease, and held out the bag of beef jerky. When I shook my head, he dug into it like he hadn't eaten in days. Mike drove the boat while Cole and Keith studied a map. Paul and John seemed to be in some kind of conversation but spoke in French. To me, it sounded personal, so I turned away to give them privacy.

"Here." Paul tugged his deep green hoodie over his head and handed it to me. I appreciated that he'd noticed I was cold.

"Won't you be cold?" I had to ask, but he shook his head and said something to John in French. "Thanks, then." I plunged my frozen arms through the sleeves and pulled it on. I was instantly engulfed with his scent, and his leftover body heat felt like heaven. I crossed my bare legs and wished my bag was closer so I could change back into my pants.

A wave hit the side of the boat, and I felt like I was about to fly over the side, only to have Paul's hand automatically reach out to push down on my legs to keep me in place. *Sweet hell, that scared me!* Paul didn't even glance up. *How do these guys stay so agile?* I grabbed his arm and used him as an anchor and wiggled closer, not caring how I looked. Besides, he radiated heat, and I wanted some. He didn't seem to mind as I tucked myself to his side. I figured it was the safest place for me.

"I think I saw Jesus with that last wave." I yelped as another one hit. "He's determined to get me."

"You're not going anywhere." He chuckled at my comment then leaned back with his feet out. I was very aware of the tight grip he had on my thigh. I missed being held by someone, even if it was just to keep me from plunging to my death. I figured simply having someone who cared about me was enough in that moment.

He turned his head to me. "What's your history with Agustin Ruiz?"

"I worked with him and his family on a story that made it to the press," I yelled so he could hear me, and he nodded. "I gained their trust, you know, played their game, until Agustin wanted more from me. I had to set boundaries, which all these Cartel men hate." I rolled my eyes. "He did cause some trouble between Bruno and me. Male egos at play, and all that." I sidestepped how bad things had been back then. I wanted to prove to Paul that I was good at my job and tried never to cross any lines along the way.

"Did you and Agustin ever…?"

"Sleep together?" I laughed and leaned close to his ear. "No, and while we are on the topic, I haven't slept with Bruno or any of the Cartel families." He seemed to like that answer because his shoulders relaxed under his damp t-shirt. *Interesting.*

"Seems to me Agustin would like another try."

"He's persistent." It was true. Agustin was

dangerous and had no moral compass, but the same was true of Bruno. It was how all the men were in the Cartel world.

He stared down at me. "Guess I better keep you close."

I'd like that.

As we approached the island, a stillness came over the team as they slipped into their Blackstone roles. Cole glanced at Mark, who gave a nod, then he gave that same look to Keith, who nodded, then it went like that until each of them had done their silent check-in.

Mike jumped off the boat first, and as he tied it up, John did a quick scan to cover his back. The others followed silently. I quickly stripped off Paul's hoodie and handed it to him. He offered me a hand and tugged me up on the dock in one fluid motion. He put the hoodie in a small duffle bag.

"Stay close," he warned and put a hand on my hip to move me behind him. I shivered. The loss of the hoodie had left me with bare arms, but the warm Mexican sun would soon warm me up.

To anyone else, we looked like a group of friends out for a good time. Mark, of course, played his part like a champ, buying a fruity drink with an umbrella and a pineapple wedge on the side. He popped on a fedora and waved a map around like he was our tour guide. The best part was how he continued to give Keith a hard time for not wanting to give the hat a try. I couldn't help but wonder if he'd been a theater kid.

I chuckled to Cole when he came up behind me. "He always like that?"

"He's worse," he huffed, along with John and Paul. I laughed even harder.

"And no one minds?"

"We don't have a choice," Mike muttered from up ahead.

"Someday," Cole went on, "I'll fill you in on his backstory. He had a rough upbringing. He uses humor as a way to cope, and we all get that."

"We all give him shit," John said over his shoulder, "but he's probably our favorite."

"I'm going to pretend I didn't hear that," Paul piped in and sounded ticked.

"You're still in the doghouse." John smirked. "I still need time." I got a kick out of the fact that they all played along.

Paul looked down at me when I laughed, and I saw a lightness poke through his otherwise stressed expression. I realized I'd give my left kidney to know his and John's backstory as friends.

"Would you look at that?" Mark held up his hat and pointed it up ahead. "I see our hotel." Which was code for he spotted the boat. As fast as the guys had begun to play around, they slipped right back into military mode.

They made their way toward it slowly. I found it hard to take the time and pretend to look at things as we went. I knew we couldn't seem like we were checking out the area around the boat.

"Mark and Mike, you're with me," Cole said quietly. "Keith, John, fan out on either side, and Paul and Nicole, you stay by the ramp."

Paul positioned me by the entrance of the ramp and put an arm around me as if we were a couple. His eyes constantly scanned the area around us.

"Do you ever get scared?" I grinned up at him to look like I was flirting.

He gave me a one-word answer. "No."

I wiggled my nose to show I didn't like his answer. I needed something to focus on, but as I went to open my mouth again, I spotted Agustin as he hopped off some billionaire-looking yacht. The drug business sure paid well. I stepped into Paul's chest and used him to shield me. Without hesitation, he rested a hand on my waist and pressed me behind a large dock post to partially shield us from view.

"What do you see?"

I peeked around and saw Agustin with a few men race toward some locals. "Agustin just arrived with some men. Oh, my God." Panic rippled through me. "I see Jerry Canos and about ten of his soldiers." I took a deep breath. I really didn't like the idea of seeing any of them. This was becoming very real, very fast.

Paul quickly spoke into his tiny radio and let the team know. "What are they doing now?"

"I can't see."

He stepped into me, his knee between my legs, one hand swung around my waist, and he dipped low enough for his lips to graze the side of my neck, and where his lips were on my sensitive skin brought a rush of a hundred different endorphins to the surface. His firm hold and confidence took me by surprise. "Put your arms around me, Nic," he whispered, and I melted at the use of his nickname for me.

"Is this how you and John work as a team?" I made a poor attempt at a joke to try to rid myself of the anxiety that was building. I pulled him in closer.

"John likes to be manhandled more." He spread his hands along my back just as Agustin came into view. "Now what are they doing?"

"Jerry is about twenty feet from us, scanning the area, but Agustin is talking to some men. They're looking this way. Paul, I'm nervous he might spot me or—" He looked over my shoulder then threaded his free hand into my hair, so I'd look at him.

"Keith has him in his view," he said in a calm tone. "The boat is currently unoccupied, and Mark just gave me the signal they've planted the cameras. In just a moment, we'll move on."

"I don't think my legs will work," I admitted.

"Hey," he pulled me back to look straight in my eyes, "I know these guys. I know how they think and how they operate. Trust me when I say I won't let anyone touch you." I gave him a nod and took a much-needed deep breath. I believed him. "We just have to wait until he leaves." He took my hand and used the post to shield me until Agustin got into a car.

His head tilted slightly, and I knew someone was on the radio. "Time to move," he said. He hesitated, and I got the vibe he didn't really want to let go, but then the moment passed. He just needed to make sure to keep up the romance for show.

The hotel looked over the marina. Mark took the first shift to watch the boat, Keith kept an eye out from the balcony, while Paul was in another room on a call. Cole talked to Mike about something I couldn't follow, so I let myself zone out for a bit and finished my salad. Once I was done, I tossed the container in the trash and joined John on the couch. He was reading something on his phone, but when I sat down, he tucked his phone away.

"How ya doing?" he asked with a smile.

"A little uneasy, but all things considered, I'm fine."

"You're good at your job, Nicole. I'm impressed with how well you've hung in there."

"I appreciate that." I unscrewed the cap on my water and took a sip as I thought. "I got myself into some situations when I first started this job that I honestly wish I could forget." I grimaced. "It left scars that remind me in moments like today that I'm not as untouchable as I imagined. I constantly do research on all the Cartel families in Mexico, even the smaller ones, because what's small today can be huge tomorrow. Things here can change with one gunfight."

"Very true." He leaned back and propped his feet on the table. "I know you have history with Bruno." My stomach twisted. "Which means you probably know the Perez family's history."

"I do."

"Do you know much about Bruno's uncle, Martin Castillo?"

"I do, yes."

Paul stepped into the room and pocketed his phone. He gave John a quizzical look then sat down across from me.

I turned back to John. "Actually, I was asked to cover the story after you guys took down Castillo's operation."

John's gaze moved to the roof like he remembered something. "I didn't see any story, and at the time, we were watching the press closely."

"Yeah, that's because my assignment got pulled at the last minute. My story changed from one on Castillo to his right-hand man, Eric Noah."

Paul coughed, and I thought I saw something dark go across his face. It made me wonder if Blackstone had had a few run-ins with Eric Noah before they made their move on Castillo.

"And what is your take on the infamous Eric Noah?" John pulled me back to him, and I thought about all I knew.

"He was an American who moved to Mexico when he was in his late twenties or early thirties. No family that I could find. He ran a very successful human trafficking business out of Rosarito. Business was so good, his operation among the locals was referred to as The Tunnel to Hell." I threw a look of disgust at John, but he didn't react, so I continued. "At some point, he joined forces with Martin Castillo. I'm sure once Castillo saw what he had to offer, he was only too happy to get in on the action.

"He had an on again, off again relationship with Talya Canos, who was also rumored to be dating the head of a mafia syndicate in Vegas at the time. A guy named Grim Gates. Although I never really believed that."

Paul bit into an apple. "Why?"

"Call it a hunch, and now I know that the child is hers and Eric Noah's, I don't believe Grim Gates was ever romantically involved with Talya. Plus, when he left for Vegas, she didn't go, and later he got married to someone else. I don't know. I just don't see it."

John nodded like he could follow my line of logic. "Did you ever meet the guy?"

"Eric Noah?" At his nod, I continued. "Yes, once, just in passing, but I'll never forget it."

"What was that about?" Paul interrupted and leaned forward, resting his elbows on his knees.

"I had a run-in with Bruno and was trying to find a way back to my team before he could catch up with me. I took the side streets, and when I came around a corner, I saw him. I recognized him right away. It was Eric Noah, and he was dealing with some guy. Before I could move, he shot the guy right in the head. He looked directly at me then turned and walked off in the other direction. Bruno appeared and started yelling. I took the opportunity to get the hell out of there. I saw enough to know I never wanted to see that man again."

Paul looked at John then back at me. "Well, it's a good thing he's dead." He shrugged.

"See, that's the thing. It was said he died in the explosion, but his remains were never found. Isn't that odd? Surely, there'd be at least a tooth?"

Paul stood and snapped his back. "I can promise you, Nicole, Eric Noah is dead."

"You know that for sure?"

"Yes," both said at the same time.

I raised my hands as if to say *if you say so*.

"Well, good. Now, if only you could remove Bruno, Agustin, and Rafael, the world might sleep a little better."

John agreed.

I watched as Paul slipped out onto the patio to join Keith and wondered if I should follow.

TWENTY

PAUL

I slid the door closed behind me and leaned over the railing near Keith. "Hey, man," he said but kept his eyes on the busy marina below, "how ya holding up?"

I rubbed the back of my neck. "Ask me again when this is all over."

"Shit," he lowered his head, "I seriously understand that statement."

"Can I ask you something?" He looked over. "Do you look at me any different from when you knew me before, versus now, I mean? When you think of *them*," I meant the Cartel, "do you think of me?"

He fiddled with the wedding ring he wore on his right hand and seemed to think about his words. "You know what I see when I look at you Paul? I see a man who gave up everything for Blackstone and your country. Don't forget how many women you and Chili saved during that time as well. You played a role for a decade. Put your whole life on pause. You didn't have to do it, but you did. To me, that's a true soldier." I pushed back the emotion that had taken me over. I hated this whole topic, but knew Keith, out of all the guys had been the one who handled my return the easiest.

My son, Nicole, this whole mission played with my head, and I hated the disconnect I seemed to have with John since I'd come back. He was my best friend, my brother, and although it might be on my side, I had to find my way back.

"Thanks, man. I feel like I'm slipping backward."

Keith stood straight. "What do we do when we slip?"

"I know." I nodded and knew what I needed to do. "What about—"

"We're up, boys," John shouted from the behind the door, and we were instantly ready to move down to the boat. John handed Nicole her earpiece and told her to hang back and let us know if she recognized anyone. We headed down the back stairs to blend in with the nightlife of the marina.

Mark signaled Selena was coming up to the boat. We sank into the shadows and blended the best we could. We had no idea if we were the only ones watching the slip. I was the closest to the boat and had a good view.

We could hear the baby's cries as Selena got close.

My stomach took a nosedive, and my heart went with it. There was my son in a filthy Onesie flopping around on her hip like a rag doll. His mouth was open, and his cries echoed through the lines of boats. His face was flushed, and he looked terrified. Something inside of me shifted, and I saw red.

"Easy, brother," John said softly in my ear. "Play this out right."

"I demand to know where Arlo is!" Selena snapped into her phone in English, and I wondered who she was speaking to. From our research, we knew Arlo was her boyfriend and another one of the Canos' soldiers. "You brought me here, and I didn't sign up for this shit!" She looked at my boy. *"Cállate!"* My grip on my handgun tightened when she yelled at my child to shut up. "This wasn't the deal!"

"Let her onto the boat," Cole said through our earpieces. "Let's make sure no one else is coming."

"I don't know when he ate last." She cursed again. "All he does is scream!" She yelled right in my baby's face when she spoke. "I hate this kid. I'm done!" She hopped onto the boat and practically chucked my son on the bench seat. He struggled to sit up, and when he did, he put his head back and screamed some more. "I hate you!" Selena whirled with her hand raised to slap him, and then, to my horror, Nicole appeared next to the boat with her hands in the air.

"Everyone hold," I said quickly as I tried to process what was happening. This was not in the plan. "Nicole, what are you doing?" She didn't answer, but I knew she could hear me.

"Excuse me?" Nicole called, and Selena quickly snatched up my son and glared at her.

"Go away!"

"Sorry for bothering you," Nicole pressed, "but I heard your baby crying, and as a mother myself, I recognize the stress you must be under. My daughter has bad colic, and there are times when I think if someone could just see how I was about to lose it and take my child just for a minute so maybe I could think straight. What's the baby's name?"

Selena squeezed her eyes shut as Nicole stepped down onto the boat. "Stop!" she yelled, but Nicole didn't stop. Panic ripped through me, and I fought to stay still.

"We're only human," I heard her say through the screams. "Why don't I hold the baby for a sec, and you can take a minute to breathe." Selena shifted my son to her other hip and seemed to be considering the idea.

"Hold," Cole ordered. "See if she'll make the transfer."

Nicole took a step closer. "We mothers need to stick together. Let me help you." My boy, though still screaming, seemed to have turned his gaze to Nicole. "Hey, there, sweetheart." She waved at him and gave him a big smile, and we could hear him hiccup through his wails. She reached for him, but Selena jumped back.

"Get back!" She reached into her bag and pulled out a gun and pointed it at my son's head. John's hand clamped down on my shoulder to hold me in place. "I hate this kid! I hate this place!"

"Hey," Nicole stepped closer, and my vision blurred for a moment, "point the gun at me, not at the baby. If you want to kill someone, you kill me."

"Just leave me alone!"

"Selena." Nicole used her real name, and the woman's eyes went wide. She swung the gun toward Nicole. "That's right, keep the gun on me, drive that bullet into my head. If you're going to be a murderer, do it right."

"John…" I could barely speak, barely breathe.

"I know." He kept his hand in place. "She's got this."

"If Selena hurts her…" I couldn't finish the sentence because I couldn't believe I said it.

Selena shuffled to the side of the boat, the gun still on Nicole. "Who are you?"

"I'm a friend, just trying to help."

"I don't believe you."

Nicole reached for her phone, holding it up for her to see. "Rafael sent me."

"Smart play," John grunted.

"I was just talking to him, but he never mentioned you."

"I was late," Nicole looked around the boat then back to her, "but I'm here now. Just give me the boy, and you can be done here."

Selena started to panic, and I knew something was about to happen. She shook my son, and he screamed even louder, then she hauled back and smacked him across his face with the back of the hand with the gun in it. Nicole jumped in horror and covered her face while John kept an iron grip on me to stop me from leaping onto the boat. "That gun'll go off, Paul," he hissed, and I could feel his terror.

"He needs to die the way his mama did!" Selena screamed and awkwardly dangled my son over the edge of the boat. Everything went still inside me. John let me go, and I jumped to my feet. Nicole's eyes flew to mine, and she seemed to read my mind. I raised the gun and drilled a bullet through her temple, and as Selena's arms gave out, Nicole caught my son, mid-fall. Selena fell over the side, and Nicole wrapped her arms around his tiny body and pressed him to her.

I leapt aboard the boat before I heard Cole's command to move. John was right next to me as the rest of the guys ran toward us. I grabbed Nicole by the elbows as she clung to my son and made sure she was all right.

"I'm okay." Her eyes were glossy, and she was shaking, but she was fine. "It's okay, sweetie, you're okay now. It's okay." She worked to console him, but he was too far gone.

"Damn." I huffed and stepped back from them, at a total loss. John squeezed my shoulder and handed me my bag. He understood my need for something to do, and I started to plant some evidence that would make it look like Bruno and his soldiers had been there. They had a style when it came to ransacking a place, and I added one more thing for good measure.

"Is that a York candy wrapper?" Nicole asked.

I didn't answer her. We didn't have time.

"Let's go." Keith stepped onto the side of the boat and plucked two out of the three little cameras we'd planted. We wanted to see if they took the bait on Bruno. "I don't trust we haven't been seen."

Nicole grabbed the bag Selena had dropped and stuffed in a few diapers along with some salted crackers she had brought.

"Let's go." I steered them off the boat and down the shoreline where we carefully made our way back toward the boat we arrived on. It wasn't easy with my son still wailing, but who could blame him?

I hopped into the boat first and reached for my son, but he had a fistful of her dress and his head was buried into her chest as he cried. I knew from working at Shadows that our 'guests' needed to be handled very carefully, and if they found comfort in one of us, we didn't intervene. Besides, now wasn't the time. Instead, I reached out and practically lifted them both into the boat and down to the seat.

Within seconds, we were idling away from the shore and into the open water. My head spun with how everything went down, and I found myself getting upset with Nicole and how she put herself in danger. At the same time, she'd saved my son from likely drowning.

The guys were on high alert, and I checked to make sure I had a bullet in the chamber. We were far from being safe.

"It's okay, sweet boy." Nicole gently rocked him as he held on to her for dear life. "I've got you. You're okay." She kissed his head then looked at me. His cries seemed a little less loud. "Paul? Can I have your hoodie again?"

"Sure." I pulled it free and handed it to her. I thought she was going to put it on since her skin was broken out in goosebumps, but instead, she made a makeshift sling and tucked him inside. She positioned him so he was on her hip and protected from the cold. His hand popped out and grabbed a piece of her dress again as if to anchor himself as he screamed some more. A few times, he'd stop and cough. His lungs were probably congested from being so upset. "Okay, you want to stay in the front, you can." She twisted the hoodie around, and he pressed his head against her bare skin. He seemed to like that, and his cries softened. It broke my heart at how much he'd been neglected since Talya died.

"Shit," Mark pulled my focus, "we got company, boys." I looked over my shoulder and saw the lights of three separate motorboats coming our way fast.

"Nicole," I spoke louder since the baby's sobbing grew louder with the sudden disruption, "get down on the floor." She wasted no time and dropped then curled herself around my son. A bullet zipped over my shoulder, and Cole made a sharp turn. Nicole yelped and grabbed my ankle.

Zip-zip-zip, more bullets came, and we ducked. Once we returned fire, we knew we'd be rained on.

All but Cole ducked so it looked like he was the only one in the boat. "I see it up ahead," he called, "but we have to deal with these guys first. I'll let them get close. Be ready."

"Hey," I said into Nicole's ear, "get a grip on him and your bag. We're about to switch boats in a few minutes."

"What, we're separating?" Her eyes bulged. "Why didn't I know this?"

"You know now."

"Don't leave us." Her voice shook and outed how nervous she was. I loved that she accounted for my son and wasn't only worried about herself.

"I'm not," I promised then made a motion to stay low.

One of the boats was almost behind us and gained ground quickly. Within seconds, the boat pulled close. Cole waited until they tossed a rope over the side and raised his arms. When the guy started to climb in, we opened fire and sprayed them with bullets until all were killed. I jumped in their boat, zip tied the wheel to steer slightly to the left, then rigged a pole so it would press on the throttle when we were ready. I jumped back into our boat and pushed the pole to move the throttle forward. The engine roared as it took off away from us.

Cole raced off as the other two boats gained on us. I looked back at Nicole, who had her cheek to the baby as she spoke softly to him. He'd exhausted himself from crying and now just gulped, wide-eyed, with his hand tightly fisted around the fabric of her dress.

I waited for Cole to take a hard right and cut the engine behind a large concrete pillar from an old bridge. "Let's go!" I hauled Nicole to her feet and helped them onto the fishing boat we'd arranged to be left for us.

John grabbed my arm and made me look back at him. He didn't have to say it; I knew what he was thinking.

"See you on the other side," I assured him.

"You better," he grunted and then they sped away.

I pressed Nicole and the baby down then joined them. I prayed it had worked. It had to seem as though we were all still on the same boat. When the other two boats roared by in pursuit of Cole and the guys, I breathed a sigh of relief.

I looked down, and Nicole was shaking. I wasn't sure if it was from nerves or the fact she was in only a cotton dress. "We need to get inside the cabin and out of sight. If he starts to cry again, he might out us."

"Yeah." She rushed inside the cabin with the child, and I grabbed a blanket to cover her shoulders.

"You might want this." I lay the blanket down next to her.

"Thanks," she said as she looked around the old fishing boat. Her hand rubbed my son's back. I tried not to stare at him, but he looked a lot like me. "He's cute." She looked at me, so I turned away and picked up my rucksack. I pulled out the small bag Savannah had given me.

I pulled a chair over to sit in front of them and emptied the contents next to her.

"Is that baby soap?" She smiled at me. "You thought of baby soap?"

"Savannah did."

"Savannah?"

"Cole's wife." I reached in and brought out a pouch and read the label. "Once Upon A Farm, squeezable carrots." I turned my nose up at it and thought how gross it sounded.

"It's no different than your MRE." Nicole slowly undid the side of her sling.

"I beg to differ." I leaned over. "Here, let me help." I helped her tug it off, and she spread out my hoodie on the padded bench seat with her free hand, then carefully laid him on top of it. He didn't like it, but when she started talking to him, he relaxed a little. His tiny hands clenched and tears welled in his eyes, but he held it together. I felt a little proud.

"You need to be changed, and you really need a bath, don't you, sweetheart? Yes, you do." I handed her some water and a clean shirt of mine to use as a washcloth, and she started to clean the dirt off his face. "No one is going to hurt you now." He kept his eyes on her the whole time, except once when I got close. His bottom lip stuck out as he stared at me, and I looked at Nicole for help. "Just talk to him," she suggested.

"It's okay, buddy." I kept my voice low.

"Don't be scared. That's Paul. I know he's big and scary looking, but he's a big teddy bear." His eyes got wider, and I wondered how many men hurt him in the time he'd been taken. "He's nice," Nicole said calmly. "He's a good man."

Her words pricked at my core. I rather liked that comment. I couldn't remember the last time someone called me a good man.

"See," she wrapped her arms around me, and I didn't even think about it and hugged her back, "friend." Now, that comment I didn't like. His hand came up and reached for her, so I let go, and she went back to his sponge bath. "Now, what's the plan?" she asked over her shoulder as she eased his diaper off with an unhappy sigh. "When were you changed last, sweetie?" She went to work.

"For now, we take this boat to a spot along the shore where a car is waiting for us. They'll take us to a safehouse. Once we're there, the chopper will come for us."

"Good. Wait. Who's driving this boat?"

"I am."

"Oh, okay." She started to tuck his feet into what

looked like footed blue PJs and ran the zipper carefully up his front. "There, you're all set in your
jammies. Look how handsome you are, Eric."

A cold feeling rushed over me. "Don't call him
that," I snapped.

"Why? That's his name."

"Just don't." I wasn't about to get into a conversation over it.

She didn't push it. "Then what do we call you?"
She spoke to him as I searched my brain for a better
name. "What about Chase?" She chuckled. "Seems to
suit, don't you think?" She looked up at me, and I
had to admit it was good. She took his hands and
helped him stand, but he dropped back down on his
butt. He gave a little whimper and wrapped his arms
around her neck. He seemed to just want to be held.

"Chase," I repeated and gave a curt nod, and she
stepped toward me with him, and my stomach
knotted.

"See, we like Paul." She took his tiny hand and
placed it on my cheek. My insides melted, my heart
squeezed to the point of pain, and my breathing
stopped. *My son.* He held it there for a moment but
then buried his face in her chest again and gave a
whimper.

"I don't think he likes me." I wished I was better
at this.

"He's tired and most likely hungry. Give him time
to warm up. Women tend to be more who they want
at this age."

I handed her the carrot mush. "You feed him. We need to get moving."

"Copy that." She sat down and began to feed him, as I continued with my internal struggle.

I decided to have it out with her and squatted in front of them, "Hey, I need you to promise me something."

Chase wiggled in her arms, not overly interested in the food. "Okay."

"I appreciate what you did on the boat, but you can't do that again. You hear me?"

Her sharp green eyes moved to mine, and I saw her jaw lock. "I will if someone tries to hurt a child again."

"Nicole," I growled from somewhere deep inside my chest and leaned forward with a hand on her leg to drive my point home, "I mean it."

She leaned forward to mimic me and stopped an inch from my face with her eyes fixed on mine. "So do I."

Her warm breath brushed over my face, and I fought not to kiss her, but it wasn't the time. I hated and loved that she fought me on things. The tangled emotions she brought out in me were confusing. I blamed it on the situation. My world had just been shaken like a snow globe, and I still waited for all the flakes to settle. I wondered if I'd ever see things clearly again.

"We'll discuss this again later." I squeezed her thigh and stood.

She kept her gaze on me. "And I know how it'll end."

I clamped down on my tongue and started the engine. I scoped the area and hoped like hell there was no one around.

We made it to shore without any problems, and as I tied up the boat, I was happy to see car lights flash as we stepped off the dock. Our ride had arrived. I grabbed the bags, and Nicole followed closely with little Chase.

"*Hola,*" the driver greeted us, and I helped Nicole in the back seat then climbed in after her.

"*Gracias—*" Nicole started to speak, but I put my hand on her thigh. I seemed to like touching her there.

"No names, no talking, just let him drive," I warned. That was how these operations worked. It was much safer for them not to share anything with us, and us with them.

She let out a sigh. I knew it was engrained in her to establish contacts, but it wasn't the time for that.

My head was on its normal swivel as we drove along the back roads to the safe house where we'd spend the night. My weapon burned at my hip, ready to fire if need be. My nerves were so much more on edge now that we had my son. I saw danger at every turn. I wondered if anyone had taken the bait that it might be Bruno who took the baby, and they searched for him somewhere else.

Nicole's body sank heavily against my side, and I

knew she was way past exhausted. Chase lay awake, and I was glad he was quiet. His tiny hand played with a piece of her hair as he sucked away on a pacifier. His cheeks were red, and his eyes looked kind of glossy as he lay there. Poor kid was probably so messed up with all that had happened, his little mind must be blown. I'd have to worry about that once we got him home.

I was incredibly thankful for Nicole. If she hadn't hooked up with us, I wasn't sure how the whole thing would have gone. I thought of all the times she helped us as we tracked him down and how she used her connections with the Cartel. She was a huge asset, and I needed to share that with her at some point. She deserved that much from me. Chase let out a little cry, and Nicole jerked awake.

"What's wrong?" she whispered, and he rubbed his eyes with his fists. "You wouldn't eat before. Are you finally hungry?" I pulled out the gooey carrots and handed them to her. She held it up and squeezed a little on his lip, but he turned away. "I'm a little worried he won't eat," she confessed quietly.

"Let's try again when we get to the safehouse." I tried to ease her concern, but I wondered the same thing. "Maybe we should try another kind?"

"Maybe."

We pulled into a long, tree-lined driveway then followed it to a house that was set well away from the road. I hadn't stayed at this house before, but I knew

Frank's team, Eagle Eye, had. Frank had set things up for us.

"*Gracias.*" I pulled out some bills and paid the man well. It was always a wise thing to overpay for services. He handed me a key without a word and left.

There wasn't much to look at, but the fridge was stocked, it was warm, there were places to sit and sleep, and there was a fully functional bathroom with a shower. That was all we needed for the night.

"I'm going to see if I can get him to sleep." Nicole turned from the entryway as if to walk toward the living room, but I gently pulled her back by her shoulder. "What?"

"Let me clear the place first. Stay put."

She looked at me with concern. "Didn't they already do that?"

"Yeah, but they're not me." I pulled my handgun and made my way through the kitchen, small bathroom, and two bedrooms. I checked everywhere anyone could hide. When I returned, I found Nicole in the kitchen balancing Chase in her arms. He looked sleepy and kept rubbing his eyes. "Is this your idea of staying put?"

"I needed water," she said over her shoulder, "plus, Chase is really warm." She picked up a clean dishcloth that was folded on the counter and wet it. When she pressed it to his forehead, he started to cry. "You're so tired, sweetie. You really need to sleep." She turned to look at me. "Can you please hand me my bag?" I passed it to her and watched as she dug around for something while Chase fussed in her arms. "There you are." She held up a small bunny with long Dumbo ears. "Is this yours?" Chase immediately pulled it to his face and rubbed it over his cheeks.

"Where'd you get that?"

"I forgot about it. The sisters told me it was left with his birth certificate. Talya must have given it to them."

I studied the little guy as he gripped the stuffed animal and felt a tug in my heart that he had something from his mother. It would help him to feel safe. At least I hoped it would bring a happy memory for him.

Nicole put a bit of another type of kid's goo on her finger from a squeezy tube, but again he refused to eat it. He just turned his head away and rubbed his face into her shirt.

"Not even applesauce, little guy?" She twisted up her mouth. "I think I'll just try to get him to sleep." She went into a bedroom, and I followed and sat in the chair in the corner as she put him on the bed and lay down next to him.

For someone who didn't have a happy life growing up, she sure was good with kids. "You seem like you've been around kids before," I said softly as she rubbed his belly.

"When you've been skipped over time after time to be adopted, you tend to focus on the kids around you to help fill the emptiness that brings."

I watched as she smiled down at Chase with gentleness and compassion. He was no one to her, just someone's child. She was a pretty impressive woman.

"We should eat while we can. I'll go round us up something." I figured while we had a down moment, we should refuel.

"I'll be here." She stroked his cheek with the back of her fingers, and I could see he was slowly drifting off to sleep. "That's right, sweet pea, give in to it. You need it." I stood there another moment, and like magic, the little guy was out cold.

"Wow, that didn't take long," I whispered.

"He's so tired, poor thing. I'm hungry, but I think I'll have a shower first. I'll meet you out there."

"Sounds good." I checked my gun again and made sure there was one in the chamber. Call me OCD, but I wasn't taking any chances with my son or Nicole.

I stared in the fridge and instantly missed Abigail's and Savannah's cooking. I wasn't much of a cook, but I could make a mean barbequed steak.

Thankfully, there was some already prepared taco meat and enchiladas, so I tossed them in the microwave and pulled two plates from the cabinet. I did my best to add all the fixings then questioned where we should eat. I hated not to be in the same room as Chase, so I headed to the bedroom with the food. We could use the little table I'd seen in there.

I used my foot to open the door, and I paused

when I saw Nicole standing in the open bathroom. She was in a pair of panties and had her back turned to me. Her slender spine arched when she slid her shirt off the counter and tugged it on then let it fall. It hit her mid-thigh and looked incredibly sexy. She must have felt my eyes on her, and she turned to look over her shoulder. "I wanted to keep an eye on him." She pointed at Chase.

"Food." I stumbled to find my words. "You should eat."

"You don't have to tell me twice," she said softly, and I put the food on the table. She joined me and sat with her bare legs crossed. She flipped her hair back then dove in.

"What will happen to Chase when you get him back to the States?" I thought about the way she worded that.

"When *we* get back to the States, you mean?"

She shifted uneasily. "Yeah, well, both of you."

"You're not coming back?" I pulled my chin in and studied her face. The woman was mad. Everyone and their crazy cousin was on the hunt for us. All of us. They'd kill her to get the location of the Canos' grandchild. My son.

"My job is here."

"Nicole," I laid my fork on the side of my plate. I knew I had to tread lightly here, "aren't you worried about how Bruno will deal with you if he thinks you helped us get Chase over the border? What about Rafael, Agustin, Sully?"

She thought for a moment. "I'll think of something, but my work is here. It's my life." She thought again. "Rafael's gross, it's true, and I know he's going to be furious when he realizes I've worked against him, but I'm sure he's already got his money for that poor baby twice over. He's probably double-crossed more than one family, so he might not be long for this world, anyway.

"That leaves Bruno." When she saw I was about to say something, she held up her hand. "I know we have history, but I'm not going to let my fear of him ruin my work. He knows I work for a powerful news network, and he's smart. He was counting on getting his hands on the Canos' grandchild to have power over them, just like the rest of the Cartel. He'll get over the loss of his chess piece. I just need to come up with a new story to make him look good, while I work on a much larger story for later."

"Nicole, I know you're a smart woman, but I don't think you realize how bad things are. It's not just Bruno. Every Cartel family is looking for that child. He's become a prize they all want. It's about pride and bragging rights, let alone the chance to dangle him over the Canos family to have them give up territory to get him back."

"I know that."

"Do you, though? Are you really willing to risk your life on that? Things have changed here."

She tilted her head and looked toward the sleeping baby. "Can I ask you something?"

"Maybe."

She studied me with her pretty eyes. "The guys are all married, right?" Her change of topic threw me. "I know Cole is married to Savannah, thanks to you, and I heard him talking about her with John, but who is John married to?"

"Sloane."

"Sloane, right, and Mark is with Mia." I nodded, and she went on. "Mike is with Catalina. Is Keith married?"

My stomach clenched as I remembered my final days in Rosarito.

"Was. She passed." I cleared my throat uncomfortably.

Her nose wrinkled like she felt bad for not knowing that. "I'm sorry."

"It was complicated." I pushed the meat around my plate, suddenly not hungry.

Chase whimpered, and she looked at him again. "And what about you? Married? Ever been? Girlfriend? I'm hoping not, since we kissed twice."

Instantly, I thought of how she felt in my arms, how she tasted, how she smelled. My pants grew tight.

"No to all." I slit my eyes at her. "Nicole, you completely changed the subject. I'm not going to allow you to stay here and get yourself killed, you know."

She stared at me, and when I looked up, she didn't move her gaze off me.

"What?" She shook her head and went back to her plate. "Say it," I ordered, a little harder than I meant to.

"I guess you just puzzle me. You try to be so commanding. I know it's the way you have to be in your job. You're attractive, a bit moody," she smirked, "but kind when you want to be, and you're a great kisser." I looked at my plate. "Are you shy?"

I let out a laugh. "No, hardly shy."

"Good, because shy guys drive me nuts." She put a hand over her mouth. "That came out rudely. I just mean, in our world, there's no room for shy, nervous men."

"Your last boyfriend, what did he do?"

She leaned her arm on the table. "Justin worked a corporate job. Something I tried to get on board with, but—" She shrugged. "Let's just say he couldn't hang here, that's for sure."

"What attracted you to him?" I figured if she could dig, so could I.

She held a smile for a moment, then it fell, and I knew I hit a nerve. "At first, he seemed like he was a take-charge kind of man. Driven and knew what he wanted. Confidence is everything for me in a man, but over time that fizzled away. He didn't like that I was always here, and he often had to attend his company's work dinners and parties alone.

"He tried to do all the things to get me to marry him. He told me he loved me and that I'd never be without family again." She looked away. "Then I found out he'd been cheating, so he obviously never did love me at all. There it was again. I was destined to be alone." She pushed her plate away. "People like Justin use your most vulnerable insecurities to hit you with when you don't do what they want. They want to control you."

"Seems like a real ass." I didn't have anything more to say about the guy; she was better without him. "Why don't you date soldiers?"

"Because there's no future there. They do a job too close to mine. Always moving to the next place, no time to settle down."

"So, you've never dated one?" She shook her head. "Never kissed any?"

A smile tugged at her lips. "Just one."

"Well." I drank some water as I dragged out the moment. I rather liked this conversation, and I enjoyed that she answered my questions. "Why me?" I leaned back in my chair and spread out my legs to get more comfortable.

"Why me?" she challenged and leaned back to mimic my movements.

I reached forward, grabbed the arms of her chair, and slid her silently across the smooth floor. I wedged her between my legs and leaned forward to rest my elbows on my thighs.

"Because you're strong, assertive, smart, and *painfully* beautiful to be around."

She arched her brow with intrigue. That hungry

twinkle she got in her eye right before we'd kiss was back. "Painful, huh?"

I played along. "Excruciating."

"I wouldn't want you to be in pain around me." She rubbed her hands up my forearms, and a rush of adrenaline coursed through me. "What should we do about this situation?" She pushed to her feet and moved forward to lower herself onto my lap.

"I can think of a few ideas." My hands went up under her shirt then slid around to her smooth back. Everything inside me coiled tightly, and for a moment, I hesitated. I hadn't been with a woman in well over a year, and Nicole brought a rush of all kinds of feelings to the surface.

I pulled her to me and kissed her neck while I pressed my erection against her. Her heartbeat pounded against my tongue, and all I could think of was I wanted to do the same inside her. Our hunger for each other intensified, and my hands ran up her sides to graze her plump breasts. I wanted to savor every moment, but at the same time, I felt the need to throw her on the bed and show her how hard these past few weeks have been.

"Nicole," I gasped as I pressed my lips to hers, "I haven't forgotten our earlier conversation."

I heard her chuckle as I lost myself in her. "Why am I breaking my rules with you?" She moaned as I pushed her harder into my lap. "I hate that I know how this will end."

"I want more," slipped from my mouth as I controlled the kiss. "Give me more."

"*Mamá, mamá*," Chase suddenly cried and then gave a cough.

Nicole flinched and she broke contact with my lips. "He's hurting my heart." I felt it too. I hated that his mother was taken from him, and me too. I shook that thought out of my head, because it felt wrong to think of Talya when I wanted Nicole so badly.

As Nicole stood, my hands fell from her silky body. "To be continued." She gave me a quick kiss as she moved over to my son. "It's okay, little guy, you're not alone."

"*Mamá, mamá*," he repeated and rolled onto his stomach. He began to crawl toward Nicole, and she scooped him up so he wouldn't fall off the bed.

"Paul," the tone in her voice made the hair on my neck stand, "he's got a fever. He's burning up."

PRESS

NICOLE

When I pressed my cheek to the baby's, I could feel the heat. There was no doubt he had a fever.

"Here," Paul pulled out a Tylenol and used the bottom of his glass to crush it, "put this in his cup."

I looked at him like he had two heads. "He can't swallow that. That's for an adult." He looked down and removed a little of the white powder.

"There."

"No, Paul, he needs baby Tylenol. He would never swallow that. Besides, it could kill him."

He brushed the whole thing onto the floor and headed for the bathroom. "Nothing in here. Let me check the other."

Chase stuck out his bottom lip, looking insanely pathetic but unbelievably cute. "*Mamá*," he cried helplessly. I swore Paul could hear my heart break from the other room.

"I know. I'm sorry, sweetie, *Mamá* isn't here." I hated that he could feel what I had growing up. The empty feeling of not having a parent to hold you when you were sick or sad. Those were the times that left a scar that could never truly be healed.

"There's nothing here," he ran his fingers through his hair as he looked through his phone, "but I think there's a place I can get some down the road a little way." I looked at him nervously, and he seemed to read my face and gave me a worried nod. "I hate to be split up, but it would be a risk taking him out in public, plus he could be quite sick."

Paul rubbed his face, and the stress lines from earlier deepened around his eyes. He studied Chase, then me, and Chase again. "It's against everything I've been trained for, but I think I should go."

"Oh, God." I started to panic but I knew he was right.

"Look, it'll be okay. Just stay here, lock the doors, and stay quiet." He seemed to run things through his mind. "Just in case, if anything happens and you need to run, you have my number and Cole's. Do you remember the plan and where we're supposed to meet up for the chopper?"

I nodded. "I do." I had to show him I knew how to handle myself.

"Good." He patted Chase's back, turned, and gave me a quick kiss. "I'll come through the front door. If you hear anyone, or if someone tries to come in from any other way, grab him and run."

"I promise."

He checked his gun, grabbed his rucksack, and headed for the door. "Nicole?"

"Yeah?"

"Promise me, if anything happens, use whatever means necessary to get him over the border."

"Of course."

"Promise me."

"I promise." I watched him hesitate, then he stepped out the front door and closed it. I quickly locked it and went back to the bedroom and locked that door behind me too. I balanced Chase on my hip and began to fill the sink with lukewarm water to try to cool him down. I peeled him out of his jammies and couldn't believe how hot he was. "You need to sit, sweetie." I tried to get him to sit in the water, but his legs went stiff and refused to bend and he started to wail. "Okay, okay, you can stand. I held him close with one arm and cupped my hand to scoop some water up over his back. He looked so miserable I changed my mind, and I patted him dry then quickly got him dressed again then sat and held him. I popped a straw in a drink box and held it to his lips and was happy when he drank some.

As I soothed him, I thought I heard a clicking sound. "Paul?" I called and listened, but he didn't answer. I stood and struggled to keep my grip on Chase. I heard another click. Was it someone trying to turn the knob? My heart raced, and I knew immediately something wasn't right.

I snatched Paul's hoodie and remade the sling. Footsteps outside the bedroom had me rethinking that idea, as the intruder was already inside the house. Chase was fussing in my arms, and I knew he was about to cry. If we were going to survive, I'd have to lure whoever it was to him and hope I could overpower them. I felt physically sick when I put the baby on the floor on top of Paul's hoodie. I tucked his bunny beside him and looked around the room for a weapon.

A heavy glass candle holder shaped like a lotus flower caught my eye. It had nice, pointy tips. It would do. I glanced back at Chase, who was upset that I had put him down, but he wasn't crying too loudly. The handle of the bedroom door started to turn, and I dashed into the closet and watched in horror as a man burst through the door.

The loud sound scared Chase, and the little guy began to scream at the top of his lungs. The man caught his balance and rubbed his shoulder then glanced around the room. He moved toward Chase and leaned over him as if to pick him up, and I flew out behind him and swung the candle holder at his head as hard as I could. He must have sensed something because he started to turn at the last second and deflected the hit with his hand. He yelped in pain then whirled completely around as he reached for his gun.

"No!" I jumped over Chase and slammed my body into the guy. We tumbled into the wall, and his gun flew across the room as we both cried out. Before I could react, he shoved me to the side and my head hit a chair. I saw stars. He jumped up and grabbed Chase roughly by the arm. I lost it as the baby screamed again.

Paul's words echoed in my head. *Use whatever means necessary.*

With all my might, I scrambled to my feet, grabbed the candle holder again, and smashed the heavy thing with its sharp, pointy petals into the back of his head. His body jerked, and he dropped Chase. Luckily, he landed on my bag. Blood poured from the man's head, and as he dropped like a stone, he hit the table hard with his head before he hit the floor.

I wasted no time and grabbed Chase and stuck him inside the homemade sling. I searched around for the gun. It had slipped under the bed. I tucked it in my bag and swung it over my free shoulder then grabbed Chase's little black backpack and headed for the bathroom, afraid more would be coming through the front. I locked the door and opened the window. I bundled Chase in the hoodie, placed him out the window, and climbed out after him.

After I got Chase tied around me and the bags in place, I peered around in the dark. I moved to look around the side of the house and saw a car a little way down the drive. I figured it waited to hear from the guy inside, so I headed in the opposite direction. I wondered if I'd killed him, but I wouldn't waste a tear over him.

Without a flashlight, the ground was tricky. It was uneven and there were holes everywhere. My knees and ankles took a beating, but nothing registered. I lost track of where I needed to go, and when I hit the road, I almost cried with relief.

Chase had a death grip on his bunny with its ear shoved in his mouth. His terrified eyes were huge, and tears streaked his cheeks, and I felt like the worst human ever that I was just happy he was quiet. Headlights lit up the dusty road, and I ducked into some bushes. I wondered if I should wait out Paul or try to get to where the chopper would be at daybreak. I remembered my phone and pulled it out with shaky hands to call Cole.

"Nicole?" Concern was evident in his voice.

"Cole," I didn't wait for him to ask what was wrong, "the baby got sick. We made a call for Paul to go get meds, and after he left, a man broke in. I think I killed him." I sucked in a deep breath. "I'm running. I'm at the road trying to figure out what to do next. I think I should go try to meet up with the chopper. There's no sign of Paul."

"Good, Nicole, that's just what you need to do." Then he went over a few contingency plans, should something go wrong there. "I'll contact Paul and let him know what's happened."

"So, you haven't heard from him?"

"Not yet, but I will. Your job now is to get you and the child to the rendezvous point for the chopper. We'll find our way to you as soon as we can. Nicole, listen to me carefully. If something happens and you can't get to the chopper, your next move must be to get to the El Paso border. Once there, look for a gray Toyota parked in lot two with a mismatched black trunk cover. We have a guy there. His name's Manuel, and he's a paid border agent who helps us cross the border when we need him. I'll let him know there's a small possibility you might need him, but hopefully all will go as planned if you get to that chopper. Keep me in the loop, and I'll help you navigate through this."

"Gray Toyota, black trunk, lot two, Manuel border agent," I repeated.

"Good."

"Okay, but Cole—" Silence. "Cole?" I pulled the phone away from my head and saw it had died. "No!" A new level of fear settled in my chest as I looked around at the darkened nothingness and quickly realized that it was now just the baby and me.

"Gray Toyota, black trunk, lot two, Manuel border agent. Gray Toyota, black trunk, lot two, Manuel border agent," I repeated so it'd stick in my memory.

"All right, buddy, we need to focus on getting us out of here." I spoke out loud to calm myself down and knew it would be good for Chase to hear my voice. I'm sure my rapid heart was thumping against his little ear. "I promise you'll be safe with me," I assured him. "We're going to get you to where you'll be loved, and you can run free like a little boy should. You're not going to be a pawn in their chess game for power. Those monsters aren't going to get you as long as I'm alive. No way."

"*Mamá*." He whimpered so sadly I started to cry. It was my turn, after all.

"I know I'm not your *mamá*, Chase, but I'll try to be the next best thing." I wrapped my arms around him and held him tight. He seemed to like that because he nuzzled close and repeated the word *Mamá*. We hurried along the side of the road, constantly on the lookout for anything scary, and I checked to make sure I was headed in the right direction. It was cool out, but Chase's fever hadn't let up, and his hot little body kept me warm.

I searched my brain and pulled at some memories from when I used to watch the kids at the orphanage and remembered how baby Jackson loved to be sung to. "I've sung a few times on stage, you know," I said to him, "but that's not saying much." I chuckled as I thought about the few fun times I'd sung in a pub in Billings, "But I'd do anything right now to help you feel safe, so here it goes." I closed my eyes for a moment and focused on the lyrics. The last team I worked with used to sing *Nose on the Grindstone* by Tyler Childers, and before long, I'd join in with them. I had a cry in my voice that worked well with the song as I tried my best to soothe the little guy in the only way I knew how.

The sounds of insects seemed to join in on the song and provided company for me while I continually scanned the horizon for trouble. It was just us and the moon, and I was happy it provided me with just enough light to see the ground.

Soon, Chase's eyes grew heavy, and I felt like somewhere in the universe Talya was smiling.

My feet ached by the time I hit a major road, and the side of my head felt wet. I figured I had a gash in my hairline from where I'd hit the chair. At least I was still standing.

Headlights from behind cast my shadow in front of me, and before I could hide, I knew I'd been seen. My heart was in my throat as the stake-bed truck slowed to a stop. I moved the bag to my front and wrapped my fingers over the handle of the gun and kept my hand out of sight.

"*Hola.*" A man waved. "*Necesitas un disco?*"

I stepped back nervously. "*Sí.*" As much as I was scared, I knew we needed a ride. Time wasn't on my side anymore.

"*Vamos.*" He waved for me to take the front seat, but I didn't move.

"No," I pointed to the open back of his truck, "*me sentaré atrás.*"

He shrugged. "*Bueno.*"

"*Señor?*" I called him back to make sure he understood what we needed to find was a bus stop. "*Parada de autobús, por favor.*"

"*Sí.*" He waited for us to climb in, then once we were settled, I raised a hand for him to leave.

He never asked about the baby, and I wasn't about to offer any information.

I had to shift Chase up to lie on my chest so I could wrap my arms around him like a seatbelt.

After a bit, the vibration of the road made it hard to fight sleep, and whenever my eyes grew heavy, I'd mentally kick myself for letting my guard slip. I constantly had to ask myself how Blackstone would deal with the situation, but I couldn't find the answer.

When the truck finally stopped, it took everything for me to lift my exhausted body. I did a quick check that Chase was okay, that I had my bag, and the weapon. I was satisfied I had everything.

I swung off the side of the truck and waved a thank you to the man. As he drove off, I felt a sense of relief that there were still nice people left in the world. That feeling left quickly when I looked around the busy Merida bus station.

"When is the next bus to Costera?" I asked the ticket booth operator in Spanish. I didn't waste any time buying a ticket.

"One leaves in an hour." She paused. "Actually, I have one seat left for one that leaves in five minutes."

"I want that one, please." I handed her some cash, and she eyed Chase, who was glued to my chest. He was awake, but his fever made him lethargic. I took the ticket and raced to find bus number four. I made it just in time and plunked my exhausted body down onto my seat.

"How are you doing, big guy?" I rubbed his back, and he made a little whimper. "I'm sorry you're not feeling well." I dug out a drink box, and he drank almost all the juice. Then, once he settled, I closed my eyes.

I jerked awake and nearly panicked when I realized the bus had stopped. I saw a sign and realized I'd slept the whole way there. Chase hadn't moved a muscle, but his breathing was good. I was thankful for that, but it also made me worry more about his health.

I checked the time on the man's watch in front of me and saw the chopper would be at the landing spot in forty-five minutes. I needed to get going.

I knew the dangers of hitchhiking in Mexico as a single woman, but the locals I met were nothing but wonderful and kind. One even knew me from TV and took me a little farther out of his way.

The spot where the chopper was supposed to meet us was at a tiny private airstrip. I had been there a few times before and felt pleased to be back in familiar territory.

I entered the building where a skinny man with a wiry mustache sat behind a desk, nose deep in a novel. I felt like I knew him, but I couldn't remember.

"*Hola.*" I waved, and when he granted me a

gummy smile, I instantly remembered he was the assistant manager to this place.

"Ms. Winter," he seemed pleased to see me, "it's been a while."

"It has." I shifted Chase, who felt like he'd doubled in weight since we'd left, and gave him a little pat on the back. "We are supposed to meet an American chopper here anytime now. Could you tell me if anyone else is here?"

"No one is here." He flipped open the logbook and ran his grease-stained nail down the rows. "*Si*, there was supposed to be a chopper, but it says here he was diverted north due to a technical problem. Looks like nothing has been rescheduled." My eyes prickled as hope left my body. I covered my mouth as a tired cry escaped. "Oh, Ms. Nicole, I'm sorry." He raced around the counter and patted my arm and looked down at Chase.

"I need to get to the El Paso border." I felt helpless. "Please tell me someone is heading north that I can catch a ride with. I can't hitchhike anymore."

His wide eyes moved over my head, and I followed his line of sight to a small cargo plane being loaded with crates.

"*Si*, they're heading to that border, but you don't want to go with them." He shook his head.

"What family are they with?" I knew they had to be Cartel.

"They don't have the tattoos." He pointed to his wrist. "But they work with someone not good."

"I don't care. I made a promise, and I don't know how much farther I can walk."

He closed his eyes, and when he opened them, he looked like he'd made a decision. "I will make sure they take you. You stay here. I'll be back."

"Wait," I pulled out some cash, "use this." He nodded and took it then headed over to the men loading the plane.

I set my bag on the chair and dug for my dead phone, but it was gone. It must have fallen out at some point. *Shit!* I didn't know the guys' numbers by heart, and both Jack and the asshole would be wondering why I hadn't checked in. It felt like everything was against me. I gave myself a mental shake. It wasn't an option to give up.

I fingered my GoPro strap and made the decision to strap it on in case something happened. I finagled it on, being mindful of Chase. It sat high up on my shoulder well away from his face, and I strapped in two battery packs in case the current one died. Thankfully, my GoPro was the newest one on the market, and with my extra batteries and SIM cards, I could film for a week straight. Plus, it switched to dark mode automatically, so I never missed a shot.

"Ms. Winter," the fellow, I couldn't remember his name, came back, "they agreed to let you fly with them. I still do not recommend it." He shrugged.

"I have no choice." I smiled then ripped a piece of paper from my notebook. "If any of these American soldiers call or show up here," I scribbled down some very vague descriptions of Cole and Paul and wrote a cryptic message explaining I had to find my way to the border, "will you give them this message?"

"*Si.*" He took it and tucked it in his pocket. "Good luck."

"Thank you." I squeezed his arm and hoped he didn't notice my slip in memory as to his name.

I didn't risk another moment and hurried out to the plane. I looked it over and said a silent prayer it could even get off the runway.

One man smiled at me with a set of black-lined teeth. He made a crude comment but shut his mouth quickly when I shot him a look. He stood back from the step so I could climb up to the door. It was barely more than a tin cage.

A big, burly man motioned at me to sit, and I sat where he pointed and strapped the belt around Chase and me, then he left the plane and shut the door. Two men, one of them the rude one, jumped in the front without a word while the other fellow gave me a mock salute and settled into the pilot's seat. He turned back and studied Chase briefly. I quickly pulled the hoodie over his face and gave the pilot a defiant look. These types of men had very little respect for women or children, but he simply shrugged.

A short time later, we managed to take off, and as we lifted into the sky, I felt the plane shake. I'd flown countless times before, but this hunk of junk felt like it was held together with glue and tape. I didn't want to know what was in the crates they'd loaded because with my luck it was either cocaine or spare body parts.

I kept my eyes shut for most of the flight. It was very long and uncomfortable with Chase glued to me like paint on a wall. A few times, he shifted about but soon was asleep again. I knew I had to get the child to a doctor.

We stopped three times for fuel, and I barely had enough time at each stop to stretch my legs and give Chase a drink before we were back in the air. Another sign that we were more than likely carrying drugs. I saw the weapons they carried before we boarded, and I didn't care, and I made sure they knew I didn't care about what they did by not acknowledging the crates, not even when they moved some of them around to give me more room after the second stop.

Finally, I saw we were close to the border. It had been what felt like a lifetime in the sky. I didn't have a firm plan, but I'd gone over everything Cole had told me on the phone. The fact I was that close to my home country gave me a burst of energy I so desperately needed. When the tires hit the tarmac, I said my Hail-Marys that we survived.

When I climbed out of the plane, the pilot asked if I needed a lift to and across the border. Even as he spoke, his partners were loading the crates into a truck with potted palm trees. They tucked the crates among the pots and surrounded them with loose straw.

I didn't want to be associated with Cartel anywhere near a border, even if they didn't have a tattoo to show their alliance with a specific family. I thanked him but refused the offer, and he merely shrugged and let us go.

The air strip wasn't too far from where I needed to cross, and my legs were dying for some kind of activity, so we started to walk. It took me about forty-five minutes to get there.

I immediately headed toward the car lot and searched section two. But as my luck had been, there was no gray Toyota with a black trunk that I could find. After a few stress tears, I decided to head to the bus station. What I really needed was to get the attention of one of the border agents and ask for Manuel. Problem was there was always a chance of getting a dirty one, and any border crossing always crawled with Cartel soldiers.

I reached the bus station, and a man held open a door for me, but just as I was about to step forward, an arm hooked mine and I was spun around to come face to face with Bruno Perez.

"No!" I cried without thinking and instinctively wrapped my arms around Chase.

He dragged me around the corner and out of sight of the hustle and bustle of the border. Two of his men stood guard as he pulled me behind some garbage bins. I wanted to scream, but the place was so loud between kids, tour groups, dogs barking, and engines, I knew it would be useless.

His hand wrapped around my throat, and he pressed me against the wall and leaned in. He drew in a deep, controlled breath. His glare was as cold as ice, and it chilled me to my core as his hand tightened against my vocal cords.

"I warned you." His voice wavered, and I knew he was past all chance of reason. "You broke your word to me." He smelled like expensive brandy, and it mingled with his cologne. I wanted to vomit. I'd only seen him this angry once before, and I'd promised myself I'd never get there again, but there I was.

"My word," I fought to speak, and my temper fought to rise against my fear, "was never given." I ripped his arm away, and he released my throat, then he went to do it again. "You ordered me. There's a difference."

His chest puffed out, and I knew I was playing with fire. "Here's how this will go." He stuck a finger in my face, and Chase started to cry from all the erratic movement. "You and the child will come with me. I will make my deal, then I'll throw him to the *callejeros* so there's no chance the Canos family will ever have an heir." I pictured Chase being torn apart by wild street dogs and never felt more protective in my entire life. Something clicked inside, and I knew if there was ever a time to make a big play, it was at that moment.

"You're mad," slipped from my lips, and his eyes flared with anger.

"You have no idea." He grabbed the tops of my

arms and shook me, and Chase began to wail. "I look forward to the many punishments I've been conjuring up for you," Bruno shouted over Chase's cries. He shoved his finger into my chest, and I flinched at the pain. "You sent me on a wild goose chase up to Rosarito because of that article you released. You cost me thousands of dollars, and now you will spend the rest of your life making it up to me." Then how did he know I was here in El Paso and not Rosarito? What kind of game was being played? Was it all Rafael?

I desperately tried to play this smart and pretended my temper took over my brain. I let my mouth fly.

"You're so blind, Bruno," I snarled and slapped his hand away again. "Don't you know who I am working with to get this baby over the border?" His brows went up. "Wow, you really have no idea?" I laughed to deepen the blow. "Your mother was right. You're so clueless."

Whack! He slapped me across the face, but I barely registered it as I carefully slipped my hand down into my bag and felt around for the hard steel handle. I angled my hip. "I was working with Blackstone." I made sure to enunciate each word and watched as his penis-sized brain swelled to absorb it all. "They offered me a much better deal than you." I smiled and watched his face. It felt good to rub salt into the wound.

"I'm going to kill you—"

Pffft. The gun fired and barely made a sound. I was thankful for the silencer; not even his own men would hear it. Bruno's eyes flickered as his brain registered his pain and he looked down at his bloody boot. I stepped back and pointed the gun at his face.

"No, you're not."

"You better run, Nicole, because if I can find out that baby's father was Eric Noah before this fucking witch hunt started…" His face had turned white, and he held up his foot, unable to stand on it. "Mark my words, I'll find you and their safehouse. Ben was only the start." He suddenly lunged at me and grabbed the gun, but I didn't let go. We both wrestled with it, and Chase's shrieks made me fight harder. It wasn't just me anymore. The gun flew out of my hand and landed against the trash can, and in desperation, I drove my heel into his injured foot. He cried out, and I kicked him in the stomach, and he fell to the ground in agony. His eyes were tightly shut as he cried and held his leg.

I dropped into a squat and balanced Chase on my thigh as I snatched his phone where it had fallen from his pocket. "I'm coming for all of you," he moaned.

"Yeah, you do that." I kicked him in the leg one last time and ran off before his men showed up. I rounded the corner and almost got to the bus station again when I spotted Agustin.

"Holy…!" I spun on my heel and saw Rafael and some of his men. He had his phone to his ear. I froze behind a post and saw Elva, Jerry's Canos' wife, as she scanned the area. I was done. We were surrounded. I desperately looked toward the border, and something caught my eye. A gray Toyota Camry with a black trunk, my getaway car, pulled away from its spot and drove across the border. My stomach took a dive as all hope faded. What chance did we have now?

I looked at Bruno's phone in my hand, and an idea came to me. I knew what I needed to do. I slipped inside the station and entered the family restroom and locked the door. I was thankful it was a private room.

"It's okay." I soothed Chase's whimpers and pulled out a cookie, and he sucked on it and stopped his cries. I bounced him gently as my body trembled. It took me two tries to recall *his* number from memory. I was so rattled.

"Where the hell have you been? Tell me you have something for me," he snapped.

"I need your help."

"Tell me what's going on first."

"I'm at the El Paso border. I've got the child, the one I've been helping Blackstone retrieve. We got separated, and now I'm surrounded by multiple Cartel families. I need a way to get us over the border."

Silence.

"You did what?" he yelled in my ear, and I had to hold the phone away. "Are you fucking crazy? That's not your fucking job!"

I closed my eyes and knew I was about to lose it

myself. "I don't need you to remind me what my job is. I need you to remember how long I've worked for you and how good I am at my damn job. So, work your magic and get me some help!"

"You want some help?" he growled. "Ditch the fucking kid, head back to your own area, and find me the next lead."

"They'll kill him." He was heartless.

"And? Think about what you're doing! Think about what this means. If you do this, we're finished."

"If I don't do this, the child is finished. Glen, please—" I cringed when I realized I used his name. I'd never slipped up before.

"Strike two." He hung up.

"Oh, my God!" I slapped a hand over my mouth as things went from bad to horrible. *He really is an asshole!* We were as good as dead. I covered my face and took a few deep breaths, and when I opened them again, I saw a wide purse hook on the wall.

"Screw it." I used the last ace I had up my sleeve.

"Jack, *Washington Post*."

I could cry, I was so unbelievably happy to hear his voice. "Jack, it's Nicole. I'm in trouble. I'm going to go live, right now, and I need you to blast it everywhere."

"Oh, shit," he started typing, "how bad is it?"

"Take the credit, get the promotion, and if I make it out alive, I'll treat you and your wife to a steak dinner at Finnegan's."

He puffed out a breath. "Sending the link to the number you're on now."

"Thanks." I sniffed and tried to prepare my head for what I was about to do. "Jack, I'm at the El Paso border. Set up a line, and if anything credible comes in, text me on this number."

"El Paso and this number," he repeated. "Nicole?"

"Yeah?"

"You're scaring me. You sure about this?"

I squeezed my eyes shut as tears leaked out, and I fought the ringing in my ears as panic tried to take over. Chase coughed, and his little hand reached out for my necklace, and suddenly everything inside me said to do it. I needed to do it.

"I am."

"Then go for it."

"Thanks, Jack." I hung up, clicked the live camera link, propped the phone on the double hook and stood back a little to get in focus. I pulled Chase out of the sling and angled his lethargic little red face away from the camera. I used part of Paul's hoodie to conceal his face in case he moved during the live. I wouldn't risk that one of the Cartel had someone with enough computer skills to create some crazy AI footage of the child. God knew how it could be used later. I'd seen it happen before, and the possibilities were scary.

I waited for the light to turn red at the top of the screen and hoped to God this was a good idea.

"My name is Nicole Winter, reporting live from

near the El Paso, Texas border, and I need your help," I started and allowed the tears to stream down my cheeks. "This poor, innocent child is the target of an ongoing manhunt by the Cartel." I kissed the top of his head through the fabric.

I saw that Jack had posted his number on the bottom of the screen with a message to call if anyone was able to help us. I signaled Jack a thank you by scratching the side of my neck. I knew he'd see it, and that if something happened to me, I would be thankful for everything he'd done for me. I often communicated with him in that way; it was our secret language that only Ben was in on.

"This baby is nothing but a pawn in their chess game of power. The child's parents are dead, and it only has me for protection right now." I made sure not to reveal Chase's gender for his own safety. I rubbed his back as he let out a wet, congested cough. "The baby is also very sick, and I have no way of help-ing." I gulped for air. "We're surrounded at this very moment by multiple Cartel, the Perez family, the Canos family, and the Ruiz, to name a few.

"We've been beaten, chased, stalked. You name it, we've been through it. I'm begging anyone who can to help me get this little one to safety. If you do this, I'll make it worth your trouble." I felt defeated, and the weight of it all took its toll on my sanity. "I know what I'm asking is huge, and getting involved with the Cartel is a whole different level, but no baby should ever go through what this little one has." I fought back my emotions. "Please," I broke into a sob, "I've got no other moves here."

Suddenly, a text popped up from Jack.

> Jack: Someone told me to tell you to head to lane two and wait. I think it's a credible source. I'd do it.

I spoke to whoever had connected with Jack. "Thank you, thank you." I quickly ended the live feed and thought, even if it was a trap, it was our only chance. I tucked Chase back into the sling where he seemed the happiest and opened the door to see if the coast was clear.

"Oh, look at that face!" an older lady with a bun in her hair cried with delight, and I almost fainted. I took a breath then and saw the opportunity.

I waved for her and her friends to come over and see Chase, and as they cooed over him, I thought how Mark would have loved them. They were all dressed like a Florida retirement home.

"Hello there. I'm Lucy. We've been down here on vacation, and Elvira was just saying the one thing we were missing was a little baby to gush over." She looked at my puffy cheeks, red eyes, the gash on my forehead, and the cut from Bruno's latest hit and gave me a sad smile. "Everything all right, dear?"

"Not really." I sniffed, as I hoped they'd be my ticket out of there. "We're trying to get away from my ex." I lied, but I didn't care. "Would it be too much to ask if and you and your friends could walk me over there toward lane two? I'm meeting someone there."

She and her friends stood straighter and linked arms like they were their own little army. "We'd be happy to. Come stand in the middle, and we'll create a barrier." For once in my life, I was pleased to be a little shorter than most as we were swallowed up in a sea of pastels.

Every step was terrifying, and I couldn't help the near panic at the thought of who had called Jack. It might have been Cartel, but I had to try. I had to try for Chase.

As soon as we got close, a tall man with aviator sunglasses and a faded Green Bay Packers ball hat homed in on me. He was dressed in a black button-up shirt and a dusty pair of jeans with cowboy boots. If he'd worn a black cowboy hat, he'd be a perfect knockoff for Rip from *Yellowstone*. He gave me a small nod then tilted his head toward a parking lot of big rig trucks. I nodded to let him know I understood.

"There's the person I need to go with." I pointed at the stranger. "Thank you, ladies, from the bottom of my heart for your help."

"This is what women do. We stick together and protect ourselves and our young." Lucy placed a hand on my arm with a smile. "You take care of that little one, now." She smiled down at Chase.

The man nodded at the ladies, and they gathered around us in their protective shield.

"Nicole Winter?" he said quietly to me.

"Yes."

"Put this on." He handed me an oversized coat. "Up over your head too." I followed his instructions, as I knew it was my only option.

"Thank you so much, Lucy, all of you." I beamed at the ladies to show I was okay.

"Only too happy to help, dear. Be safe, now." Lucy smiled back. "Look after these two." She gave the stranger a stern look, but he didn't react.

"You ready?" He looked at me, and I nodded. "Good. Now, follow me and keep your head down." I did but scanned the area like it was my next breath, maybe because it kind of was.

He took me around a corner away from the hustle of the car lanes. Then he stopped at a blue eighteen-wheeler. He opened the huge rolling door at the back and nodded. "I can get you across if you hide in here."

"There?" I repeated and looked inside the long, dark box as I lowered the coat from my head.

"Yes."

"Okay. Wait! Can I at least know your name since you know mine?"

Suddenly, something moved inside the box, and I locked eyes with… My heart dropped straight to the ground, and I turned back to him with my mouth open. *What the hell?*

"My name's Chili."

TWENTY-TWO

PAUL

The smell of damp earth found its way to my senses and drew me from my groggy state. My head pounded behind my eyelids. A nasty pain ripped through my chest, and my lungs burned like my flesh was on fire. I dug my fingers into the ground, desperate to ease the pain. It took a few seconds to realize I was on my back, and I rolled around to try to orient myself.

I screamed, but the vibration brought on a whole new level of pain. Every thought that managed to get through swirled into the next, and I couldn't get a clear handle on any of them. The only thing that made sense was that I was seeing white from the pain.

Sunlight pierced my eyes when I opened them, and my body felt like a ton of bricks hung off it as I tried to move my legs to stand.

"Ah!" I felt the cycle of pain, confusion and a foggy head again. The only thought that managed to push through was my watch. I clicked the button on the side of the face twice to activate my signal for help. Although if my blood pressure had dropped, it would have alerted the team already. My right arm moved better than my left, so I felt around and jolted when I ran my hand down my chest and felt a hole.

A flashback of when I died the first time came screaming back to me, and I knew I must have been left for dead, but by who?

An engine noise stopped my thoughts, and I blinked at the dust cloud on the horizon. Company was coming. I felt around for my weapon, but it was gone, and so was my backup I kept on my ankle. *Shit, fists it is.* The world tilted when I lifted my head and tried to make out anything else, but all I could see was that the dust cloud was bigger.

I tuned in to a different noise, like a fan cutting into the wind, and I leaned awkwardly back to see the sky. Our beloved military chopper was headed in my direction. I dropped my head into the dirt with a sense of relief as a Jeep appeared out of the dust and stopped a few feet from me.

"You better be fucking alive, brother." John rushed to my side and ripped the gear from my chest. "If I didn't know it was you," he tapped my watch, "I wouldn't've recognized you with all that paint on your face."

I tried to get my eyes to focus on him. "Stop

moving, will ya?" I groaned. "I kept," it hurt to speak, "my promise." I tried to sit up and couldn't stop my cry of pain.

"Stay down, brother. You've taken quite a beating." John pressed my shoulder. "Help's on the way."

"My son?" I managed to get the words past my thick tongue. "Have I had too much tequila?"

"How is he?" Cole asked.

"He's been drugged with something." John's fingers touched my neck. "Looks like he put up a good fight, but they probably took him down with this." I felt him touch my chest. "He got a stab wound here and here, but it doesn't look like they got the heart or lung, or he'd be gone. They probably figured he was done and left him."

"Look at his arm." Cole sounded pissed. "They marked him. It was the Ruiz soldiers who did it, and they might be back."

"My son," I repeated as the wind from the chopper whipped around us. *Why aren't they answering me?*

"Let's get him in the chopper," John shouted, and I felt myself being lifted.

"You're gonna be okay, Paul." Keith's voice was muffled.

"Keith." It took all my strength, but I pulled the memory of what happened forward. I had to tell them. "Safehouse. Tylenol. Got jumped." Things made sense in my head, but I knew I was all over the place when I spoke. "Nicole, Chase."

"Who's Chase?" John leaned over me. "You'll be fine, Paul. We're gonna get you fixed up and you can tell us everything." I focused on his face. "Paul, when did you last see Nicole?"

I couldn't answer. My mind swirled again, and my tongue wouldn't work. I felt a jab in my arm and closed my eyes. I could feel that we'd lifted into the sky, and I felt relief that I was safe.

"I got the IV in him." John's voice again. "Shouldn't take long now. We need to flush whatever the hell they gave him from his system."

Another sharp prick, and I felt the warmth of morphine go through me, easing my pain immediately. At least this time I didn't see a white light like all those years ago when death tried to take me. My head began to clear a little.

"John," I managed to grab his hand, "where's my son? Where's Nicole?"

"What happened at the safehouse?" John leaned over me, and I focused on his face.

"I was jumped after I left the safe house to get Tylenol for Chase."

"Who's Chase, Paul?" John looked confused.

"My son." I shook my head to clear it. "They shot me up with something. I tried to fight them, then someone stabbed me. They thought I was dead. One of 'em got a call, and they all took off. Fuckers were gonna leave me there for the jackals. Now, answer me. Where's my son, where's Nicole, and are they okay?"

He squeezed my hand and didn't say anything. I

knew every line of my friend's face, and his expression said it all as his brows pinched and his lips thinned into a straight line.

"Tell me."

He pulled out his phone and handed it to me, and I watched in horror as I saw Nicole put my son on national TV to try to get help to cross the border.

"Frank sent Chili to get them, but we haven't heard anything yet."

"She put my son on fucking national TV. Is she out of her mind?" Anger pushed the drug aside, and I fought not to lose my shit. My son was supposed to disappear and start a new life free of his ties to Mexico.

"I know," John nodded but kept a heavy hand on my shoulder to keep me put, "but it might have been her only play."

"She used him for a damn story." I was so angry, and suddenly the phone was too heavy, and as my arm dropped, John grabbed it. "There's low, and then there's that," I moaned in anguish.

"Oh, shit." Mike's voice made the hair on my neck stand up. "Like father, like son." He turned his phone around, and my eyes widened in horror as I watched another video. "Paul, looks like you're the newest chess piece."

TWENTY-THREE

BRUNO

"Where is she?" I screamed at my men as they scrambled like fools all around the place trying to find her. Why was the border so damn busy? "You're all fucking useless!" The pain in my foot radiated from extreme to unbearable. She was fucking dead. I was going to rip her from scalp to ankle, let her bleed out while I watched, and just before she took her last breath, I'd do the same to the boy.

I limped over to Armondo, who was on the phone. "Well?"

"She was last seen talking to some women who took a bus over the border. Maybe she's with them?" I whirled and spotted where the buses stopped before they crossed. "*Ey!*" I pointed at two of my soldiers. "Go!" They rushed off in that direction.

"*Señor,*" Armondo stepped into my murderous view, "look." He held up his phone as a video played, and I closed my eyes to steady my rage as I read the headline.

"How am I losing control?" My voice boomed and made a whole bus line of people look at me. "Ahh!" I kicked a trash can and sent things flying. My ears rang from the pain, and it only fueled my temper.

All right. Think. I pressed my palms into my eyes to try to stop the pounding behind them. *Okay.*

I wiped the sweat from my face and placed a hand on Armondo's shoulder and moved him closer to me. "I want them found, alive."

"*Si.*"

"No." I could literally feel my brain start to unhinge, then a sudden calmness went through me as realization came to the surface. "Wait." I held up a finger in front of his face. "Not just Nicole and that fucking kid, I want them all. Every one of them. It's time, Armondo."

"Yeah?" His face lit up as I pulled out my phone and sent a quick text.

Bruno: It's time.

J: Understood.

"Spread the word, it's time to wake the embedded." I shivered as I stood and ignored the pain. "And start in Montana, at Camp Green."

The End

ACKNOWLEDGMENTS

To my mother, for diving deep into this new story
with me.

Veronica and Kasey, for again digging deep into this
storyline
and keeping things in check.

To Rachel and Lyle Womack, for always being there
when I need help with research
or some "family time."

To Jamie and Elizabeth, for allowing me to spoil the
story
for you and relishing in my evil ways.

To my beta readers, Elizabeth Clark, Jamie Johnson,
Rachel Womack, Maggie Savarese Rro, Kasey Griffin,
Veronica "Vern" Nelson, Deb Peach, and I'm sure
there are more!

To my editor Lori Whitwam.

To my street team and fact-finding group for all my
random questions.

To my reader group, I just love that you've created
a safe
place for me.

To anyone who has taken a chance on my books, I
thank you!

J.L. Drake, born and raised in Nova Scotia, Canada, later moving to Southern California. Though she loves the weather in Cali, she would sell her left kidney for a good rainstorm. Jodi's love of the seasons back home in Canada definitely appear in her books.

When she's not writing, you can often find her sitting somewhere along the coast of Huntington Beach, reading, or at home curled up on a couch with her two children and husband, binge watching a good movie.

AUTHORJLDRAKE.COM

FOLLOW ME ON SOCIAL MEDIA

facebook.com/JLDrakeauthor
x.com/jodildrake_j
instagram.com/j.l.drake
tiktok.com/@authorjldrake
bookbub.com/profile/j-l-drake

BROKEN TRILOGY

Broken

Shattered

Mended

BLACKSTONE SERIES

Honor

Escape

Freedom

Courage

DEVIL'S REACH TRILOGY

Trigger

Demons

Unleashed

QUIET MAFIA SERIES

Quiet Wealth

Quiet Secrets

Quiet Power

Quiet Empire

DARK WATER SERIES

Shadows

Whiskey

Alpha

Tango

<u>HAVOC OF SINS</u>

Grim

Havoc

Sins

<u>DARKNESS SERIES</u>

Darkness Lurks

Darkness Follows

Darkness Falls

<u>STONEWALL SERIES</u>

Extraction

Embedded (Coming 2025)

<u>STANDALONE BOOKS</u>

Behind My Words

Christmas At The Cabin

Omerta

For the suggested reading order, please scan the QR code: